The Night Tony Shot the Lights Out
and Other Stories

BY J. LEIGH HIRST

Suite 300 - 990 Fort St
Victoria, BC, V8V 3K2
Canada

www.friesenpress.com

First Edition — 2016

ISBN
978-1-4602-8661-6 (Hardcover)
978-1-4602-8662-3 (Paperback)
978-1-4602-8663-0 (eBook)

1. BISAC code 001

Distributed to the trade by The Ingram Book Company

Table of Contents

1 That Good Cahors Wine

26 Interlude

59 My Former Yugoslavia

146 Short Haul

158 Rhymes with Love

217 The Shed

246 Annie Crook

318 The Night Tony Shot the Lights Out

370 Acknowledgements

372 About the Author

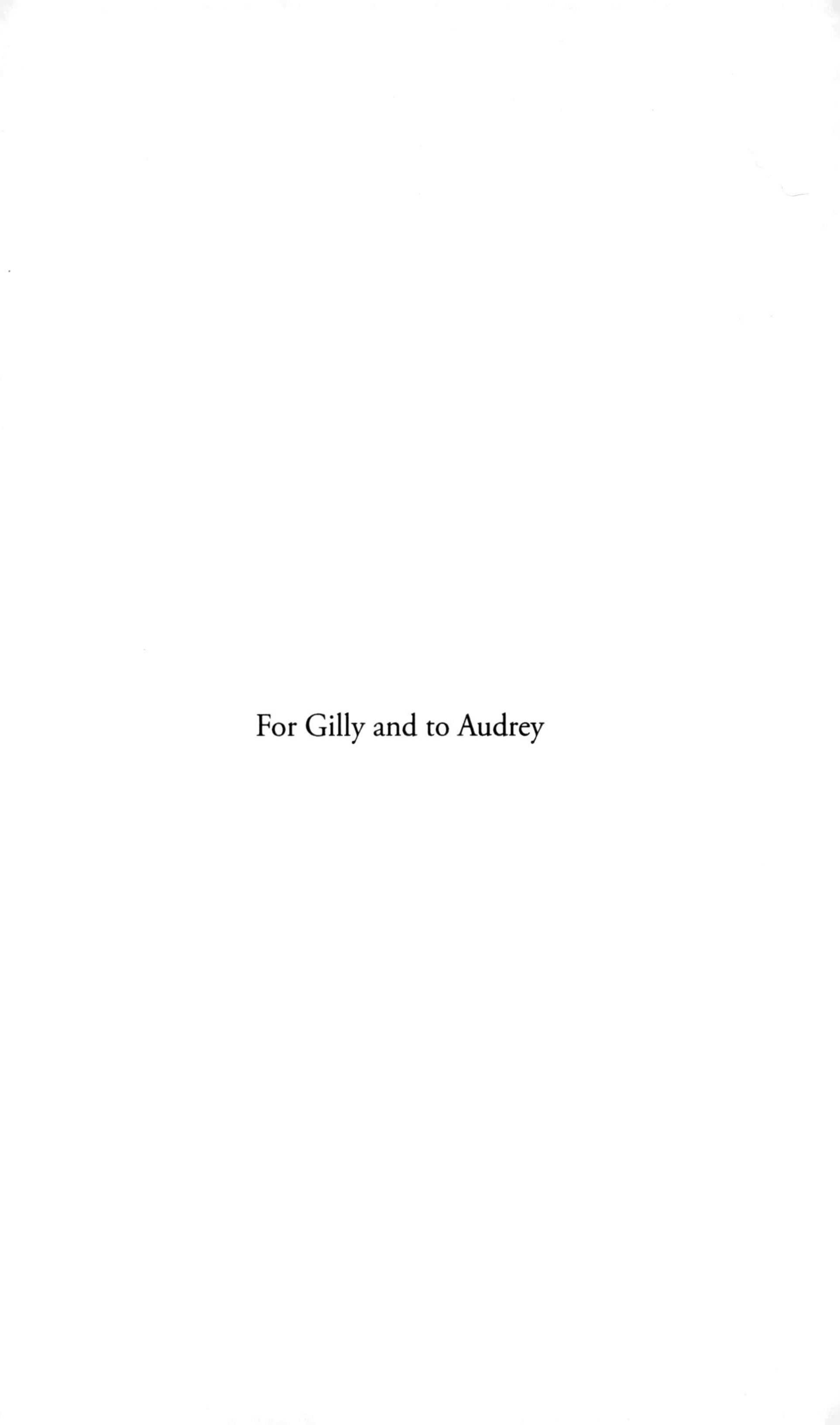

For Gilly and to Audrey

That Good Cahors Wine

"Intense involvement with living things is involvement with death. If you follow nature you have to accept whatever is capricious and twisted in nature. If the capricious is beautiful it is also tragic."

The woman at the launch ramp wanted a contact number. "In case you don't come out. We want to know who to bill after we find - or don't find - you." Mitch gave her his cell number. She wouldn't be as glib when, if, she heard his voicemail.

"You might find this handy." She flipped him a photocopy of a map that showed the trail snaking inland from the head of the lake. It roughly tracked the course of Drinkwater Creek and crossed a number of smaller tributary creeks. An X marked each of three campsites. Della Falls was at the end, ten miles into the Park. From the trailhead to the base of the falls, the trail rose 1200 feet.

"Anyone in there?" he asked.

"No, not that I know of."

She would know. The trailhead was at the far end of the lake and this launch, at Ark campsite, was the only access.

"Two guys came out by canoe last night. They were the last to go in. Haven't seen anyone else. Most nobody goes in alone and…" She eyed him. To himself, he finished it for her, "…specially sixty-something old men."

"How much for the launch?"

"Ten bucks."

Mitch looked at the map. A note at the bottom of the page read: *Della Falls is the highest waterfall in Canada. It flows in a pristine, natural environment and, due to difficult access, remains isolated and relatively unknown. Joe Drinkwater discovered it in 1899 while prospecting for gold. As a tribute to his wife Della, he gave the falls her name.* Mitch knew this. And there was more to the story, which told him something about Joe.

Mitch studied the ramp. Built for smaller boats than his, it lay at a right angle to the road which ran parallel to the dam at the end of the lake.

Launching a 22 foot, three-ton runabout from a trailer was tricky enough for one person. This looked to be a real challenge. He wasn't going anywhere if he couldn't get the boat in the water. A retaining wall restricted the trucks turning radius. He had to closely watch the nose of the truck as he backed around. He was relieved when, after careful manoeuvring, he had the trailer submerged on the ramp. He secured the bow line to the adjacent float, giving it plenty of slack, got into the truck, accelerated it in reverse down the ramp and hit the brake. The boat resisted, then slid down the rollers and split the surface of the lake, torpid under the July noonday sun. He drove the rig up to the parking lot, locked the truck, and walked back to the boat.

Mitch was sweating. He rolled the canopy forward to expose the cockpit, started the motor and in seconds had the boat up on the plane. It traced a white crease across the blue skin of the lake. Behind him Mount Arrowsmith, miles distant, was underscored by the boat's foaming wake and framed by the steep, green hills that descended into the lake. Except for a few cabins and houseboats at this, the east end, the shoreline was uninhabited. For twenty-five miles, on both sides, the hills rose up out of the water. They had been logged nearly a century ago. Now, covered with second growth timber, they looked like huge, humped animals with wavy, green fur. Mitch stood in the cockpit and felt the rush of cool air on his face and on his sweat-soaked T-shirt. He removed his hat and sunglasses. Traces of moisture seeped from the corners of his eyes. Ahead he saw the white peaks of the mountains in Strathcona Park.

An hour later the boat was at the shallow west end of the lake drifting through a forest of snags - trees drowned when the level of the lake rose after it was dammed. Grotesque, they stood silent in the water - bleak, headless sentinels with sharp, pointed necks. Scabs of black rot festered on bleached trunk-skins. Limbs drooped akimbo like fleshless, bone-white arms. Menacing, the snags flanked the mouth of Drinkwater Creek. Mitch nudged the boat through this maze of deadness, careful to avoid the submerged wooden corpses embedded in the bottom mud. The estuary stretched a good two hundred feet across and the current pressed firm against the boat. This is a river, Mitch thought, not a creek. On the north-east side lay the float at the trailhead.

It was now early afternoon. The sun stood over-head. There was no breeze. The lake shimmered in the heat, reflecting the snag-pierced sky. Those twisted pillars cast scant shadows. Mitch looked up along the estuary, past their serried ranks, and saw the mountains, snow-crested and stacked against each other as they receded back into the park. A jagged horizon. Mitch watched them as if they were alive.

Another hour and Mitch had the boat unloaded and moored to the shore in the lee of the float. He secured the bow rope to a vine maple that grew horizontally from the bank, threw out a stern anchor and then waded ashore. Mitch looked at her. She lay there, twenty-two feet of gleaming, white fiberglass, reflected in the mirror surface of the lake. *Runaround Sue* was inscribed above the outdrive on the transom. She was too sleek, too crafted, to be bound to this wild ragged shoreline. Too alien.

His hat and shirt were now rinsed in a fresh layer of sweat. A canopy of evergreens shaded the trailhead but he left his wet shirt on. It would keep him cool during the hours of walking. He shucked his sandals, secured them together by their ankle straps, hung them from a limb near the boat, and put on his trail runners. The trail lay out before him, sun-dappled, silent, beckoning, through a forest corridor. Mitch was at once excited and apprehensive. He hoisted his rucksack onto his back. There is always that first step. "Feets," he muttered, "do your stuff."

The trail meandered through tall stands of second growth timber, mostly fir and hemlock. Except for decaying stumps, disguised by decades of epithetic growth, there was scant evidence of the earlier logging. Barely visible were the notches hacked into the stumps that had, a century ago, held the loggers' springboards. As Mitch crossed a chasm spanned by two logs that lay side by side, he avoided the rotten patches that scored the smooth surface of each log. A misstep here would mean an unscheduled descent and a hard landing onto the rocky creek bed below. Above him, a raven *gronked.*

The initial three or four miles of the trail rose gradually; first a soft, fir-needle mat, then a dry, rocky creek bed punctuated with black stretches of muck. There were a number of blow-downs. Mitch found it easier to crawl under them after removing his pack than to climb over. This lower section of the trail followed what was once an ancient logging road, now almost completely encroached by the possessive forest. He settled into a rhythmic pace. His bear bell jangled on his rucksack, which clung to his shoulders and rested on his hips. Thirty-five pounds' worth of survival strapped to 160 pounds of flesh and bone. To his right, down a steep embankment and out of sight, Drinkwater Creek rumbled. He walked steadily, pausing only to drink from his canteen which, after an hour, he had drained. He stopped at Margaret Creek and knelt in a cold, shallow pool beneath a fan shaped waterfall to refill his canteen. Joe Drinkwater had named this creek after his mother.

Into the third hour the trail steepened into a protracted incline. The straps burned into Mitch's shoulders. He trudged upwards, imagining his legs to be the connecting rods driving the piston that was his pack-laden upper body. Sometimes you have to fool an old body. His initial adrenaline rush was now a trickle. Rest stops became frequent. Eventually the trail emerged from the forest and hit Drinkwater Creek and then disappeared. Mitch found himself in a small canyon. He scrambled upstream amongst huge boulders and rock outcroppings, guided only by the occasional, strategically placed, rock pile - like Inuit *inukshuk*. Drinkwater Creek splashed and crashed, throbbing through the gorge below, to rest in clear pools before squeezing into a ruffled, white ribbon again. Looking up the canyon he could see tree-clad ravines and grey, granite bluffs.

Mitch saw the glacier. It peeked at him through the cleavage of the canyon, gleaming on the face of Big Interior Mountain. He slipped the straps of his rucksack and sat on a rock shelf above the creek - his pack a backrest - and watched the raven circling in the thermals. Black wings in an azure sky.

Mitch looked up at the glacier. It would make an interesting run. If you could get to it. In the deep winter when it was dusted with a fresh skiff of powder. You'd have to be good at it. It looked steep and there would be crevasses. Ella was good. She skied like she was born to. Mitch rode in her slipstream.

Once, right after a World Cup Downhill race at Whistler, they sneaked onto the course. They skied it from start to finish, the whole 7000-foot fall, carving wide turns, fast, barely in control. For that few glorious minutes they had the whole mountain all to themselves. At the bottom, as he followed her, Ella wheeled around, cutting her ski hard into the groomed surface, spraying snow that arced into a rainbow flash of sunlight. Her face glowed, her eyes danced. "Is it better than sex?" he joked.

That fall they went to France for the vendange. It ended there. They kept in touch but Mitch never saw Ella again. He had no bad memories. It was all good. Never ever a harsh word. She was still in love with the memory of her dead husband. Mitch thought she would get over it but she never did. He thought he would find another woman as fine as her but he never did. Still the memory of her had stayed through all the years. Somewhere in there like background music. Now the volume was turned up. Now came back all the old feelings. Looking up at that white river of snow, he missed her. That was thirty years ago.

Back then everything was visceral. A hike in the forest was intense and physical. He remembered the blood-pumping rush of a sprint at the end of a 10K run and how good it felt to take the man off the puck in the corner with a hard, clean check. Now he felt more of what he could see and hear. Especially if it had grace and was natural. And what he could touch. Like the silky feel of a good red wine on the back of his tongue. Now he saw beauty in things that, in that earlier time, he would never even have noticed.

Mitch moved on up the canyon, finding the trail again where it probed back into the dense forest and then re-emerged out onto a patch of sand beside the creek. A tiny beach formed by a rare, quietly-flowing, stretch of the creek that turned into a back-eddy. Good Camp - the second of three X's marked on the map. There was a fire pit surrounded by a ring of fist-sized rocks across which lay a rusted iron grate. Nothing else. Mitch gathered up driftwood from the creek shore and lit a fire. He strung a line between two trees, hung his shirt and socks to dry, and changed from his shorts into a pair of jeans. Then, using a length of plastic rope, he slung his pack to a tree limb high enough to be out of the reach of bears. He scooped a pot of water from the creek and set it on the fire and then lay back against a log. Cool air flowed down the canyon from the snow-packed alpine. Mitch felt it swirl around him as it met the warm air rising from below. The heat from the retreating sun was still embedded in the sand and it warmed his bare feet. With a stick he traced lines in the sand - intersecting vertical and horizontal lines that made a pattern in the white sand. He'd seen a Mondrian once in a museum in Spain. A man's vision of nature distilled into hard, geometric shapes. The shapes were squares and rectangles placed asymmetrically. The colours in the squares and rectangles were red, blue and yellow. They were separated by straight, black lines. There was also a lot of white. The white meant nothing. Nada. Mitch dragged his foot across the sand, erasing the lines he had drawn.

The pot boiled and he stirred in a freeze-dried stew. He watched a dipper - a strange, little grey bird with a fat belly, a stub for a tail and long, spindly legs. It stood bobbing up and down on a log. An avian version of push-ups. Mitch watched it dive into the transparent water and, steadied by its extended wings, probe the creek bottom for grubs. It surfaced, hopped back up onto the log, and resumed the push-ups to the rhythm of a cheeky, shrill call. *Dzeet, dzeet, dzeet.* Mitch ate the stew straight out of the pot. The first spoonful was too hot. Not the pepper hot that Mitch liked, but fire hot. He didn't want to ruin that pepper taste by burning his tongue so he removed the pot from the fire. He let the stew cool enough so he could sooth it down with the cold, sweet creek water.

Mitch felt drained from the journey. Emptied. A good emptiness. A relief from all the noise in his head. He had come a long way for this. Good Camp was aptly named. He was now settled until daybreak. The stew would taste just right. Just right for the occasion.

Before dusk he lay in his sleeping bag and listened to the insistent hiss of the main stream which was punctuated by the throb and gurgle of the back-eddy as it nuzzled along the shore near his feet. His body, prone and at rest, spoke to him. The sciatica in his lower back protested, abetted by the bursitis in his left shoulder. One of his toes joined the chorus. His legs were quiet, not tired, still strong. "Built with bands of steel," Ella said once, tracing her fingertips down his thigh.

Mitch watched the sky turn black. A darkness like he'd never known was lit up as sparkling stars punctured it. He slept. And in his dream, she came to him. She lay on the sand beside him, one elbow bent, her head propped up. Very close to him. He felt her moonshadow cross his face, her warm breath. He felt her, with her forefingers, gently draw his eyelids down across his eyes.

As the sun seeped over the ridge and spilled into the canyon, Mitch made coffee and toast on his Primus stove and watched the dipper on the log watching him. "Relax," he said to it, "I'll be out of here soon." Refueled, Mitch stowed his gear in his pack and strung it back up onto the limb. Then he set out, with his canteen and camera, up the trail beside the creek toward Della Falls. Within half an hour he caught his first glimpse of the falls, high in the alpine, beneath a crest of snow. From then on they would appear gradually closer each time the trail provided a vantage point as it struggled up through the rocky ravine until it entered a flat, narrow valley. Mitch sifted through thickets of salmonberries and blueberries. Bear country. Part of the trail was worn ankle-deep into a soft marsh and was bordered with wild heather. Sword ferns grew in the shadows beneath the cedar canopy. Near the falls were the remnants of an old sawmill beside a clearing used by campers. Huckleberry bushes sprouted from rotting stumps.

He could hear them and after a short climb from the campsite he was at the base of the falls. He stood in sensory suspense - in awe of the plummeting wall of water as it pulsated against immutable granite. He was enveloped by a cool, rising mist. Fourteen hundred feet above him the main cascade poured over the lip of the precipice - a flowing white veil which crumpled onto a ledge and then thrust outward to become an angry, ragged mass of water tumbling down to a massive outcrop that split the torrent, splaying it to the left and right so that it continued in two streams over a series of jagged rock faces to finally pound into the pool where, its energy spent, it gathered itself to flow obediently into Drinkwater Creek.

Mitch stood in a cacophonous solitude. Exhilarated, he waded waist deep into the pool. The cold torrent splashed down onto his head and shoulders. Shivering, he climbed up onto a flat rock. He stripped and laid his shorts and T-shirt out to dry. He lay back on the warm stone, luxuriant in the morning sun, gazing up at a spectacle of nature's lifeblood - seeing it flow forever, remaining remote, detached, known only to an enchanted few - never just another roadside attraction. He lingered there. The sun arced higher, heating the little valley like a crucible. He put on his nearly dry clothes, snapped some photos of the falls and headed back down the trail to where he had seen the remnants of the sawmill.

Joe Drinkwater's sawmill. Mitch poked through the heap of timbers and rusted cables and saw blades in a corner of a clearing that was surrounded by huge boulders, scattered randomly at the edges, moss-draped and cleft-ridden and shadowed by an evergreen canopy. He stepped over fresh bear scat and then suddenly stopped twenty feet away from a black bear sow standing in his path, her shoulders braced forward. Behind her were two cubs. He reached for his bear bell and then drew his hand away. They both stood immobile. The only sound was the roar of the falls. "Here we are," he murmured, "your move." She turned and Mitch watched her furry, black behind disappear into the salmonberries, followed by the cubs. The thicket undulated in waves away from the clearing.

Mitch found footing in the clefts of a boulder and climbed it. He sat and watched as the sow reappeared and sniffed her way around the clearing. Above him the falls rumbled and, looking up, he could see where the cable system had once descended down to the base of the falls. That would have been a project. The only practical way to get the ore out. You would need big timbers for supports and for the crusher up at the mine. That was why Joe built the sawmill.

Mitch watched the bears with their noses now poked into the thicket, snuffling at the salmonberries, and his thoughts drifted back to a story as remote as the place that it tells of. Mitch smiled to himself. There would have been no gold and the falls would have had another name if the geologist, Sutton, hadn't said that it was impossible to cross Vancouver Island from Bedwell Sound. That was good enough for Joe Drinkwater. A challenge. And to prove Suttton wrong to boot.

That was how it happened. How Joe Drinkwater discovered gold on the shore of a lake high in the mountains - that no white man had ever seen before. How he paddled a canoe from Tofino up into the Clayoquot to the head of Bedwell Sound and then beat his way through the bush up along the Bear River into the alpine where he found outcroppings of copper and gold and staked his claims. From Bear Pass he could see the lake below him. He worked his way down and explored its shoreline. At the outlet of the lake he heard a thunderous roar. Looking down he saw the falls. He found gold and he developed a mine on the lake and he built an aerial cable system to carry the ore in buckets down 1440 feet to the base of the falls. From there he cut a pack trail down the canyon to transport the gold to Great Central

Lake. It was the trace of this century-old trail that Mitch had followed.

Mitch watched the sow bear. Her snout nudged the cubs along by their backsides as they left the clearing. He reflected on how Joe would have weighed the cost. Joe loved the wilderness but for too long he left his other love alone back in Alberni. While he was rambling around in those back-country mountains his friend Ward was helping Della keep his bed warm back at home. Joe was straight-up. Not stiff. Straight. He could have had his wife back. He might well have. She, at least, gave him the choice. Maybe he saw the gold as lustre in Della's eyes. He gave her name to that alpine lake and that monumental waterfall. A grand gesture? Mitch was doubtful. Maybe Joe figured it was the least he could do. That was a hundred years ago. All that remains is the rotting ghost of the sawmill.

By late morning Mitch had retraced his climb and was back at Good Camp. He repacked his gear and the sleeping bag, loaded up the rucksack and hoisted it onto his back. Two hours of walking were behind him and four hours lay ahead. He descended from the high country to the initial section of the trail which, as it rose gradually on the way in, was now a comfortable down-slope coming out - the old logging road, mostly overgrown and shaded by tall pillars of new growth forest. It was hot in spite of the shade. He had refilled his canteen several times at small streams that cut through the trail. He could hear Drinkwater Creek rushing, unseen, deep in the ravine below. Sweat dripped from his forehead into his eyes. The raven flew toward him, its wings *whisp, whisping* in the still air.

Ahead two large logs stretched across a tributary creek. They lay in a shaft of sunlight, remnants of an old logging bridge. Mitch remembered crossing on them on his way into the falls. And he remembered the smaller log, lying slightly lower and tight against the other, was pockmarked with lesions of rot. As he stepped onto it his eyesight was blurred momentarily in the sunlight. His foot sank into a rotted groove and he stumbled. All in an instant he felt the forward motion, his body a catapult driven by the weight of the rucksack, and he saw the smaller log coming up to meet him, his arms thrust forward, and then he bounced sideways. That was about all Mitch knew. He found himself lying in a shallow creek on his back, the wind knocked out of him, struggling to breathe. He could see the log bridge maybe twenty feet above him. His head was clear. He figured he must have landed on his back, the rucksack cushioning the impact.

Mitch sits up and shucks the pack. The stream meanders to either side of him. He is soaked and suddenly feels very chilled. When he tries to stand he discovers the damage. His left leg won't move and, looking, he sees the jagged end of the tibia protruding through his jeans. Blood flows into the creek. The blood stains the water pink as it courses quietly along. Strange that he feels no pain. But he is very cold. Alarm, like a mute triphammer, ripples up his spine. He reaches out and grasps the branch of an alder growing out of the creek bank and drags himself out of the water. Now there is pain. With one hand he pulls his knife from its sheath and slits the leg of his jeans. With the other he tries to stem the blood flow, which pulses with every beat of his pounding heart. Mitch removes his belt and cinches it tight above his knee. The blood flow slows. He retrieves a rope from his pack and winds it around his leg beside the belt, ties it tight and releases the belt. The blood still flows, now not gushing, but seeping, crimson across his pale skin. He knows that the tourniquet won't tighten enough to completely stem the flow.

Mitch lies prone beside the creek and with his good leg he nudges his lower body and immerses the shattered leg into the cold, lazy water. He looks up at the moss-scabbed underside of the log bridge. Sunlight slants down, illuminating a white wildflower that grows defiantly from a crack in the granite wall of the creek chasm. He lies back, grimacing, and lets the sunlight bathe his face.

Presently Mitch sits up and swabs the wound with gauze from his first aid kit, slathers it with Polysporin, and then binds it with the gauze. He cuts a branch off the alder beside him and fashions a splint which he binds to his broken calf with the last of his roll of gauze. Then, holding his broken leg tight against his good leg, he manages to manoeuvre his body around so that he faces downstream. He can see where the creek enters the lake. And, farther out, he sees the grove of snags; that sepulchre of dead trees that had greeted him yesterday on his arrival at the trailhead. "Goddam!" Mitch blurts. He had thought, before he fell, that he was getting close to the trailhead. Now he knows. The Drinkwater Creek estuary would be to his right and the trailhead, and his boat, a couple of hundred yards the other way. He'd almost made it. He still could.

The rucksack is waterproof and Mitch reckons it would float. He removes the solid stuff, including the Primus stove and cooking gear, leaving only his extra clothing, towel and the sleeping bag. Then, for good measure, he encloses the pack in a heavy-gauge garbage bag and seals it with a twist-tie. He feels for, and finds, the boat key in his pocket. The broken leg is now numb from the knee down. Mitch eases into the stream and crawls on one knee in the ankle-deep water, pushing his pack before him until he reaches the lake. Then, buoyed by the pack, he pushes out into the lake and begins paddling with his arms. He can see the boat farther along the shoreline, its white fiberglass hull bright in the sunlight. Mitch paddles into the plume of Drinkwater Creek and for a brief minute it carries him toward the boat. Then the current turns. Mitch paddles harder but he is losing. The current carries him back into the forest of snags. He reaches out and grabs a drooping, naked limb. Exhausted, Mitch clings to it and tries to think. He can only guess that the warmer, deeper, lake water absorbs the cold, flowing creek water and causes the current to swirl. He stares down into the water, fixated on the graveyard of trees decaying in the mud beneath him.

The boat beckons, some two hundred yards away. The distance between life and death. It seems so banal. So ordinary. This deadly, placid, awkward stretch of water. Mitch gives a hollow laugh - and gets a mouthful of lake water.

Somehow his body gets twisted such that one eye is submerged. Mitch scans the still surface of the lake with the other eye. Like a Cyclops. The surface of the lake is now the horizon of his waterborne world. The sun beats down. Spectral images shimmer on the surface of the lake. A float plane appears. A Beaver. Mitch tries to paddle towards it. It remains just out of reach.

"It's a mirage, you dumb bugger." More floating images appear but Mitch resists. "Can't keep chasing ghosts. Too tired anyway." He raises his head and gazes down into the clear lake and watches the tendril of red flow from his wound and become a rosy bloom that stains the reflection of his face in the water. Then he lets his head fall back and his face becomes half submerged.

So Mitch doesn't believe the kayaks. He lies motionless and watches them - two water skimming bugs with wings that rise from the glassy surface and dip back into it in a lazy rhythm. They grow within the visage of his Cyclops eye as they draw nearer. Then, fully realized, they turn in toward the trailhead beyond the boat.

"Groak!" Mitch garbles. With his good leg he pushes away from the dead tree and tries to paddle toward the kayaks. He has no strength. He barely moves. He tries again to call out and gets another mouthful of water. The first kayak has now disappeared behind the shore-tethered boat. Mitch raises one arm and slaps it down onto the water. *Slap*! And again, *slap*! And again, slowly, rhythmically, *slap - slap - slap*! He thinks he hears the echoes reverberate back, splitting the deadly water-bound silence.

Now he can see only one kayak. Its paddle becomes still. Resting horizontally. Then, as Mitch watches, it rises up and inscribes an arc above the distant horizon. And then, up and over again. Then it dips into the lake with purpose, and the water skimmer turns toward the flailing, one-arm, slapping sound.

Then there are two kayaks again. Mitch hears the *slish, slish* of their paddles in the water grow louder, closer. *Slish, slish.* In rhythm. Like breathing. Like a heartbeat. Like life. He hears a voice. "Is he alive?" And an answer. "Yes, his arm is moving." And Mitch hears Ella. How she used to chide him for his misadventures.

"Mitchell, Mitchie, Mitch!"

Interlude

Back in the late eighties, when I was working in Vancouver, I used to run in Stanley Park during my lunch break. The YMCA on Burrard Street was a ten-minute walk from my office. I would change there and then run along Barclay Street to the Park and then lose myself in its myriad trails. I ran about eight miles three days a week, leaving the other two for a light workout in the gym.

In those days most of the city's derelicts - the rubbies, bums, druggies, boozers et al - hung out in the tenderloin down around Hastings and Main. But a few, panhandlers, had moved uptown and I had to pass through them as I walked along Robson Street, behind the art gallery, on my way to the Y.

I ignored them. Was deaf to their begging, until the day I encountered Roland. Or, I should say, he encountered me. He had been standing in a doorway and as he stepped toward me, he stumbled and fell at my feet. I tried to walk around his crumpled form but was blocked by a passing pedestrian. Then, as I stepped over him, I felt a tug on my pant cuff. At that point another stranger bent over him to help him up.

I stopped, out of propriety I guess, not wanting to appear callous to the small knot of people now gathered around us. His grasp on my pant leg might have, for a fleeting second, annoyed me. He struggled up off the pavement as if, like a puppet, strings were attached to his shoulders. First one hoisted, pulling him erect, then the other jerked up to be in alignment. He wore a Hitler moustache plastered to his upper lip, black, in sharp contrast to his shock white, rough shorn hair and the stubble on the rest of his face. But he was no Hitler, instead more a Charlie Chaplin; a pathetic, deadly serious, slapstick clown. Everything about his shambling countenance was in defeat - except his eyes, which fixed on mine, not (as I could have imagined) like a cobra's, but rheumy, as if they were weeping, yet still clear blue and sincere.

His lips began to move but there was no sound. He inhaled and then it all came out in one gravelly gust. "Sir, I humbly request a donation of two dollars toward a sandwich for my lunch."

I was conscious that we, he and I, had become a sort of sidewalk tableau; dual, stationary postures on the pavement around which pedestrians streamed by in both directions. Behind us a crowd had gathered to listen to someone, standing on the back steps of the art gallery, bellowing something about the Komagata Maru. I had the strange sensation that, for a brief moment, a scruffy sidewalk Svengali had taken me right out of time.

"Donation" brought me back. No muttered, '*Hey mister, can you spare a quarter for a cup of coffee,*' accompanied by a vacant stare for this guy. He wants a contribution to his project - the procurement of a sandwich.

Somehow this performance melted the edges of my refrigerated heart and in the sweet absurdity of it all I heard myself saying, "Listen buddy, how many *donations* have you got so far towards that twenty-sixer of Wiser's Special?"

His eyes fell and he mumbled something. I continued, "I'm not going to finance your boozing but if you really want a sandwich I'll buy you one. Follow me."

His eyes widened in disbelief. “Yes, yessir.”

“Let’s go,” I said.

I took him, skipping along to keep up, to the Oasis cafeteria on Burrard which, back then, was just down the street from the Y.

The owner, Enrico, was behind the cash register. He knew me as a regular because I would often stop there for a salad or a sandwich after my workout.

“Hey Rico, I’ve got a customer for you. This is…” I turned to Roland. “What’s your name?”

“Roland.”

“G’day mate.” (Rico was your typical Italian-Aussie). “Pleased to meet you.”

I handed Rico a ten-dollar bill. “Roland’s hungry.” I pointed to a scrawled notice on the board behind Rico: *Grilled ham and cheese on rye, Vegetable soup, Coffee, $6.50.* “That looks good for starters. Right, Roland?”

He nodded vigorously, “Yes. Of course. Certainly.”

This formal, sometimes archaic, way of speaking, I learned, was normal. It was a clue to Roland. I left him there and went on to the Y. After my run, as I walked back to the office past the Oasis, I looked for him through the glass storefront but he was gone.

The next day, a Friday, as I again walked along Robson Street, Roland fell in step with me. "Greetings, kind sir." He attempted a smile, which was more like a grimace. It revealed one gleaming gold front tooth under his furry moustache. The other front tooth was missing. "Please forgive my bold intrusion but I wish to advise you that yesterday, as a result of your generosity, I enjoyed a nutritious repast for the cost of six and one half dollars." This came out all in one breath.

"Wonderful," I said, trying to anticipate what was coming next.

"And so," he continued, "there is a balance remaining on the ledger of three dollars fifty."

"On the ledger? You mean what's left of the ten bucks I gave Rico?"

"Precisely."

We had stopped walking. He stood there, looking as much like a forlorn vaudeville comedian as he had the day before - again so seriously persuasive it was amusing, almost endearing.

And again, as I had gathered, the subject was another sandwich.

"It would be a boon if you could find it in your heart, kind sir, to top it up, so to speak. The balance, I mean, by three dollars, thereby financing lunch again for me this fine day."

When I look back on it I marvel that I actually listened to this but it has since dawned on me that his affected rhetoric was part of it. It was camouflage making him able to beg without sounding too obsequious. And, as I said, I found it funny. I agreed.

As we continued on to the Oasis, I noticed that Roland walked with more purpose. He even had a bit of a spring in his duck-walk step.

That weekend Erica and I went to Gabriola to open our cabin for the summer and didn't return until Monday evening. When I told her about Roland she laughed. "You of all people getting sucked in by someone like him. Maybe you're getting soft." Then, as if as an afterthought, "I'd welcome that." (In those days I was in the investment business and was continually fending off scam-artists and stock-jockeys who try, and too often succeed, to infect the culture.)

What happened next I can only explain with the notion that, when I didn't appear as usual on Monday on Robson Street, Roland must have figured that I was avoiding him. Because on Tuesday he greeted me at the entrance to the YMCA. I won't try to describe the buzz in my brain at that moment except to say that on the one hand I felt that I was being stalked and on the other, I felt intrigued by such a bizarre intrusion into my daily routine and actually into what had become a habitual, if not necessarily boring, life. And Erica's remark was lingering back there as well.

So, not to belabour it, I took Roland back down to the Oasis. Rico agreed to let me run a tab not to exceed $10 a day to feed Roland. I left him there and, though I'm not religious, at that moment he looked to me to be as would, I imagined, a supplicant - which left me feeling uneasy.

Most weekdays I left my office for the YMCA at 1 pm (after the markets closed) and then, after my workout, I stopped at the Oasis for a salad or a sandwich. I therefore missed seeing Roland who, according to Rico, showed up around noon and was gone by one, which he did every day that week. So, when I settled up with Rico that Friday the bill was $32.50, not including the tenner I'd given him originally. Roland was spending $6.50 each day, not $10. That impressed me.

"This is no problem for you, Rico? He's not your normal clientele."

"Naw. He's orright. Polite, quiet and he doesn't smell. He's even spruced up a mite. Ain't it amazin' what a bowl of soup and a sandwich will do."

I nodded. Amazing was a good word.

"I put him back there in the corner where he don't bother anyone. I learned you gotta mind the boozers. Used to run a bar in Melbourne. Anyway, I reckon he's off the grog. Just sits back there, eats his lunch, reads a book and nurses his coffee. Sometimes comes up for a refill."

"He reads a book?"

"Right mate. Amazin' ain't it. You want to keep this up?"

I shrugged. "Might as well. As long as he keeps showing up." I don't know why but I felt good, sort of chuffed. And curious.

Rico said, "Well, at least it gets him off your back."

Off your back. That sunk in. I could have told Roland to get lost, and threatened him if he didn't. But I didn't.

The next Monday I left the office early and found Roland in the cafeteria with his coffee and his book. He rose to greet me. His gold tooth, gap-tooth, smile lit up his face. "Oh, my dear benefactor! What a pleasure indeed."

"I thought I'd check up on you, Roland. See how you're doing."

"As you can see, splendid. Certainly better than before I found you." He lowered his eyes. "My humble thanks."

I said, "Don't they feed you down at the Mission? The one on East Hastings? "

"They do. One meal a day. Provided I'm sober."

"You look like it now."

"Yes. Presently I am well victualed, thanks to you. And considerably less irrigated. My beverages are purely water and coffee."

"You haven't had to go somewhere to dry out?"

"Not yet." His eyes drilled holes in the cover of his book. It was Dickens' *Martin Chuzzelwit* (I'd expected a pulp novel or a murder mystery) from the library.

"You like Dickens?"

"I do. Who wouldn't?"

"No one reads him anymore."

"Yes. Tis a pity."

We talked, lubricated by successive cups of coffee, well into the afternoon. Looking back, I still don't know whether I simply found Roland interesting or that I was taken with the incongruity of the relationship - probably a bit of both. In any event, that afternoon, I missed both my workout and my lunch.

He said, “You seem interested. How novel. My memory fails in its attempt to identify a time when anyone had any interest in anything I had to say.”

I asked him how he got his gold tooth.

He couldn’t remember. “It was in an ancient time when I possessed a fine abode and a loyal spouse. Before I exchanged them for a sojourn in Her Majesty’s penal emporium.”

Erica said, “You didn’t tell me about this.”

She was looking at a framed document, a “Certificate of Merit” awarded to me by the Vancouver Police Commission in 1969. It read, in part: *In Recognition of His Outstanding Courage and Disregard of Personal Danger in Grappling with and Subduing an Armed Man….*

“It happened a couple of years before I met you. When we moved in together it got packed in a box and I guess I forgot about it. I had other things on my mind.” I grinned.

“So what’s it got to do with this Roland guy? This drunk?”

“He was the gunman.”

"Come on, Michael. I've known you too long for that."

"It's true. At least I'm pretty sure of it."

"Ye-e-s? You remember what he looks like? After nearly 20 years? I'll bet his face is a couple of miles of bad road."

"It is. And I don't remember. That's not the point. There are other clues that fit with what's in that newspaper article that I attached to the back of that thing."

She turned the citation over. "Is his name Roland Breton?"

"Yes. And he told me when he went to the Pen. And when he got out. He got five years in 1969. That fits with that article."

Erica looked less skeptical. No more wrinkled brow. "Well my dear, if you're right it wins the prize for this year's biggest coincidence."

"There's more. The key to it, what got me thinking, is his gold tooth. It's one of his front teeth. The other one is missing. If it weren't for that I wouldn't have rooted around for that old citation. His name meant nothing to me back then."

“Ok,” she sighed, “tell me about the gold tooth.”

“Why don’t you get yourself a drink? And one for me. This will take a while.”

She went into the kitchen and came back with two gin and tonics. We went out and sat on the balcony.

“I was in a menswear shop, the Brandywine, a small haberdasher on the corner of Howe and West Pender, picking up a new suit. There’s just me and the clerk. Bob. Bob Hamilton, and the Greek tailor behind the curtain in the back room. This guy comes in. I remember him being about my height, nondescript, didn’t take much notice until I heard him say something like, ‘gentlemen don’t move.’ He reached under his sweater, a shaggy, rust-colored crewneck, and pulled out a pistol stuck into his belt. It was a very large revolver and it looked to be too heavy for him, wavering in his hand, like it might go off all by itself. Strange the things you remember, but I remember thinking that when he pointed it at me and demanded cash.

“I had some small bills in one pocket and a fifty in the other. I didn’t know which was which. I put my hand in the wrong one and out came the fifty. He took it and stuffed it in his pocket. Then he turned the gun on Bob and told him to open the till. Bob said, 'I have no authority to open it.' I remember, at that moment, feeling my sphincter tighten and muttering to myself, '*Bob, open the goddam till.'* I hadn't taken my eyes of the guy since he'd produced the gun and now I noticed how unsteady he was, rocking back and forth. He looked as scared as I felt."

"Drunk probably." Erica said.

"Or wasted. Drugged up. He stood there for a few seconds, looking at Bob, but not seeming to focus and then he suddenly said, "Ok." He put the pistol back in his belt, pulled his sweater down over it and, with my fifty bucks in his jeans, turned and started for the door.

"I jumped him. We went down with me on top and him kicking and flailing his arms. And, on the way down, we crashed into glass shelves that held shirts, ties and socks. I reached under his sweater for the gun and threw it across the floor. Out of the corner of my eye I saw Niko, the tailor, scurry out from behind the curtain and grab it and disappear out the door. One of the glass shelves shattered and I got a gash in my forehead." I touched a scar above my right eyebrow.

Erica said, "That's news. I've always figured that was just another wound from your old-timers' hockey. Like that one on your jaw."

"This is where it starts to get goofy," I said, "like Keystone cops. There was blood everywhere, most of it on the robber. So when the cops arrested him they sent him to the hospital (in handcuffs) where I reckon they couldn't find any injury except maybe a sore neck.

"I had managed to get my elbow under his chin and I pressed hard into his windpipe. Right away he croaked, 'Stop! I give. You're strangling me.' I eased the pressure and we both lay there on the floor and waited for the police to come, which seemed to be forever. I had literally embraced him, face to face. Greasy hair, stunned eyes, whiskey breath. But what has stuck in my mind all these years is that gold front tooth. This was before the other one went missing. For at least ten minutes, until the police came, and as he quietly gasped, mouth open, it glinted into my eye.

"Like I said, Keystone cops. When they finally came they drove right past us up Howe Street. I remember feeling relieved when I heard their sirens approaching and then pissed right off as their wails receded up the street. They drove, two cars, around the block and somewhere en route they spotted Niko running along with the pistol. So they arrested him. And that's how they found out where we were.

"They frisked the robber, searched him, and came up with my fifty-dollar bill. I asked to have it back and one of the officers replied, 'No, we need that as evidence.' I never saw it again."

"You never saw it again?"

"No. When I think of all the absurd events in my life, this one has to be high on the list. I risked my life for fifty bucks and in the end it disappeared into the bowels of the downtown police station."

"If you hadn't shown me this," Erica held up the citation, "I would have listened politely because it's a great story. But I wouldn't have believed a word of it. You must have been nuts."

"Fifty dollars was a lot of money in those days and I wasn't all that flush. I'd just started my business."

"Ha! Some business if you're dead." She had a point.

"Anyway I waited to be called as a witness and heard nothing. Then I saw in the paper that

Roland Breton (I didn't know his name until then and had since forgotten it until I dug up that citation yesterday) had pleaded guilty and had gotten five years. I even had a hard time finding the prosecutor and when I did he, at first, couldn't remember the case. Apparently it was in court less than ten minutes. He gave me a note and sent me downstairs where Roland's belongings were locked in a wire basket. The money wasn't there."

"The cops stole it?"

"Who knows?"

"Maybe you should ask Roland."

I laughed. "I doubt he'd remember. And I'm not sure I even want to bring it up."

"Why?"

"I don't know."

"You are a strange one." She sat down beside me on the chesterfield, leaned over, and put the tip of her nose up against mine. "How'd I find you? Are you an illusion?"

She stood up and looked at me with what, I'd like to believe, was an affectionate smile. "Speaking of absurdities, here's one for you."

"What?"

"You're spending a couple of hundred dollars a month to feed someone who, once upon a time, robbed you at gunpoint."

I got into the habit of arranging my workouts so that my lunchtime coincided with Roland's. Noon, once a week, generally on Fridays. He always seemed to have a different book, sometimes a copy of the Sun with an article he would mention and we would discuss. He had a basic understanding of economics and the free trade deal with the US was a hot topic that year. I was impressed at how well he understood the arguments. At some period in his life he had read a lot. He said he still spent his mornings at the library.

I said, politely, "When you are able."

"Yes, and I have been able, sober, you mean. For some number of weeks now."

The obvious attraction to me was simply interesting conversation mostly about books and literature, and he was good at it. Especially since I figured that he, in that street environment, wouldn't have the opportunity. In fact, I could imagine there were days when he didn't speak much at all, except perhaps to say yes, no, please and thank you. And I found it refreshing to talk to a man about subjects that weren't guy talk - business, hockey, football, cars - which I got plenty enough of the other six days a week, particularly on Sundays in the fall and winter, which was football day on the tube.

With me Roland would become quite loquacious and at the same time he toned down the rhetoric. In prison he had been in a drama programme and, he said, had read all Shakespeare's plays as well as others. At my encouragement he would recite some of the more famous passages, including Hamlet's soliloquy and MacBeth's "Tomorrow and tomorrow and tomorrow," which generally provided entertainment for other Oasis patrons sitting at tables close by. Sometimes there would even be applause.

I told this to Erica when she asked me, "What do you two talk about?" That was news to her.

I asked her, "Do you know of any male book clubs?"

"No. But you can come to mine."

"Yeah, me and eight women. Be nice. So long as you don't get jealous. How many guys in your

CanLit classes?" Erica was in the English Literature department at UBC.

"Not enough."

"Get my drift? So here's a guy, a bum, a rubby-dub who would be a star if he was in your class - and might have been if his life had been different. You know I walk past them on the street and I just see hollowed out, vacant-eyed zombies that clutter the sidewalk. He's not. There's a real person in there. I can actually have a conversation with him. Good conversation. It's an enjoyable way to pass the time for a couple of hours each week. And he gets something out of it too."

"What about me?"

"You're not a pastime."

So my attempt to identify Roland with her discipline didn't catch on. Funny, because that was the one thing we all had in common; love of literature and good conversation.

"By the way," I said, "is *Under the Volcano* part of your curriculum?"

"No, it's not CanLit."

"I thought it might be. Lowry wrote it when he lived here. In North Van."

"Why?"

"Roland was reading it the last time I saw him."

"Did you talk about it?"

"No. It's too close to home. The main character, Firmin, is a hard core alcoholic. As was Lowry. Both drank themselves to death."

"I know. I've read it."

"Well that might give you a window into Roland."

One Friday, in mid-July, Roland was reading an article in the Sun when I arrived. The front page lay on the table and the headline read: **Man Shot During Bank Hold-Up. Robber Still at Large.** I'd read the story in my office. The gunman filled a brown bag full of bills from a teller at a Royal Bank branch and, as he left with the loot, a customer tackled him. He got a bullet in his shoulder for his trouble. The robber got away. The bank manager was quoted as calling him, the customer, stupid and endangering the lives of others in the branch.

I said to Roland, "Did you read that?"

"Yes. A sign of our desperate times."

"Not often someone gets shot, though."

"True. Seems the populace has grown wiser."

We paused as he folded the newspaper and then he looked at me with an enquiring grin. The change in him was palpable. He sat across from me, comfortable and confident, no longer a pathetic clown.

I said, "That happened to me once." I glanced at the newspaper.

"What? You were shot?"

"No. But I might have been."

"Dare say, sir. Not you? How so?" He was still smiling, as if I was putting him on.

"It's true. I foolishly tried to get my money back from a robber."

"When was this?"

"Twenty years ago. I was in a men's wear shop that he'd decided to hold up. Instead he got *my* money. Fifty dollars."

"My goodness!" His curiosity now seemed uncertain. For a brief second he stared at me then away. The smile was gone.

"Funny thing, though." I shrugged. "I tackled the gunman and held him for the police. But I never got my money back. My fifty bucks."

"You did that? How brave. Bloody cops!"

I laughed. "Ironic, isn't it. Even funny, although I didn't think so at the time."

"Certainly not. I would never have imagined you being so unfortunate."

"It's history. I'd forgotten about it," I lied. "That headline made me think about it."

Roland had slumped back in his chair and his eyes wandered. He had no more questions. I had jogged his memory and then immediately regretted it. I changed the subject.

From that day on our relationship changed. He became quieter, less forthcoming. And he began to speak more 'normally', dialling down the rhetoric. We continued to enjoy good, interesting, conversation but it was clear to me that we had reached a point where the imbalance in our personal situations - the beggar and the benefactor

- was hard to ignore. It was a contrived thing, say, a 'summer friendship.' One day winter would come. In the meantime, it was complicated by what was unspoken between us. What neither of us wished to acknowledge. And with this too, I held the advantage. I knew what he knew but it didn't work the other way round. He could only suspect and, I suppose, hope he was wrong.

Then what? Was I feeding Roland so that he'd stick around so I could be amused? That didn't sound right. But what did? What does happen when winter comes? Do I continue buy him lunch and do we keep on meeting on Fridays forever? At some point, somehow, it would end and I hadn't given a second's thought as to how that would happen and where that would leave Roland. Nor, I figured, had he. As Erica has said, more than once, "There are always consequences."

I was involved once with an 'older' woman - I was 25 and she was 35. Prudence. A dedicated social worker and a very controlling woman. We got along well physically. I was living in one room and was tempted to accept her invitation to move into her comfortable bungalow on Point Grey Road. But I'd gotten to know her well enough to be wary. Her clients were poor families, mainly single mothers. She thrived on them. A mother hen nurturing her brood. Only I likened her to a Lamprey eel. She was their formidable advocate which meant keeping them dependent on her. She intuitively resisted any programme designed to get them off welfare. These people were her constituents. If they weren't there where would she be?

Was I another Prudence? As long as I helped sustain Roland, met with him, befriended him, I was keeping him dependent. I could rationalize this because there was no other alternative to his situation short of detoxification and rehab which, in the past, had proven futile. But still the question loomed. What next? I had no idea. So I became resigned to continuing to buy Roland's lunch indefinitely, while gradually winding down our weekly meetings. And wait.

The last time I saw Roland he was reading a book by an author I'd never heard of; *The Book of the IT*, by Georg Groddeck.

Roland wasn't surprised. "Groddeck," he said, "was a German doctor, a physician, a contemporary of Sigmund Freud. He wrote four books. Only one was fiction. The others were about sickness and the psyche."

"He wasn't a psychiatrist?"

"No. but he was considered a pioneer in psychosomatic medicine. He and Freud shared theories." Roland leaned toward me across the table as if he was about to reveal a secret. "Before I went to prison, I was a hard core addict. I inhaled anything with alcohol in it, even tried to squeeze it out of shoe polish. Shot up heroin. Pills. You name it. Inside, they put me in detox. There wasn't much rehab back then. But there was one chap, a counsellor, Dutchman, name was Hank. He came once a week. You could book time with him and just talk to him. There was no structure."

He paused. He squinted into the sunlight refracting through the soapy-streaked window glass and then said, "Passing strange, isn't it? The way the mind works. I'd forgotten about Hank. Only lately he's been on my mind. Fine fellow that. Perceptive."

"What did you talk about?"

"I surmise, because I read voraciously and was a thespian, prison version, he brought me books. Mostly novels. Nothing directly therapeutic. Looking back, I'm thinking that perhaps that was the point. But one day he brought me one of Groddeck's books."

"Is that it?" I gestured to the book on the table.

"No. It was *The Seeker of Souls*, his only book of fiction. I found it fascinating. It's an allegory. Satirical, humorous, and rather bawdy for the time. Groddeck uses the main character, whom he portrays as both a genius and a fool, to present his ideas on illness and the IT."

"The IT?"

"Groddeck perceived the IT to *represent* that unknown awkward thing inside one that controls what one does, good and bad, positive and destructive. Includes primal emotions, like anger, or fear. To him it was the cause of disease. To consider it personally - my alcoholism."

"Your counsellor…?"

"He thought it would give me some insight. Groddeck believed that it was possible to gain some influence over the IT. And Hank felt that my sense of self was strong enough to control my demons. I had to accept my addictive personality but not give in to it, and get proper therapy when I got out. AA was one option."

"But it didn't happen."

"Obviously. I remained clean for a few months but, as many ex-cons find, the world had turned on me. Had become strange place. It was too real after the isolated and controlled life behind bars and, before that, my rat hole existence with booze and drugs. I got a boring job, drifted into a social life with the wrong compatriots and renewed my acquaintance with John Barleycorn."

"So you went back down the rat hole?"

"I did. But with some impermanence. Otherwise I wouldn't be here. Would be dead. Indubitably. At times, over the years, I've managed to pull myself together. Stay sober. Even hold a job."

"And this would be one of them?" I was going to add, 'and maybe this time for good,' but thought better of it.

"Yes. I've been able, these past many weeks, to recognize myself again, thanks to you. Forgive the sentiment, my friend, but this has been a most pleasant interlude. This, the Mission, the library, and my welfare cheque," he ticked off his fingers, "is an adequate life. I dread the alternative." He looked at me, knowingly. "Still it beckons and I doubt I'll survive it. But, is it not a common fate that *time and chance happeneth to us all*?"

So much had changed. I was struck by how much his sensibility about his future echoed mine. And how ominous that sounded.

The following Monday I flew to New York on business. When I returned at the end of the week Erica persuaded me to take advantage of the fine weather. On Labour Day I went to the office to set things up for my staff and then Erica and I spent the next two weeks at our cabin on Gabriola.

I unwound a bit. It was the first time in months that I'd taken time out to relax and reflect. Naturally, Roland drifted in and out of my thoughts, particularly that last conversation. His prior references to his past had been brief and anecdotal. And I, not wanting to change the script, didn't pursue them. (I could say that I didn't want to pry and I wouldn't be lying.) He was real to me as I found him. Sordid details about his past would only have been a distraction.

His description of his prison experience, and his sense of it, implied more. He didn't come right out and say it, yet it seemed that the Pen had been a sort of sanctuary for him; a place where he learned to become a 'silent witness' to his condition. And that, for me, made him become even more real. His interest in Malcolm Lowry and, particularly, in Groddeck fit with this.

So, for three Fridays in a row, I missed my customary two hours of coffee and conversation with Roland. On a Monday afternoon in mid-September I walked into the Oasis to bring my tab up to date and enquire about him.

Rico seemed uncomfortable. Initially no eye contact. Then he faced me. "You been out of touch, Mike. So I reckon you wouldn't know. Roland's dead."

I didn't, couldn't, reply but my reaction must have been obvious.

Rico said, "Steady mate. I figured I'd end up givin' you the news. And I don't know any other way to say it except straight out."

"What…?"

"He was here every day for two weeks. Asked me about you on the Fridays. I told him you were prob'ly takin' some break-time. No worries. I'd keep the tab runnin'. Then he didn't show up at all last week, 'cept on Friday, three days ago. And then it wasn't for food. He'd tipped over the milk cart. Looked awful crook. Worse than I remember him that first day you brought him here."

Rico opened the till and took out a folded, crisp, fifty-dollar bill. "He handed me this and said, 'give it to Mike.' I said, 'where'd you get fifty bucks?' He said, 'I stole it.' Then he walked outta here through that door, across the sidewalk and straight into the traffic. I heard a *screeech* and then a *thump.*"

We just stood there, looking at each other. "Sorry Mike. That's all she wrote. You want me to put this fifty toward your tab?"

"No. I'll take it. Use this." I handed him my Visa card. "Thanks, Rico."

Erica and I were able to retire at the same time. Some twenty years ago. We live on Taylor Bay on Gabriola Island, facing west toward Nanaimo harbour. The sunsets are spectacular. We moved the cabin to the back of the property and built the house close to the beach. I try to devote two or three hours most mornings to my writing. Erica has a part time contract, a couple of days a week at Vancouver Island University in Nanaimo. And I have roots there. Gravesites. We still have a small apartment, a 'pied-a-terre', on False Creek in Vancouver, where we spend some time in the winter. But as the years go by, I recognize the place less and less. It has grown away from us. Many of our friends, my hockey buddies and business associates, have either died or moved away. Downtown is now a mass of high rise buildings. It looks and feels different.

I'm no longer a member of the YMCA but I walked over there the other day. Speakers still harangue you from the back steps of the art gallery. That hasn't changed. But the Oasis is gone, replaced by an apparel shop, and the Y has been renovated, although the exterior still looks the same. On my way back, along Robson Street, as I passed three or four panhandlers, I found myself staring at them, searching their faces. They, each of them, met my gaze. Blank. Nothing there.

I haven't laid eyes on a fifty-dollar bill in years. I don't carry a lot of cash and, these days, the ATM machines just pump out twenties. But last Sunday I was selling my books at a craft fair here on the island and I had to make change for a fifty - a small, pink, piece of paper with the image of a former Prime Minister (the séance King) on it. It has an assigned value. It is worth whatever you can exchange it for. For me, that would be a memory.

My Former Yugoslavia

He rose up out of Genoa through fog-shrouded, silent, switchback streets to where, from the crest of the escarpment, he looked back and down. The city lights glowed lazily through the veil of mist - phosphorescent in the twilit dawn. Turning east into the oncoming November morning he found the secondary road that ran roughly parallel to the Autostrade and he stuck out his thumb.

A Deux Chevaux, a rattling contraption of tubes and tin, it's wild-eyed driver sucking on Gauloises after Gauloises, transported him as far as Tortona where he languished by the roadside until he gave up and boarded a day train bound for Milan. From there he took the overnight train to Venice. He sat in a stuffy compartment and conversed with an old bearded Jesuit who spoke heavily accented English. When the priest nodded off he slipped out into the aisle and bedded down on the floor using his rucksack for a pillow. Through the night the train stopped at Brescia, Verona, and Padua and each time he was conscious of newly boarded passengers stepping over him as they proceeded down the aisle.

The next morning he rambled around Venice. In a steamy bar he ate his first meal in 24 hours - a bread roll, fruit, and espresso. He explored dank alleyways that often led to a small verdant cortile. He toured the Grand Canal in a motor launch and dozed on a bench in the Piazza San Marco, with the wan November sunlight warm on his face. Thus ended his time as a tourist.

By noon he was across the Freedom Bridge and in Mestre where he found a road to the northeast and got lucky when a transport truck swerved suddenly and stopped in a plume of dust on the gravel shoulder. As he climbed into the cab, the driver, glancing at the flag on his rucksack, shouted above the din of the idling diesel, "Canadese?"

"Si."

"Bene." The driver grinned as he rammed it into gear and the truck lurched out into the traffic. Three hours later it was crawling through Trieste's narrow streets en route to the Centrale railway station.

He discovered that there was a night train to Zagreb and he bought a ticket and then he walked to the harbour where he found a restaurant. He ordered a bowl of pasta and a carafe of wine and he lit a cigarette. From his table by the window he watched the evening dark rise across the gulf toward the lights of Venice.

PART ONE: TRIESTE, NOVEMBER 1963

Parker lay with his head propped and resting against his rucksack on the concrete floor of the platform in the railway station in Trieste. Out in the darkness a dim bead of light, like a low distant star, appeared to grow and creep closer, the locus of the converging lines of the tracks and the borders of the platform as if set in the deep perspective of a surreal Dali painting. Then he heard the train, lugging and creaking toward the station.

Lamps on the platform stanchions made halos of dirty yellow light. Beneath them huddled lumps of humanity. Peasants. With children and rope-wrapped cardboard boxes for luggage. A goat on a leash. This was the first time Parker had encountered people who were akin to what his image of a peasant was. He had been with poor rural people in Italy and in Spain where he had worked picking onions. He never thought of them as peasants. He felt an affinity with them, with their resilience, with their rough, sardonic optimism. They did not seem oppressed, even in Franco's Spain.

These people had the look of the oppressed. The owner of the goat was a small man, probably in his late twenties considering his young children. Haggard, pinchfaced, he looked twice that. His shoes had no laces. His wife squatted, immersed in the greasy grey pool of her ankle length skirt. She was pudgy. Her head was shrouded in a faded red babushka that framed a face that reminded Parker of a potato, which might well be the staple of her diet. He could smell their damp mustiness. And, perhaps, a mixture of stale sweat and onion breath which might even be his own odour after days on the road.

The overhead lamp bathed their dark forms in a sepia tone. It set them up against the blackness of the enveloping night, creating an image from another century. That from which they had yet to emerge. Similar groups, families, extended families, he reckoned, clustered silently at the bases of the stanchions that marched, serried, along the platform. He shivered and rummaged in the rucksack for a sweatshirt. The train arrived and the huddled groups began to stir. He waited to join them on their night journey.

The Australian swung down from the railcar and picked him out directly.

"You a Yank?"

"No. Canadian." Parker nodded toward the Red Ensign sewn on his rucksack.

"Sorry mate. Must be the Levis and the jumper." He looked along the platform. "Bit of a contrast to this lot." He shrugged his pack off his shoulders, grinning. "Sight for sore eyes. Haven't seen a white man in months."

"What's it like in there?"

"Where? Yugo?" He flipped two cigarettes out of his breast pocket and offered Parker one. His pale face glowed in the match flame. He stood a head higher than the crowd, which was now milling about them. He looked to be as strange in this place as Parker felt.

"Hell, mate, it's different. Like I said, there ain't a bunch of us swags on walkabout in there. Don't cater to tourists, specially hitchers. Except maybe down on the coast. No youth hostels. Pensions, mainly flophouses."

"Where were you?"

"Got as far as Belgrade. Serbia."

"Hitchhiking?"

"Not bloody likely. Waited three days once before I got smart and took the train. Got picked up once by the Ozzies."

"The who?"

"Ozzies. Tito's Gestapo.* Took my passport and put me in a room all day in some dump I can't even remember the name of. Kicked me out after dark. Ended up sleepin' in a field behind a farmhouse. Only good thing was the farmer found me and his wife cooked me breakfast."

"They're good people?"

"Mostly. Suspicious at first. Like you just arrived from the moon or somewhere. Warm up when they find out you're human. Don't like each other much either. Serbs, Croats, Slovenes, even Muslims further south. All dirt poor. Like this mob. Where you headed?"

*Organ Zastite Naroda Armije (OZNA)

"Teslic."

"Teslic? Where's that?"

"Somewhere in Bosnia. A small village. It doesn't show up on a map, at least not on the one I looked at."

The Aussie squinted at him through the cigarette smoke. "You might want to find out where it is, matey. Before you end up wanderin' around chasing shadows. That's no country you want to get yourself lost in." He produced a map from his hip pocket - sweat stained and moulded to the curve of his butt and worn through at the corner folds. Gingerly he peeled it open and set it on the platform floor.

"This here's a camper's map. Couldn't find a railway map. I got the bloke at the train station to connect the dots for me. And by crikey, there's Teslic. Must be a campsite near it." He stabbed his finger near the centre of the map. "Now all you gotta do is find out if a train goes there. I know one goes to Banja Luka." Parker could see that it was the nearest large town.

The Aussie folded the map. "I won't be needin' this. What's in Teslic?"

"A woman. She's…"

"Right!" He winked. "Must be some sweet Sheila. To get you goin' when you don't even know where you're goin'."

"She's the sister of a friend back home. I don't know her. If I find her it'll be a surprise to both of us."

The Aussie looked skeptical. "Sounds like an expedition, doesn't it mate? Yeah, well maybe the destination's less the point than the gettin' there. After you been bangin' around these parts for a while you get to thinkin' that way. It's just puttin' one foot in front of t'other. See where they take you." He handed Parker the map. "This here's just a bunch of lines on a piece of paper but it might help. It ain't no secret chart. There ain't one." He turned and threaded his way through the crowded platform until he disappeared.

Parker hoisted his rucksack up onto the luggage rack and then sank back into the soft sponginess of the compartment bench. The train lurched forward, ground to a halt and then lurched forward again before settling into a rhythmic, rattling, *clickety-clack* out into the night. Two brittle blonde women wearing short white skirts, heavy make-up, and bored looks sat across from him. He hadn't noticed them on the platform. They would have stood in contrast to the assemblage there.

In the compartment window he saw his reflection framed by the black night beyond. The outer darkness. He shrugged at it and watched it mimic him. He closed his eyes and it disappeared. What the hell. The Aussie was right. It gets to be a habit. And anyway there's only ever the one destination. And you never know what you'll find along the way, like these two bimbos, probably hookers, perched on the bench opposite.

Another night train. It wears you down. But there's an upside. It's more direct than waiting to be picked up at the side of an autoroute and you save the cost of a night at a hostel or pension. And on this one, at least, Parker wouldn't have to sleep in the aisle. He and his two companions had a compartment all to themselves. Once, months ago, he rode on the Loreley Express out of Rotterdam. He sat on the floor in the aisle, resting against his pack, opposite a full compartment which included a young, fresh-faced couple who were holding hands. Dozing, Parker felt a hand resting lightly on his shoulder.

The young man spoke softly, with a Dutch accent. "Would you please exchange places with me?" He gestured to the empty seat in the compartment. The woman looked out, smiling.

Parker stared up at him.

"Please," the man repeated, "it would be my honour."

Parker pinched the bridge of his nose, attempting to clear the cobwebs, and shook his head. "No. Why?" He looked at the smiling woman.

"You are Canadian, ya?" He pointed to the flag on the rucksack.

"Yes."

"You saved my country."

You saved my country. The light went on. "No, no, not me. That was a long time ago. I was just a kid. Still in grade school."

"I was just in school too, when the soldiers came. The Canadians. We were starving. They saved us."

"I know what they did. But I wasn't there. Like I said…"

"You must let me do this. It is important." Again he gestured toward the seat in the compartment. Its other occupants were now watching. So Parker got up and went and sat beside the young man's wife. She and her husband were from Delft and on their honeymoon. They talked and she told him how the people of Holland would never forget the men who liberated them. Later she went and sat in the aisle and he talked with her husband as the train wore down the night, slipping swiftly along the Rhine.

This happened early in his experience. After, and often during those long stretches of solitude, even loneliness, as he made his way, passing through stations where once certain others had passed and then disappeared forever, feeling strange, deliberately resisting the want of warmth and shelter, he would conjure up the image of that man and woman and reflect upon the power of their goodwill, that was sustaining, that was honourable, that healed.

They crossed at Sezana into Slovenia, the northernmost state in Yugoslavia. The train was shunted onto a siding where the Italian diesel engine was detached and a steam locomotive brought in and then the thump and he felt it as the impact shuddered in succession down the line of cars like falling dominoes. A customs agent in a black suit, escorted by a soldier in a grey uniform, cradling a sub machinegun, studied his passport then handed it to the soldier. He felt his chest tighten. The soldier shrugged, handed it back and the agent stamped it with a visa. He glanced at Parker and then he turned to the women and spoke to them in Slav. They got up and, smirking at each other, followed him and the soldier along the aisle. They didn't return.

The night passed and a grey dawn crept across the rail yard before the train began to move. Alone in the compartment, Parker stayed awake in a half-stupor as shallow green hills, some studded with stone or white stucco buildings, slipped by the window. It was now more than a full day and night since he'd slept. He felt let down. Numb. He'd had no idea of what to anticipate except that it would have involved maybe a sense of an objective being met, a barrier broken. Instead it was nothing. Literally nothing. Not one word had been spoken. It took less than 30 seconds to grant him access to the dark side of the curtain. To the bloody Balkans. To Tito's paradise. He figured there was a more pressing issue of the moment;

the opportunity for that lecherous functionary and his dull-eyed bodyguard to carry out a bit of passport inspection with the girls privately.

Should he blame Old Conway? But for him would he now be here in this place that appeared, at the moment, to be no place? Parker thought not. Decisions it seemed, especially important ones, often had tangled roots and it took time and reflection to sort them out, to discover why he had done what he had done. Sometimes there was no answer. Then there was Goldie's reaction. She told him that if he was going to leave her to go tramping around Europe he might as well go into Yugoslavia and find her aunt Maya. That would give her reason to, at least, talk to him when he came home.

He didn't get Old Conway until his last year in college. And then, when he took his MA, he became the professor's teaching assistant. Old Conway was the *eminence grise* of the History department and his lectures were popular due, not only, to his erudition but also because he entertained. He was that rare specimen; an intellectual who could teach. The focus of his courses was 20th Century Middle Europe; in other words,

Germany. He would stride across the lecture hall stage, his black gown flowing, slam his armload of books down on the table beside the lectern, and then unwind his skeletal, six and a half foot frame as he turned to face his audience. With his right arm and index finger accusingly extended he'd bellow, "Do I have your full attention?" Then there would ensue an engrossing examination of the subject at hand supported with photographic slides and other props.

But there was a sidebar. He, Dr. Basil Conway, had been in the British Intelligence Service during the war and had spent most of 1944 with Tito's Partisans in southern Yugoslavia. This intrigued Parker and old Conway was happy to oblige - in private conversation (often in a pub) and with references, including his own book: *The Sublime Taste of Hatred: World War II in Yugoslavia.* He had Parker's full attention.

This was Parker's introduction to a horror that lurked relatively unnoticed in the shadow of the Nazis' overarching achievement of mass annihilation. He discovered the Yugoslav bloodbath to be unique in its unsophisticated savagery, especially when compared to the sleek efficiency of the German murder machine. And unique, as well, for its internecine quality. It was a Slav-on-Slav affair. Still, while the story held a morbid fascination, he was otherwise unmoved. There was too much to do and see in other, more interesting, places. And only so much time. Yugoslavia was not a compelling destination.

But then, one cool November day in Genoa, Parker bought a smaller, lighter rucksack and a pearl-handled switchblade knife, stashed his superfluous gear in a locker at the Stazione Maritima and then, early the next morning, he took his leave - heading, not south toward Rome but east. Destination Zagreb.

In one way, thanks to Old Conway, he was prepared. But in another way, Goldie's way, he had almost nothing to go on. Goldie's father, John Starich, had emigrated to Canada in 1926. He left his pregnant wife in Croatia with his sister Maya (supposedly a chaperone). He would send for his wife once he was settled and working. That didn't happen. His wife had the child, a daughter, and then married another man. Parker didn't know, or care to know, the details of this sorry episode. He simply knew about the 40-year estrangement. John remarried and raised a family in British Columbia. He had never seen or heard from his Croatian daughter who was now thought to be married and living in Uruguay. And he refused any contact with his sister Maya, whom he blamed. Goldie was curious and she snooped around. Then she beat on Parker.

"Where is she?" he said.

"Teslic," she answered.

"Teslic? Where's that?"

"Bosnia."

"Where in Bosnia? Show me the map."

"It's not on the map."

"What the hell?" He turned away. "You don't expect much, do you? There's this problem and it's bigger than your family. They lock up strangers. Sometimes they kill them. And I'm supposed to mosey on in there and dig up someone who's been holed up for the last 40 years in a place that maybe doesn't even exist. Huh?"

"It's near Doboj." She held out the map. "Doboj's on the map."

Parker knew about Doboj. Mihailovic's Chetniks operated from there. After the war Tito executed him.

He left her with a vague promise. He'd consider it after he'd seen the places he wanted to see. When he got to Italy. If he had time. Now he sat alone in a slowly moving railcar in the dark on the dark side of the curtain and he thought about what it was that got him there. Something was leading him on and surely, old Conway and Goldie were part of it. But there was something else. Something that moved, ever so subtly, down there in those tangled roots. Maybe it was simply curiosity. There was a woman out there somewhere and she had a story to tell.

> "When Winston Churchill met with Josip Broz Tito in August, 1944 the deal had already been done. Earlier that year Ivan Subasic negotiated the agreement whereby Tito would become the President of the new Yugoslavia after the defeat of the Germans. This meeting, at an historic hotel in Naples, was ratification - personal recognition by the great patrician statesman of the revolutionary peasant guerrilla. The conversations were amicable, the mood relaxed yet imbued with a strong sense of irony. Churchill, scion of the House of Marlborough, aristocratic leader of one of the world's great powers and defender

of the free world, sat in deference to Tito, the seventh of 15 children of a Croatian peasant family, a man with barely five years of formal education who had spent more of his adult years in prison than out. And, as a communist, Tito was aligned with Russia, Churchill's anticipated post-war problem.

But Tito was in the catbird seat. Ivan Subasic, the Prime Minister of the Yugoslav government-in-exile, had been Churchill's choice to lead the new government. And Draza Mihailovic, the leader of the Chetnik guerrillas and Tito's military rival, his choice for military commander. Instead, the success of Tito's Partisans in preventing complete Axis control of Yugoslavia had created his dominant power base. Thus Churchill gave Tito his blessing. With the defeat of the Germans in 1945, Tito assumed control of Yugoslavia and Ivan Subasic became Foreign Minister. In the ensuing months the fledgling Royalist/Partisan coalition government gave way to a communist dictatorship. Tito crushed all opposition with a campaign of terror, particularly against the remnants of fascism in Croatia. Political enemies were imprisoned and some, including Mihailovic, were executed. Ivan Subasic resigned." *

*B.G.Conway. The Sublime Taste of Hatred, Foreword, p. X11

At Ljubljana Parker stepped out onto the platform and bought, from a kiosk, bread, sausage, and a beer which he ate and drank before falling into a deep sleep as the train rumbled and swayed its way into Zagreb.

The city was as he'd imagined. He walked several blocks past squat grey buildings that hunkered over streets devoid of shops, passing people who moved purposefully, their eyes on the pavement. It was dark when he found a hotel. The room was cold, the windows without curtains, the floor dirty ceramic tiles. But there was a fluffy duvet on the bed and the sheets were clean and crinkly to the touch. He showered and shaved and then he slept again.

In the morning the desk clerk, who spoke English, directed him to a building that defied Zagreb's otherwise drab countenance. It rose, in stages, ten stories out of an expanse of manicured lawn and bore the symmetry of the Viennese Jugendstil. He entered a room, passing a female soldier who stood, expressionless, with a submachine gun slung over her shoulder. Another woman sat behind a desk and muttered in Slav while she inspected his passport and then handed him a document to sign. She held up three fingers and said "*tri*," which he took to mean he had three days before he was to report again to some official office somewhere.

At the train station, he found an agent who, like most Croatians, spoke some German which Parker also spoke enough of to enable them to communicate. They, with the help of the Australian's map, were able to build an itinerary. The agent sold him a return ticket first to Banja Luka, where he would change trains, and then to Doboj where he would have a six hour wait for the train to Teslic. He felt a ripple of relief and affection for the ticket agent who was smiling proudly. The awareness of having been lost seemed more acute now that he'd found his way. He paid for the ticket in German marks and then went back to the hotel to check out, where he also settled the bill with marks.

> "In Zagreb, in the spring of 1941, Ivan Subasic prepared for his evacuation to London. As the last Ban of Croatia (roughly the equivalent of provincial or state leader

in Canada or Australia) he attended to procedures to effect the dissolution of his government as the invading German army approached. There were many details. One, which he neglected, was the release of the communists, many of whom were Serbian, from Croatian prisons. Dr. Ante Pavelic stepped into the vacuum left by Subasic's departure to create the fascist Independent State of Croatia. Pavelic's paramilitary, the Ustashe, executed the communist prisoners and began to cleanse Croatia of ethnic minorities. This included the annihilation of whole villages with the attendant atrocities such that even the Nazis were impressed. In May, 1941, Pavelic received a private audience with Pope Pius XII in Rome.

"The basis for the Ustashe movement is religion. For minorities such as the Serbs, Jews, and Gypsies, we have three million bullets. We will kill a part of the Serbs. Others we will deport, and the rest we will force to accept the Roman Catholic Religion. Thus the new Croatia will be rid of all Serbs in its midst in order to be 100% Catholic within 10 years." (Mile Budak, Minister for Education

and Culture, Independent State of Croatia, July, 1942)

Between 1941 and 1945 the Ustashe killed over half a million Serbs, expelled a quarter million and forced 200,000 to convert to Catholicism. The main extermination camp was at Jasenovac. There were no gas chambers at Jasenovac. The killing was done less efficiently - one death at a time. It was there, one evening in 1942, that one of the guards, Petar Brzica, won prizes, including a gold watch, in a macabre contest. Within a few hours he killed 1360 prisoners by slitting their throats with a small curve-bladed knife." *

*B.G.Conway. The Sublime Taste of Hatred, Foreword p. X

PART TWO: DOBOJ AND TESLIC

The train rolled south and east through an undulating plateau, its landscape draped now in fall fallow and peppered with livestock. Cattle and goats. Crossing into Bosnia it entered forested hills that grew gradually into mountains. Once or twice, to the northeast, Parker caught a glimpse of the white peaks of the Transylvanian and Balkan ranges, those so deeply embedded in the violent mythology of the region. Through them flows the legendary Danube, the access route of an endless succession of invading armies that over centuries laid siege to Belgrade, each time destroying the city. Small wonder that civilization has shallow roots in this place.

It was late afternoon when he arrived in Doboj, which appeared at first to be nothing but a vast rail yard animated and energized by arriving and departing passenger and freight trains. Several locomotives chugged and thumped and belched steam and acrid smoke as they shunted railcars onto sidings. In a distant corner, well separated from the main terminal, stood a small building. After wandering about Parker discovered it to be the station for the train to Teslic. The train had not yet arrived and it would not leave again for Teslic until eleven. He had six hours to kill - then another hour out into the darkness. After that? Well, he'd slept outdoors before, including once in a graveyard beside a church in Munich during Oktoberfest. He figured he'd be ok if it didn't rain and the Ozzies didn't find him.

> "It was at Doboj, in April 1941, that Serbian Colonel Draza Mihailovic disobeyed orders to surrender to the invading

German army. Mihailovic, with a group of loyal officers, created the Free Yugoslav Army, the Chetniks. The Chetniks can be considered the natural heirs of the Black Hand, the Serbian nationalist movement behind Gavrilo Princip's assassination of the Austrian Archduke Ferdinand in Sarajevo in 1914 – the spark that ignited World War I. Tito's communist Partisans did not join the resistance until Germany invaded Russia later that year. Initially the Chetniks were the only effective opposition to the Nazi invaders. Mihailovic established radio contact with the Yugoslav Government-in-exile in London and was appointed military commander. But as Tito's Partisans became the dominant guerrilla movement, the two groups fell into internecine conflict, mainly along ideological lines; Serbian nationalist Chetniks against communist Partisans. Tito prevailed, usurping Mihailovic's preferred position with Winston Churchill and the Yugoslav government-in-exile. With his assumption of power at the end of the war, Tito executed Mihailovic." *

*B.G.Conway. The Sublime Taste of Hatred, Foreword p.XIII

Parker crossed the network of tracks to the town which clustered around a dominant medieval fortress. Lights along the main street were coming on and shops were closing. He'd not eaten since Zagreb. He passed several cafés and bars, all closed. There were few vehicles on the street.

Gradually the town emptied of pedestrians including Muslim women who, in their distinctive headscarves and full-length robes, seemed to glide, footless, as they moved. Near the end of the street he found a small café tucked, as if in a cave, into the ramparts of the fortress. Everyone in the place was smoking, even the waiter. He found a table and set his rucksack on the chair opposite and sat down and lit a cigarette. The waiter appeared from behind a curtained doorway and set a jug of red wine and a glass tumbler on the table. He said nothing. Before Parker could speak, he turned and disappeared behind the curtain. The couple at the next table was eating what looked like small white dumplings soaked in a red sauce.

"Was ist das?" Parker asked, pointing to the food.

The man gave him a blank look. The woman continued to eat.

He tried again. "Sprechen Sie Deutsch?"

The man shrugged and resumed his meal. Parker drank the wine and waited for the waiter to reappear. When he did he ignored him. Parker got up and followed the waiter behind the curtain into the kitchen where he encountered three startled faces. One, the cook, stood square to him, legs apart and holding, almost casually, a large knife.

"Ich habe hunger." Parker tried to remember the Slav word for food.

The cook stepped toward him. Parker raised his hand and forced a smile.

"*Hrana.*" He pointed to his mouth and rubbed his belly.

The cook and the waiter grinned and then guffawed in unison, "*Dobro, hrana!*"

Parker returned to his table and watched as the waiter, tall and lithe, slid effortlessly between the tables, depositing plates laden with food. Dressed in black, he melded into the surrounding gloom. Patrons sat, in twos and threes, at more than half of the dozen or so small tables. Some silent and motionless except for the mechanical raising and lowering of their arms and hands as they ate and drank. Others, equally unanimated, conversed quietly so that all he could hear was a low, toneless drone.

Virtually everyone, male and female, was smoking. On each table a candle, stuck in an empty wine bottle, burned. These formed the major source of light in the room, each flickering in its own aura within the enveloping, smoky haze. They were augmented only by dull electric light bulbs mounted in wrought iron sconces attached to the walls. These lights blurred eerily through the smoke, as if masked with gauze. And they cast ragged shadows across the windowless, rough-hewn, stone walls. The timbered ceiling was barely visible above an undulating layer of cigarette and candle smoke. Parker tilted the candle toward him and lit a cigarette and sat waiting in this strange room. He felt no company with these mannequin-like beings consigned to a smoke-filled cellar. Doboj's ante-room?

But the room was warm and Parker removed his jacket. And the quiet settled him. He let the shadows enclose him as he poured the wine into the tumbler. It overflowed and traced a rivulet across the table to drip over the edge onto his jeans. He drank from the brimming glass. Then he refilled it, taking care this time not to spill. He turned the glass on the table and watched the swirling blood-red liquid. It was a dense, coarse, country wine that was warm and familiar in his throat such that it leavened the strangeness of the room. There was a red splotch on the leg of his jeans, dramatic on the sand-bleached denim. Goldie's father made wine like this. In his root cellar beside the sawdust shed behind the house in the town in British Columbia where Parker grew up.

Presently the waiter set down a plate of what tasted like *kartoffeln* in a spicy red sauce. Parker ate quickly and the waiter reappeared with more wine and a steaming bratwurst with bread and mustard which he also ate quickly. The waiter stood over him, grinning, and said "*hrana*" as he rubbed his belly.

The hand resting on his shoulder roused Parker from the torpor he had drifted into following his meal. He sat up in his chair and the waiter, gesturing toward the door, spoke to him in Slav, the only part of which Parker understood was "*prijatelj*" (my friend). He looked around. The candles on the tables still flickered but the room was empty. He stood and took two 10-mark notes from his wallet and handed them to the waiter. He shrugged as if to say, "How much?" The waiter, his former grin now subdued to a smile, folded the notes twice over and deftly inserted them into Parker's shirt pocket. Parker sensed that there was more to this than simply the gift of a meal so he did not protest. The waiter followed him to the door and as Parker stepped out into the night, his rucksack slung over one shoulder, the waiter murmured, *"Sigurno putovanje."*

The street was deserted except for three boys who stood on the corner as if they were waiting for a bus. School kids in their early teens. One had books and papers bound by a belt and slung over his shoulder. Another, the biggest boy, had a deranged look to him. As he drew closer Parker discovered that he had a wall-eye. The night was still and very cold. Street lights, sparkling in the cold air, formed a corridor in the darkness. At its end was the rail yard.

The boys' eyes followed him as he passed. Lightly dressed without jackets, they stood against the cold with their shoulders hunkered down into their chests. Parker crossed to the iron gate on the ramp that led to the entrance of the fortress and shook it. It was secured with a chain and a padlock. Deterred, he headed along the street-lit corridor toward the train yard. By the time he reached the tracks he had attracted a procession of children, some 30 or so and mostly smaller and younger than the original three who had assumed the lead and were now close on his heels. They streamed behind, chattering and whispering, in a bizarre cavalcade led by a reluctant Pied Piper. Parker felt like he had been cast into a morality fable that seemed more like a film noir movie.

He also felt crowded. There was no one else in sight. As the group grew in size it grew bolder. The wall-eyed boy, who was as tall as Parker, spoke to him in Slav and when Parker didn't answer, he turned to his audience with a grin and a dismissive wave of his arm. His next remark, more direct, sounded like a challenge. Parker was now surrounded in the middle of an expanse of intersecting railway tracks. The earlier activity, the passing and shunting trains, had quieted. He slipped his hand into his jacket pocket and felt the smooth bone handle of the switchblade he'd bought in Genoa. Who are these kids? What are they doing hanging around these deserted streets late at night? They weren't urchins dressed in rags. Some of them carried schoolbooks.

In the distance he saw the train to Teslic had arrived at the station. An ancient steam engine with a potbellied funnel that looked like something out of a Western movie. Attached to it were three small passenger cars and a caboose. Smoke and steam from the engine drifted across the rail yard. He stepped toward it and as he pushed through the crowd he felt a sharp nudge below his ribs. An elbow.

Parker heaved his pack before him and clambered up into the coach. It was Spartan-bare with simple wooden benches aligned forward, on either side of an aisle, like pews in a rough country church. The children followed, scrambling in helter-skelter like hobbits in anticipation of some strange encounter. At the end of the aisle a fire burned in a black iron stove bolted to the floor. The stove had a hinged door in front and there was a small glass portal on it and the flames, curling and dancing behind the glass, cast an amber glow into the dark recesses of the coach. This was the only light. Around and behind him shadowy heads bobbed and curious eyes stared.

The windows were fogged from the moisture of breaths and bodies come in from the cold outside and crammed shoulder to shoulder on the benches. The wall-eyed boy sat next to him on the front bench. He stared and grunted questions in Slav and then turned to shrug and smirk to his audience when Parker didn't answer. Was it menace he saw in that contorted visage, or simply vacancy?

Parker was sweating. The closeness of the room, its awkward intimacy, was claustrophobic. He gripped the switchblade, finding reassurance in the button on the spring trigger which if pressed, would snap the six-inch shaft erect from its cradle in the handle. He visualized the knife released. A miniature sword. A deadly cross, the blade separated from the handle by the transept of the cross guard.

A small boy crept out of the shadows and sat cross-legged on the floor in front of Parker. His garments were barely better than rags. His coarse woven shirt hung listless across bony shoulders. The stove light burnished his sallow, raised-up face. The reflected flames flickered in his eyes. He reached over and ran his fingertip along the inseam near the hem of one leg of Parker's Levis. With one hand the wall-eyed boy grasped the child's hand and he raised the other, threatening to strike. Parker rose and stood between them. He gripped the unleashed knife. There was no sound. Nothing spoken. The children remained frozen to the benches, and as he stared down into that one focused eye a chill rippled through him.

And then that eye was looking past him. He turned and saw a soldier enter the coach followed by the conductor, who pointed to him and beckoned with the flattened palm of his hand, fingers upraised. He led Parker out into the cold night. The Australian flashed through his mind. He had a brief vision of himself alone in a windowless room. He glanced back to see the children, his erstwhile retinue, immobile on the wooden benches, their eyes fixed on him. He followed the conductor two cars forward and into a compartment in what appeared to be a first class car. The conductor nodded and then disappeared. Parker stowed his rucksack on the rack above and settled into the plush seat. It took a few minutes for him to adjust to the abrupt transition from the tense encounter with the children to the relative calm of this compartment. By now he had lost the sense of anticipation that had been building since Genoa. Teslic could still be a whole continent away, not just 23 clicks down the line. He shivered as if he were cold, vaguely aware of the cool night air that wafted in through the half-open compartment window.

The compartment was full. Across from Parker a young woman perched eagerly between two older men who, like crumpled puppets, dozed while propped upright, their fleshy chins each collapsed onto their chests. Beside him sat a young man dressed in a suit and tie and cradling a briefcase on his lap. He spoke to Parker in German.

"They have been watching you."

"Yes?"

"Yes, since you arrived. No one comes here alone in the night with a rucksack and can not speak to go to Teslic."

"How do you know this?"

"The conductor." The man nodded toward the compartment door. "He spoke with the agent and they decided it best for you to be in this car." The man smiled and offered his hand. "I am Dusko. Dusko Peresic."

"Parker. Parker Wells," he exhaled and slumped deeper into the padded seat. "It is good to be able to talk with someone. It is a relief."

"Why do you go to Teslic?"

"To find a woman. The sister of a friend in Canada."

"Who is this woman? Do you know her?"

"I only know her name. Maya Petrovic."

There was a pause.

The engine built up a head of steam and smoke and cinders blew in through the half open compartment window. As he rose to close it, Dusko Peresic said, as if in passing, "I know this woman."

Parker wasn't sure he'd heard correctly.

Then Dusko Peresic repeated, "Ich kenne diese frau."

This woman?

"Ich kenne Maya Petrovic."

Parker feels the train move. An almost imperceptible nudge. And he wonders, momentarily, if it is actually something that he feels within. His mind sifts back through a host of images in flux as passengers get on and get off trains. They come and go, each pursuing his or her own mission, pausing briefly to explain, the occasional one to become, if not a fixture in his life, then forever in his memory. As such this young stranger who, seemingly in the order of things, Parker finds waiting in the seat beside him in a crowded compartment in a railcar pulled forward by an ancient steam engine on a surreal journey through the Slavic darkness. This Dusko Peresic. Whose casual utterance speaks to his, Parker's, assumed burden of another man's forlorn, forty-year-old memory and he feels a sudden lightness around his shoulders - much like the sensation, at the end of a day's journey, when he stops to slip the straps to let the weight of his rucksack fall away. *Ich kenne Maya Petrovic.* Just like that.

He was a civil servant in Sarajevo, a few years older than Parker and married. He grew up in Teslic and was on his way there to visit his mother. His father was dead. He was animated with questions about the West, his bright eyes fuelled with interest. As the train wheezed and rumbled on into the night, Parker talked: more words in one short hour than during the previous three days combined.

It was midnight when they walked through the unlit village streets. An occasional light shone from a window. Presently, on a dark road where only the vague forms of dwellings were visible, Dusko Peresic pointed to one and said, “My mother lives there. And here,” he approached the house next to it, “lives Milan and Maya Petrovic”

He pounded on the door and a male voice answered from the adjacent window. Dusko replied in Slav. Parker only understood the mention of his name. The porch shook as Milan Petrovic thumped along the hallway. The door banged open and Parker was clutched into an almost suffocating embrace. Rough stubble cheeks, garlic breath, faint smell of stale sweat, soft flannel of the nightshirt. Hold on! Do you know who I am? Maybe you've got the wrong guy.

Then Maya. Her face wet with tears.

Dusko laughed, “They were expecting you.”

“So it seems.”

Dusko turned to Maya. “Er spricht Deutsch.”

He stepped into the darkness. “Wiedersehn.”

“Wiedersehn, und danke.” Parker never saw him again.

Maya Petrovic wrapped her night robe to her and said, “Kommen, kommen Sie hier.”

Her husband waited beside her, stubble-faced and bleary-eyed, his nightshirt drooping. Parker set the rucksack on the floor and stood silently, as if at attention. They surveyed each other somewhere within the parameters of surprise, confusion and disbelief. They exchanged glances as if trying to decide what to do next. Presently Maya said, "Sitzen Sie." She pointed to a dilapidated sofa and then she and her husband disappeared into an adjoining room. Parker could hear them in conversation beyond the wall. She reappeared with a pillow and a duvet and set them on the sofa and then took him into the bedroom. Milan was in bed under a duvet. Beside him was another duvet, folded back. "Schlafen Sie," she said. She would sleep on the sofa.

He protested, "Nein, nein, I cannot take your bed."

"Then you may sleep on the floor." She grinned and shut the door.

When Parker woke, Milan was gone. He found Maya waiting for him in the other room which, with the bedroom, comprised their dwelling. It was spare and clean. Linoleum floor, a throw rug, chintz curtains, the sofa and a matching chair, a large round table and chairs in the centre, and a wooden radio console in one corner. The walls were bare with the exception of a large, framed, colour photograph of a striking young woman. The picture brightened the otherwise drab room. Maya brought coffee and hot rolls from the kitchen which she and Milan shared with the family in the adjoining suite. Her face, her cheeks, creased with vertical lines, cheated her years which Parker guessed to be about 60. Her dark, furrowed skin was suffused with a satin patina that softened her otherwise stern, vital, Slavic visage. She poured the coffee and the interrogation began.

"Where do you come from?"

"A town in Canada. Duncan. Where your brother lives."

"You are his friend?"

"Yes. His daughter, Goldie, was my girlfriend."

"Goldie? Zlata?"

"Yes, Zlata."

"Why did you come?" She was both eager and apprehensive.

He had anticipated this question. The answer was complicated. Such that he had enough trouble rationalizing it to himself, let alone to this incredulous woman. Images of Old Conway and of Goldie flashed through his mind. But as they talked she began to relax and accept that a stranger had come a long way to seek her out simply as a favour to a friend. That was enough for her. He sensed that the possibilities inherent in that idea were almost overwhelming. She could take it as a sign that things would be better between her and her brother. That there would be healing. That a person who makes a difficult journey in the name of friendship can be nothing other than proof of goodwill. She kept smiling and shaking her head. Her warmth was palpable. She glowed. He saw no point in mentioning that his motives also included curiosity and adventure, which probably were secondary and had now diminished even further.

She produced a photo album full of black and white pictures, some old enough to be sepia-toned, of relatives, including brothers and sisters now living in North America. Her brother John appeared, as a young man, in many of them. The man Parker knew as Pop. There were several photos of a younger Maya with two men, one young, one mature, as well as photos of them individually. They looked alike, both tall and lean - typical of South Slavic men. Maya did not identify them but Parker took them to be father and son. "Wer sind Sie?" he asked.

"Miene mann und miene sonne," she murmured.

"Wo sind Sie?"

"Tot," she replied in a barely audible voice.

She turned away from him, her face suddenly featureless, no longer creased with happy animation. Fools blunder into an uninvited space and he sensed it best to retreat silently, to not even offer condolence lest it take him in even deeper. He had noticed that there were no photos of Milan, her second husband, nor any of his previous family, but now he would not ask, need not ask, why. He had been surprised by the warmth of his welcome, unanticipated, the impact that much greater when cast against the loneliness, anxiety and even fear he'd known in the getting to this place. Serendipity seemed to be the only word that fit. And there was something else. He had never seen a face so consumed with radiant wonder as the face that Maya presented to him as he stood before her in the middle of the previous night. That his mere presence could elicit such a response spoke of something much deeper. Something he could not, and would never, comprehend. He simply knew that his arrival had been a validation of his journey and that he was starting to figure out why he had come and he was mindful that it was not for him to be a voyeur to the tragedy of others.

He looked at the picture of the young woman on the opposite wall and realized that this was John Starich's daughter, the woman known to her father only in an old photograph and, directly or indirectly, one of the reasons why Goldie had sent him here. Yet now Parker hesitated to ask about her and Maya did not volunteer. So it went unsaid.

The silence lasted for a moment and then, smiling again, she returned to the album. She turned the pages, pausing long enough to identify certain people in the photos. Until one page, where she hesitated, holding it momentarily between her thumb and forefinger. Then she turned it and he was conscious of her gaze upon him as he looked at the single photo mounted in the middle of the page - and saw there a recent photograph of himself.

It took a few seconds for Parker to adjust to the presence of his smiling visage. Most unnerving was the sense that he beheld an imposter - a manufactured image of himself that had pre-empted his arrival to this place. Yet there he was, in vivid colour, captured by the camera in an instant of the past and preserved in time forever. He found it uncanny, especially in that this photograph should now be here, unexpected and waiting for him in a place that, until now, he had only heard of and had existed only in his imagination. His palms were sweaty and he rubbed them on the thighs of his jeans. He felt flushed and he glanced at Maya and wondered if she sensed his discomfort.

Parker had a thing about cameras. Mechanical eyes that could freeze time. He found the whole process fascinating, and not just the science. He considered Louis Daguerre and George Eastman magicians, if not geniuses, but there was more to it. In photographs that others took for granted, often with simply a cursory glance, quickly turning the pages of a magazine or photo album, Parker saw mysteries revealed in details otherwise missed or ignored when observed by the human eye. Especially in spontaneous photos of people. Those that were inwardly revealing. He was suspicious of portraits that disguised the subject's persona in a pose that manipulated the cast of the eyes, the tilt of the head and the symmetry of a smile. On occasion, when studying a photo of a family or a group of friends he imagined the pain that was masked by the smiles.

He avoided the camera. He could be detected in the obligatory group photos to do with events such as his graduation from high school, his subsequent undergraduate degree from the University of British Columbia and his MA from the same institution, but not much else. This quirk was part of a consciousness that was not shared with anyone that he knew, neither friends nor classmates. This included his sense of being animate, human, and that as such he was simply in transit and that there was ever only one event that could and would suspend the journey - that would stop time. So he kept it to himself. He had no one close enough to notice, or care. His parents were dead and he had no siblings. There was just Goldie. She noticed. And she cared.

Now, as he contemplated his face staring up at him from Maya's photo album, Parker recalled the scene. It was shortly before he left for Europe and Goldie wanted this one picture "to remember him by." He was sitting at a table in a room, Goldie's father's kitchen, a room not dissimilar to where he now sat. There was even, on the wall behind him, a framed photograph of a young woman blurred in the background by the close-up focus of the camera. Goldie had dangled the camera in front of him. "See Parker, it's just a little black box. There's no gremlin inside. You can play the ignorant, stone-age, Borneo head hunter shtick all you want but this thing isn't going to steal your soul. Geez, look at you. All you need now is a little pointy piece of bone sticking through your nostrils."

He smiled at that. And she snapped the picture.

Parker read the letter attached to the page opposite the photo. It was addressed to Maya Petrovic, Teslic, Bosnia, Yugoslavia and written in English. Between the lines someone had translated it to Serbo-Croatian. In it Goldie introduced herself as the adult daughter of John Starich, mentioned that her mother died years ago, and wrote, "I hope this letter finds its way to you." She continued with a brief but poignant statement of her desire to reunite Maya with her father whom she described as "mellowing with age but still too proud to make the first move."

She concluded, "Enclosed is a picture of my friend Parker. He is somewhere in Europe and before he left here I asked him to go to Yugoslavia to find you. He said he might if he had time. I believe he will and when he does please accept him as a messenger of my sincerity. I know he will come. I know him."

Parker smiled. Yes, she knows me. She knows how to pull my strings.

Maya sat watching him across the table. He looked up and met her gaze.

"Es ist Sie," she said

"Ja, es ist mir," he replied.

"Sie kam," she said, "Sie kam."

Maya took Parker into the village where a few shops clustered around a modest church. A lone streetlight was suspended above the intersection of two streets. Beyond, he could see the chimneys of the chemical plant where, she said, her husband worked. He sensed that this was not so much a tour of Teslic but more the opportunity to display the strange young man that had appeared at her doorstep in the middle of the night. And so it was with an air of bravado that she escorted him into the local men's club, a pavilion-like building where men sat drinking Turkish coffee on a wide veranda in defiance of the November chill. She introduced him to a dignified, elderly man, a retired doctor, who spoke fluent English. After a brief conversation in Slav, with gestures toward Parker, she left.

The doctor sat huddled against the raw morning in a woollen great coat and a snap-brim fedora tilted low over his forehead, from under which escaped a wisp of silver. A paisley cravat peeked out beneath his chin. He turned and with his index finger touched his hat brim and gestured to Parker to sit down. The greeting was so casual that it struck Parker that he had anticipated him. There was a sense of familiarity, as if they had met before. And yet, in spite of his seeming insouciance, he spoke with a barely restrained sense of urgency. As if he had been waiting a very long time to speak with someone, anyone, who would come from the outside. From the West. Who spoke English. This old gentleman who sat in his exile, stoic against the lingering depredations of the dead past. In front of him, on the table, red coals smouldered in a small iron receptacle upon which Turkish coffee was warming in a brass, ewer-shaped container.

"You have caused Maya a great surprise," the doctor said.

"I think shock is a better word."

"Yes. But there have been a multitude of shocks. Much tragedy. Her husband. Her son. This is a pleasant shock."

Parker was hesitant but the doctor's familiar manner had disarmed him and he asked, "What happened to them?"

"During the war they came here from Croatia and joined the Chetniks, the Serbian guerrillas. They died, father and son, at the hands of their own countrymen, the Ustashe, at the battle of Lijevce Field near Banja Luka. Do you know it? Banja Luka, I mean?"

"Yes, I changed trains there."

"There was a betrayal. The war was ending and there was negotiated a cease-fire. The Chetniks surrendered. Then the Ustashe commenced with the executions. Do you want me to continue?"

"No, thank you," Parker replied, "that is enough."

He avoided the doctor's eyes. It was all so matter-of-fact, as if they were discussing the weather. The doctor spoke in a measured, even cadence which had the effect of increasing the impact of his words. Parker thought about Maya. To him, considering what he had just heard, her estrangement from her brother seemed insignificant. But, as he had discovered, it was not to her. As the doctor had said, Parker had given her a pleasant shock.

"What became of Maya? Where was she?"

"She stayed in Croatia. In her village near the Slovenian border. She lived with her husband's sister. After the war she came to work at the chemical plant. She met Milan there. He too had lost his family. He is Serbian. The Ustashe locked his wife and children in their house and then burnt it down." A thin smile crept beneath the doctor's moustache. He poured the coffee - a thick, viscous liquid - into two small cups. "You are curious," he said, "that is good. But you may not believe what you hear and even then it may well make you ill."

They watched Maya recede along the street. A black shrouded form, shawl, dress, and stockings, diminishing with the distance, until she turned and entered the church.

The doctor did continue. He seemed compelled and Parker realized that to be able to speak with this man, in this alien place, in such a strange circumstance, was a gift.

"And so, she is very happy. This is unusual." He looked at Parker quizzically. "She is, how would you say, symbolic of this land? There are many like her. They appear on Sundays as an army in a uniform of black. For their dead fathers, husbands, sons and brothers they bear witness to their God. It is all they can do. They are powerless in the presence of the evil and violence that is done by men in the name of their God and by their God to them."

"He is not your God?"

"There is no God."

He spoke evenly, without inflection. He raised his cup to his lips and looked across at Parker. He had pale, clear, blue eyes.

"But today," he said, "I suspect she goes to the church for a different reason."

"You speak as if you know her well."

"We come from the same village. In Croatia. There were, if I recall correctly, five brothers and two sisters. The father was dead. The one brother, John, your friend in Canada, she was closest to him. It has been hard for her. His anger."

"She wants me to visit a woman in Zagreb. A cousin, I believe, named Vlasta."

He nodded. "She will use the telephone here in the club to arrange it. Her cousin is Vlasta Subasic. Perhaps you know the name?"

Subasic. "I know of a man. Ivan Subasic."

"He is the one. He was Vlasta's husband."

This was something Goldie hadn't told him. He doubted she even knew that this woman existed. Let alone that she was the wife of Ivan Subasic. Or that she was related to Maya.

Parker asked the doctor. "You knew Ivan Subasic?"

"We were in the war together. The first war. At Salonika. I knew who he was. Later I knew him in the Croatian Peasant Party. When he was the Ban of Croatia."

"That was in 1939?"

"Yes. When the Germans invaded he was evacuated with the king. To London. When he returned at the end of the last war there were those among us who saw him as a fresh wind that would breathe a new life into the corpse that was our country. But he was no match for Tito. After a few months in Belgrade he went back to Zagreb and ten years later he died. He was a good man. One of an honourable few. There has never been democracy here. Slavs feast at a table laden with hatred. They choke to death on it. It is a curse that haunts our people.

"You know of the horror of the war? Yes? The Nazi atrocities? The Jews? The Russian winters? Millions dead all over Europe. But few know how terrible it was here in the Balkans. Tito closed the history books. And I, in talking to you about it now, take a risk. But I am old and only the young are not hostage to the truth. The old are unwise to take it with them to the grave. Nearly two million people died. Many civilians including women and children. Croats, Serbs, Slovenes, Bosnian Muslims, Jews, Gypsies. One-tenth of our population. As a nation only Poland lost more. The tragedy is that, while the Nazis killed so many of us, we Yugoslavs killed each other more. It was ethnic genocidal madness. The Nazis were efficient executioners. They lined the villagers against a wall and shot them with machine guns. But the Ustashe were the worst. They indulged in an orgy of blood. They were berserk. They did unspeakable things. And the Chetniks. They forgot to fight the Nazis. Instead they fought the Partisans, the communists. And they slaughtered the Muslims. Hung them by their feet and disembowelled them, then watched them die. Once there were many Muslims here in Bosnia. There are fewer now. One day Tito will be gone. Then the killing of the Muslims will commence again. The Partisans were the lesser of the evils but only by comparison. I expect, that even in your country, at times, the line that separates justice from revenge becomes blurred. Here they are, as you would say, one and the same. Such was the case at Bleiburg-Maribor."

The morning had turned bleak. Rain rattled on the tin roof of the pavilion. Dead leaves, wind-blown, swirled and scraped around their feet. All but one of the coffee drinkers had retreated inside. They remained. The doctor said, "I apologize. I did not mean to subject you to such a rant. It must be the memory of Ivan Subasic that brings out this bitterness." His clear eyes had clouded, his tone of voice now modulated. It was as if he wanted Parker to know that there were still, like him, men of decency.

They sat listening to the rain. Presently the doctor spoke. "Did you come here only for Maya?"

"Only? I don't know. I would say mainly. Sometimes it is hard to sort it out. Why one does what one does. I was also curious."

"Yes, you are curious. What do you know about this country?"

"Only what I've read. I studied modern European history."

"The wars?"

"Yes. The wars."

"You came here from Austria?"

"No, from Italy. Trieste."

His voice rose. "Did you see Florence?"

Parker nodded. "Earlier. Then I went to Genoa. Then Trieste.

"Ah!" he said, "Florence is my great nostalgia." His smile was no longer forced. The bitter tone had left his voice. He leaned toward Parker. "Was there much damage? The war, I mean. The bombs."

"Not in the centre of the city. As far as I could tell. No reconstruction. Only along the river. All but one bridge was destroyed and they've been rebuilt. The Duomo was spared."

"The Uffizi?"

"No damage."

"And the Loggia dei Lanzi? The sculptures."

"Yes."

"They are etched in my memory. Cellini. Giambologna. And, of course, Michelangelo. I studied them. Now I have a good feeling to know they survived."

"You were a student in Italy?"

"I was. After the first war I went to the University of Bologna to study medicine. The art, the statues, was, how would you say? A hobby? Yes, a hobby. Perhaps more a passion. I took often the train to Florence. Once, long ago, in my dreams, I wished to be a sculptor."

As the doctor talked the images of those sculptures in the Loggia dei Lanzi drifted behind Parkers eyes. Cellini's Perseus standing triumphantly, his arm outstretched and clutching, by her tangled hair, Medusa's severed head. Her headless body prostrate at his feet. Giambologna's Sabine woman writhing in desperation against the torment of the Roman rapists. He remembered being awestruck by the exquisite power of these icons of the Italian Renaissance. And he remembered his feeling of unease at being so impressed. As plastic renditions of violent mythologies they seemed too real — too material to a brutal reality that persists. Ugly truths rendered exquisite in bronze and marble. The doctor's face was animated now and he seemed to grow younger. Parker wondered if he sensed the irony in his passion.

"When I first went to Italy I did not speak the language. Like you, here. I understand that strange feeling. Then I met another student. A Serbian. It was a relief to be able to talk. We became great friends. You should know this. Five centuries ago the Byzantine culture, in particular Serbia, was on the *edge*. No, I need a better word."

"On the cusp?"

"That is it. On the cusp. Of a great awakening. One could say a renaissance. Like in Italy. But then the Ottoman Turks came and the clock stopped. For over 400 years."

"And your friend? The Serb in Italy."

"Oh, he is dead." His hand drew an arc across the table. "They are all dead."

The back of his hand was like crazed, pale china in a random pattern of light blue veins. Delicate, almost feminine. Not thick and robust as one would imagine that of a sculptor grasping mallet and chisel. Parker imagined the doctor's fingertips, instead, caressing and finding the ever so subtle faults in the marble stone.

"I was young then. And free. I had been on the Salonika front with the Serbs. But the war was over. And Italy is still not far away. Just across a small sea. But I am old and cannot go there now."

"You know," he continued, "freedom is sometimes a trick that is played on you. As one man's flower is another man's weed so it is that one man's dream of freedom is another man's nightmare. Freedom can be frightening. It lacks the boundaries imposed by the tyrant. That is why, in this country, Tito prevails. He has drawn the boundaries and he enforces them with terror. Many prefer this. I prefer Florence."

He settled back in his chair and refilled the tiny cups with Turkish coffee. He raised his cup, as if in salute. "We welcome travellers. We are hospitable. It is of ourselves, of each other, that we have a deep suspicion."

Maya returned and the doctor, his name was Kristanovic, asked him to excuse them. Parker rose and extended his hand which the doctor took, but with his left hand. It was then, when he leaned toward him, that Parker saw his right forearm resting in his lap. The coat sleeve was folded back and pinned neatly where his hand should have been.

They conversed in Slav while Parker sat waiting at the table. Then Maya went inside to use the telephone. Dr. Kristanovic nodded to him as if in reassurance and Parker thanked him. While he waited he noticed, at an adjacent table, the lone remaining coffee drinker. Except he wasn't drinking coffee. He had a bottle of clear liquid, which Parker took to be Slivovitz, and he poured it into a shot glass. He was blind. He didn't sit and stare from sightless eyes. He had no eyes. His eyelids were closed and drooped into the empty sockets. But he was dexterous with the bottle and the glass. He didn't spill a drop. Watching him reminded Parker of a passage in Curzio Malaparte's book *Kaputt* where he wrote of an interview with Ante Pavelic in 1941. There was a wicker basket on Pavelic's desk which seemed to Malaparte to be filled with shelled mussels or oysters, 'as they are occasionally displayed in the windows of Fortnum and Mason in Piccadilly in London.' He asked if they were Dalmatian oysters. Pavelic had replied, 'It is a present from my loyal Ustashis, forty pounds of human eyes.'

Maya emerged from inside the pavilion and took Parker to the local Communist Party office where, in an eerie rerun of the scene in Zagreb, they entered past the ubiquitous grey-uniformed, submachine gun carrying, soldier and a severe, humourless woman registered him as a visitor to the village. He then returned, with Maya, to her home where he slept through the afternoon. He awoke to the aroma of paprika and the essence of hot food. He discovered his road-grimed clothes had been washed and were still damp. Mara handed him dry socks, jeans, and a shirt that she'd hung above the kitchen stove. The table was laden with steaming bowls of potatoes, turnip, cabbage rolls and a platter of fried chicken. Milan was already seated. For the first time since he had arrived Parker was able to get a good look at him - a round full face, bald, the impish grin of a mischievous troll. Maybe a jolly man in an earlier life. Now he looked weary. And hungry.

Maya passed the chicken. "Essen Sie. Das ist hendl."

Parker mistook *hendl* to be the word for *shirt* in German. "Nein," he said, tugging on his shirt-tail, "*das ist hemd.*"

"Nein, nein, das ist *hendl!*" She flapped her arms and clucked like a chicken. Milan, who had produced a bottle of homemade plum brandy, burst into laughter and nearly fell off his chair. They ate the food and drank the brandy. He told them about his home on the west coast of Canada. About Vancouver Island where immigrants like her brother had come to work in the coal mines and in the forests where the trees grew to over 300 feet tall. He talked about the whales in the ocean and the rivers full of salmon in the fall. Maya translated for Milan.

Parker told them about the countries he had passed through. England, France, Spain, Germany, Italy, and Austria. They listened with great interest. They had been once, singly, before the war, to Trieste.

He gave Maya a piece of Venetian glass that he had wrapped in a pair of his socks and stowed in the middle of his rucksack. He was relieved that it was not broken. And he gave Milan three packages of Gauloises. He thanked them for their warm hospitality.

Maya said, "Tomorrow you will go to Vlasta in Zagreb. She expects you."

PART THREE: ZAGREB

The taxi stopped in front of a drab four-story building that separated two parallel streets. It appeared to have once been stylish, fronted with a gently curved facade and a portico supported by four columns. Now a crumbling veneer of stucco, which had once been white, revealed the grey concrete beneath. The late afternoon light was fading. The driver gestured toward a figure in the shadows of a building entrance across the street. He spoke German.

"Gestapo," he said

"Gestapo?"

"Yes. Tito's Ozna watches this building. You will be watched."

There wasn't much about Vlasta Subasic to signify that she had once been the wife of the Prime Minister of Yugoslavia. At least not to Parker. But then, he wouldn't have known what to expect of such a woman. Her greeting was warm. She clasped his hand with both of hers, yet with a slight hesitation, a diffidence, as her eyes met his and then cast away. Petite, greying, almost frail in a black dress, loose at the waist, a single strand of pearls, black patent low-heeled pumps. It struck him that, since his arrival, the only Yugoslav women he'd seen not wearing black were the two hookers on the train from Trieste.

She led him on a creaking parquet floor through the hall into the parlour past a life-sized male bust on a pedestal. "This is my husband, Ivan Subasic," she said with a proud smile that betrayed a hint of embarrassment in introducing a statue. That was it. Otherwise there was a scarcity of anything grand or pretentious about her or her home. No plaques of commemoration on the walls. No photos of auspicious occasions with her and her husband in attendance. Nothing to indicate that they had once travelled in the highest diplomatic circles in Washington and London. The apartment was spacious and dark, lit only by small, ornate wall sconces which cast shadows across the old, perhaps antique, furniture. The place had a temporary feel to it.

She showed him the bedroom where he stood feeling awkward, in his jeans and with his rucksack, in contemplation of its genteel décor. Parker washed, combed his hair, and then joined her in the dining room where she waited with a samovar of tea and cakes. She stood at the window and glanced down before she drew the curtain. She seemed tentative. As if she was waiting for something to happen. As if she'd been waiting a long time.

Vlasta asked about Maya and he told her about his visit and the welcome reception. He also told her about his conversation with Dr. Kristanovic which had left him with questions. Questions he didn't have time to ask.

She smiled. "Maya tells me you know something of my husband."

"Yes, but there is much more that I don't know."

Vlasta, with her fingertips, brushed backed her hair. "You are an interesting young man," she said. "You came here to find Maya. That is easy for me to say but I think there is much that is more difficult to say. Perhaps you might have felt that you were a blind man, just groping your way along. Yes?"

Parker nodded. He was surprised by this woman's interest, that she should even care about how he felt.

"So you found her," she continued, "but there are many in her family who know where she is, including me. She is not hiding. Still I must tell you, this thing, your appearance out of the night, was remarkable to her. On the telephone she was in tears. Happy tears."

Vlasta poured the tea. "It is Darjeeling. My husband's favourite. Was he of interest to you as well?"

"No. But he is now. Being here. In the history books, he is barely recognized - just a brief biography, a mention of the Tito-Subasic agreement, not much else. And I didn't know you existed."

She laughed and spread her arms, palms upraised. "Well, here I am," she said. Parker lit her cigarette and then his. The laugh, the gesture, conveyed warmth and he felt at ease.

> "History is fickle. In 1944, two men met on the island of Vis in the Adriatic Sea. There they made an agreement that would seal the fate of Yugoslavia for the ensuing 34 years. One was Ivan Subasic, the Prime Minister of the Yugoslav government-in-exile. The other was Josip Broz Tito, the communist leader of the Partisans, a guerrilla army engaged in resisting the German occupation of Yugoslavia. They were to become the two most powerful figures in the post war government. They were born in the same year, 1892. Both were Croatian, both were conscripted into the Austro-Hungarian Army in World War I, and both defected to the Russians. There the similarities end. In less than two years, Tito would assume complete control of Yugoslavia and become a pivotal player in Cold War politics. And Subasic would become an historical footnote.

Before he became the Ban of Croatia in 1939, Ivan Subasic had been a theology student at the University of Zagreb. World War I intervened and he was drafted into the Austro-Hungarian army and found himself fighting Serbian forces which were allied with Russia. He defected to the Russians and then fought with the Serbian army against the Austrians on the Salonika Front in Greece. After the war he graduated from the University of Zagreb with a law degree and became politically active. He joined the Croatian Peasant Party and, in 1938, he was elected to the Yugoslav National Assembly which sat in Belgrade. When the Germans invaded in 1941 he was evacuated and became part of the Yugoslav government-in-exile, first as the emissary to the United States and then as Prime Minister. The Tito-Subasic agreement in 1944 preceded Tito's meeting with Winston Churchill in Naples. With the formation of the coalition Yugoslav government after the war, Subasic, as representative of the former government-in-exile, became Tito's Foreign Minister. The coalition lasted eight months until October 1945 when Subasic resigned." *

*B.G.Conway. The Sublime Taste of Hatred, Foreword, p. X1V

Vlasta, serious now, said, "I assume that you know, from what you have read, that my husband was, before the war, the Ban of Croatia. And that we and other officials in the Croatian Peasant Party, along with the king of Yugoslavia, were evacuated to London when the Germans invaded."

Parker nodded and she, unbidden, continued. She said that the evacuation in 1941 left Croatia to Ante Pavelic and his Ustashe who welcomed the Nazis. Pavelic even flew to Berchtesgaden to meet with Hitler.

So, she said, the invaders rolled right through Slovenia and Croatia like they were on a spring vacation. It wasn't until they were well into Bosnia that they met with some resistance. And then the Yugoslav Army surrendered. It took less than two weeks. But Draza Mihailovic refused to surrender and broke away with his Chetniks while, further south, Tito and his Partisans waited and then, after Germany invaded Russia, they joined the resistance.

"You have seen this country. It is mountainous, especially in the south. The hills can hide small armies. Other countries, France, Holland, had underground resistance. But these were conquered and the resistance was weak. Yugoslavia was never fully defeated. The guerrillas fought a running war with the Germans and Tito had political power that was recognized by Churchill, Roosevelt, and Stalin."

Her voice was steady, flat, without inflection and, as the minutes ticked by, Parker realized that he had stumbled into something much deeper than he had ever anticipated. She reminded him of Dr. Kristovanic in his almost desperate desire to talk about it to someone who was detached from it all. The desire to be understood. The irony struck him. This sophisticated worldly woman who had moved, with her husband, through the so-called corridors of power at the most critical period in history, speaking of these tragedies with sincerity and without irony to an itinerant stranger who had wandered in with no claim on the world save whatever he carried in the canvas pack that he strapped to his shoulders. And she was prepared to feed him and put him up for the night. Parker sensed that she would go on much longer so he sat back, resolute in silence, to listen.

She said that her husband was an optimist, and he was naïve. He believed in the treaty that he and Tito signed at Vis. Among other things, there was a clause that specified that Yugoslavia would become a Federation governed by democratically elected representatives. He believed, she said, that there could be co-operation between the non-communists who were mainly Croats and the communists who were mainly Serbs. But Tito had a different agenda. Her husband soon learned that Tito was a brutal tyrant determined to turn Yugoslavia into a communist dictatorship. And too, he misread the depth of hatred that Croats and Serbs feel for each other. "We weren't here during the war to witness the atrocities. Bleiburg-Maribor gave us a taste of it. That was enough.

"Ivan Subasic was one of three Royalists appointed to the new government. The others were Dr. Juraj Sutej who, with my husband, was a member of the Croatian Peasant Party, and Dr. Milan Grol, a leader in the Serbian Democratic Party. Officially they resigned but they were all, essentially, purged by Tito when he cancelled the democratic elections planned for 1946. The Ozna kept a vehicle and four armed men in front of Sutej's apartment and followed him everywhere he went. They watched us here at our home as well, but not as obviously. Tito had an abiding fear of democratic political organizations, especially the Croatian Peasant Party. Grol's magazine, Democatija, was banned and he has been under house arrest since he was purged. All three were fortunate to remain alive. Possibly because of their ties to London and Washington. And Tito was mindful of his betrayal. Since then he has worked to rebuild bridges to the West. In Russia we would all be dead. The leader of the Slovenian Old Rights Party, Dr. Nagode, was not so lucky. Tito executed him in 1947. And Milovan Djilas, who was once Tito's right hand man, is back in jail again for writing about Tito's corrupt and tyrannical regime."

Vlasta paused. She produced a silver cigarette case, opened it and offered it to Parker. She took one and he lit it and then lit his own. They smoked in silence, producing a blue haze that drifted and clung in the yellow light of the wall sconces. She seemed to have diminished. To have faded into the beige upholstery of her chair. She drew on the cigarette, inhaling deeply as if to catch her breath. He didn't interrupt with questions. He would let her continue when she was ready. When she resumed she spoke with the same deliberation, in a measured cadence. The same dull monotone without inflection, but her voice had softened to a whisper. Parker held his teacup but he hadn't tasted it. The tea had gone cold.

"The Germans created a special, you could say elite but I choke on the word, army to fight the guerrillas. The Prinz Eugen Waffen SS. I cannot imagine there could have been any Nazi division that was more brutal. For every soldier killed by the resistance the Germans vowed to kill twelve Yugoslavs. In reality it was more; and most often women and children. A popular method was to herd their victims into houses and then burn them to the ground. But because the South Slavic nature is bloody-minded, this savage retribution did not stop the guerrillas. So the slaughter continued. Eventually the tide, as they say, turned. The Germans were losing the war all over Europe, including here. As they retreated, and the Partisans pushed north, the revenge killings began. As far as the Partisans were concerned every Croatian was the enemy, whether Ustashe or not. It was a combination of bloodlust and politics. A communist cleansing of Croatia. Tito was efficient in crushing all opposition. Hundreds of thousands of refugees fled toward the Austrian border where the British were in control. These included not only Croatians but ethnic minorities as well. I doubt there were any Jews. The Ustashe had already exterminated them. They were stopped at Bleiburg-Maribor."

"On May 15, 1945, following the defeat of the Nazis, a long column of refugees fleeing Tito's Partisan army began arriving at the Austrian fortress town of Bleiburg, just inside the border with Yugoslavia. The British 5th Corps., which was in control of the area, already held about 30,000 Croatian POW's. The new arrivals were mainly civilians but also included Ustashe and Domobran (Croatian regular army) military units. The column, estimated to be in excess of 100,000 people, was stopped in a shallow valley south of the town. The Croatian General Herencic, who represented the refugees, attempted to negotiate a surrender with British Brigadier General Patrick Scott. This was frustrated by the arrival of the Partisan General Milan Basta who persuaded Scott that the refugees should be turned over to the Partisans with the assurance of humane treatment. Scott made it clear to Herencic that he would not permit further advance of the refugees. Herencic had no choice but to accept the fateful situation.

Almost immediately, in the valley below, panic broke out as Basta's Partisans began firing from the wooded hillsides. Those refugees who survived the massacre were forced back across the border into Slovenia where more were executed at Maribor. From there a death march ensued as the refugees were driven south, either dying along the way or ending up in concentration camps. The actions of the Partisans were a culmination of four years of genocidal civil war in Yugoslavia. The behaviour of the British in permitting this has never been explained. Count Nikolai Tolstoy alleges that the British were complicit for political, as well as expedient, reasons. The military establishment reacted to his controversial book, *The Minister and the Massacres.* The book was banned at universities and libraries and Tolstoy was sued by Lord Aldington, the former Brigadier General, Toby Low." *

* B.G.Conway. The Sublime Taste of Hatred, Foreword, p. X1V

Vlasta rose and went to stand by the window. Bleiberg-Maribor, she said, happened two months after the formation of the coalition government. "The number of dead is still Tito's secret, although

I doubt that even he knows. From what I have learned I believe it to be over 100,000. The enormity of the atrocity became apparent as the prisoners were marched south. My husband resigned. He was appalled and wanted no association with Tito. And he felt that the British had betrayed him and the Croatian people. He lived quietly with me here in this apartment until he died eight years ago. With Tito has come order. He imposed it with terror and he maintains it with an iron fist."

She parted the curtain and beckoned to Parker and gestured to the watcher in the alcove across the street. "Look at him. He stands there for hours on end and then another one relieves him and so on. This one is Max. I know them all. Sometimes, when I go out to shop, I bring them cigarettes or an apple or whatever. My little reward for doing their stupid job, to keep watch on me. It is to laugh and they know this. What threat am I? An old widow. But this is nothing. The real threats are in concentration camps. And even you. You have been watched since Doboj."

She left Parker standing by the window. She slumped onto the sofa and lit a cigarette, then passed one to him. "As long as there is Tito there will be order. And, by comparison with the other communist countries, prosperity. He is smarter than the Russians. He keeps good relations with the West. The old hatreds are pushed below the surface, but they still simmer. The Croats and Serbs hate each other and everyone else as well. When Tito is gone the Balkans will explode again. It is so tragic."

And, eerily echoing Dr. Kristanovic, she said, "Freedom is easy to say. In practice it is terrifying. There is no order. No certainty. To those who have not known it, it is anarchy. Tito provides certainty, however false. Like all the others, now and in the past. Hitler, Stalin, Franco. It is the freedom of chains."

Vlasta looked at the clock on the sideboard and smiled. An ironic smile. "There it is. The end of my soliloquy. It took so long. Did I make you sleepy?"

"No Ma'am. No, you didn't make me sleepy."

"I will prepare supper now."

She served chicken, not fried but sautéed in red wine and with small roasted potatoes. The wine, in crystal glasses, was a white Burgundy. "It is 20 years old, from our years in London." Parker recalled his recent meals. The restaurant in Doboj. Maya's *hendl.* He had eaten well in Yugoslavia.

Vlasta's sombre mood lifted and through the course of the meal she chatted amiably. She told him about the years with her husband in London and Washington and how different her life had been then. He sensed that she was loath to whine. Her life now was simply different. Nothing else.

"You will leave in the morning?" she said in a way that sounded like an invitation to stay. As if his presence might prolong the distillation of pleasant memories. Something to refresh a stale and lonely existence.

"Yes, the train to Trieste leaves at ten."

"I have applied for permission to leave," she said, "to go to London and then Washington. If it is granted I will not return. I have a suspicion that they would be relieved to see me gone."

The next morning at breakfast Parker asked Vlasta about Dr. Kristanovic's missing hand.

"The Ustashe cut it off."

He could have anticipated such an answer. But to him the horror was still an abstraction. A chaotic painting. An even more grotesque Hieronymus Bosch that held him fascinated but didn't involve him. He could not feel it. At the time, his attempt to shake a hand that didn't exist seemed merely a cruel absurdity. Now he felt a shudder of revulsion. He heard himself mutter, "Cut it off?"

"Yes." A sardonic smile. As if to say, 'You poor, sweet, innocent man.' "His mother was a Jew. His father was Croatian, which is probably what saved him from extermination. Instead they put him in a concentration camp. Jasenovac. You know of it?"

"I've heard of it."

"Dr. Kristanovic was once a prominent surgeon but at Jasenovac he was kept as a physician. One night in 1945, shortly before the Partisans arrived to liberate the camp, a guard was attacked by a prisoner. He stabbed him with a knife. The wound was deep, near the heart, and the knife remained stuck in his chest. I have a letter somewhere from Marko - his first name is Marko. He described it in detail. He said he told one of the guards, presumably a senior officer, that he didn't have much hope for the man's survival. He was ordered to operate. And he was told that if the wounded man died, he, the officer, would cut off the doctor's hand."

"And the guard died."

"No," she said, "Marko saved him."

Vlasta looked at him, registering his stupefied expression, and simply said, "Ustashe."

Parker arrived in Trieste in time to catch the overnight train to Genoa. There were few passengers so he shared a compartment with an Italian, the chief steward on a ship that was due to sail from Genoa to Australia, the Galileo Galilei, operated by the Lloyd Triestino line. He spoke English, explaining to Parker that he was a veteran of this antipodean passage and that while the crew was Italian, most of the passengers were Brits, Aussies, and Kiwis.

"No Italians?"

"Italians, no," he said, "Sicilians, yes. They emigrate to Australia. We pick them up in Messina."

"They are not Italians?"

"No! They pretend to be. They are Moroccans. Scum! We in the north reject them. They belong in Africa. Australia can have them."

Parker asked him if he'd ever been to Yugoslavia.

AFTERWORD

Two years after he visited her, Parker Wells saw Maya Petrovic again. She came to Canada for a reunion with her brother, John Starich. It was a tense, emotional occasion that, over the course of her stay, gradually mellowed. She continued on to Chicago, to see her sister Raisa before returning to Teslic.

Vlasta Subasic did leave Yugoslavia. She went to the United States where she remarried. She returned to Zagreb after her second husband died. Then, in 1998, it was her turn. She is buried beside Ivan Subasic in the Mirogoj cemetery in Zagreb.

In 1966, John (Pop) Starich travelled to Montevideo, Uruguay, to meet Mara Simic, his 40-year-old daughter, for the first time. Upon his return he stopped in Windsor, Ontario where he had a reunion (a gesture of closure?) with his first wife.

Dr. Marko Kristanovic did return to Florence. He died there in 1991.

Ante Pavelic escaped to Austria in 1945 and then to Rome where he was sequestered by the Roman Catholic Church. In 1948 he moved to a monastery near Castel Gandolfo where he lived for a short time disguised as a priest. From there he went to Argentina where he attempted to revive the Ustashe movement. He became a security advisor to President Juan Peron. In 1957 Pavelic survived an assassination attempt attributed to Yugoslav government operatives. He fled to Spain from Argentina and died from complications due to his wounds in Madrid in 1959.

Fascism re-emerged in Croatia following the collapse of the USSR in 1990. Until 2003, when it was restricted, pro-Ustashe sentiment flourished, represented by the Croatian Party of Rights. Ante Pavelic's memoirs became a best seller and streets in Zagreb and in other cities were renamed after Mile Budek, Pavelic's ideological mouthpiece - the 'three million bullet man.'

In 1948, President Harry S. Truman awarded Draza Mihailovic (the Chetnik leader executed by Tito two years earlier) the United States' *Legion of Merit* posthumously in recognition of his contribution to the Allied war effort, which included the rescue and safe harbour of American airmen downed over Yugoslavia. This is the highest honour the American government can bestow on a foreign national. Yet it was kept secret so as not to offend Tito's government, which despite being a communist dictatorship, had maneuvered itself into a favourable relationship with the US, in large part due to Tito's defiance of Soviet Russia that resulted in Yugoslavia's expulsion from the Cominform in 1948. 57 years later, in 2005, the American ambassador in Belgrade presented the medal to Dr. Gordana Mihailovic, the recipient's daughter.

Josip Broz Tito died in May, 1980. He had been successful in maintaining order and coherence in Yugoslavia despite the latent hostility between the ethnic groups. As well he achieved international status as the leader of a neutral, 'non-aligned' bloc of countries during the Cold War.

Vlasta Subasic's views on the fate of Yugoslavia after Tito could be considered prescient. Except that to anyone living there the outcome was obvious. The only surprise was that it took another ten years to happen. The break-up of Yugoslavia coincided with the demise of communism in Russia and the other Soviet Bloc states. In 1991, first Slovenia and Croatia, and then Macedonia declared their independence. This created the preconditions for the ensuing war in Bosnia-Herzegovina (1992-95) and in Kosovo (1998-99) - wars typified by ethnic cleansing that harkened back to the atrocities of World War II. "*Bosnia's population consisted of 4.4 million people before the war, 44 percent of whom were Muslim, 31 percent Serb, 17 percent Croat, and 8 percent other nationalities. By October 1993, some 200,000 Bosnians were said to have died as a result of the conflict; over 800,000 became refugees outside Bosnia; and another 1.2 million were displaced within the nation.*"* The International Criminal Tribunal in The Hague has indicted over 100 participants in those wars, mainly Serbs and Bosnian Serbs for war crimes, specifically the massacres of civilians and prisoners, rape, and torture.

*Bosnia-Herzegovina Human Rights Practices. US Department of State January 31. 1994.

These include the former and now departed President of Serbia, Slobodan Milosevic, and

Bosnian Serb Ratko Mladic who is accused of ordering the extermination of over 7000 Muslim prisoners at Srebrenica, most of whom were male non-combatants. Mladic was a fugitive for 16 years before his arrest in Serbia and subsequent extradition to The Hague in 2011.

Parker Wells sailed from Genoa to Australia late in 1963. The ship, the Galileo Galilei, was new and stylish, a precursor to the present day cruise ship. He travelled tourist class and shared a cabin below the waterline with three other men. The toilets and showers were in a large latrine room across the passageway. At Messina, the ship picked up 400 Sicilian immigrants. He recalled the horse drawn carriages at quayside. The Italian sailor whom he met that night on the train to Genoa wasn't joking. The ship's crew, all northern Italians, treated the Sicilians with contempt. Lest the men mistake them for urinals the crew posted signs above the washbasins in the latrine that read, "*non-piscio.*"

The woman in the cabin next to Parker had three small children. She couldn't speak English and whenever he saw her she was crying. He assumed she was on her way to join her husband who was already in Australia. She was scared and she seldom left the cabin. She reminded him of stories about his ancestors who travelled under worse conditions, in sailing ships, to North America and the antipodes 100 years earlier. He brought food from the dining room down to her.

Parker returned to Canada the following year and he and Zlata (Goldie) Starich were married that summer in Duncan, British Columbia. In 1969 they emigrated to Australia where Parker taught in the History department at the University of Melbourne. Occasionally, when the Galileo Galilei was in port, they would take their two young sons to the quayside to have a look at her and once they were welcomed aboard for a brief tour.

There are photographs on the internet of the MV Galileo Galilei. She is stylish and elegant as one would imagine an ocean liner, especially when compared to today's snub-nosed floating hotels. She, along with her sister ship, the Guglielmo Marconi, was the pride of the Lloyd Triestino Line. Commissioned in 1963 (Parker sailed on her third voyage that November) to service the immigrant trade to Australia, she was subsequently sold to become exclusively a tourist ship that cruised in diverse parts of the world. The last of the internet photos is an image of her burning in the Andaman Sea, off Malaysia, in 1999, where she sank - still striking even in her demise. There is also a picture of the Olimpia Lounge, the tourist-class bar where a four-piece dance band played every night during Parker's 23-day journey - an idyllic passage through the Suez canal with a side excursion to Cairo and the pyramids, then to Aden and on out into the Indian Ocean for ten remote days, destination Fremantle. It was a unique experience of freedom. Insular, sequestered in a separate world, even from the impact of President Kennedy's assassination.

Parker used to have a recurring dream in which that bar band fades, as in a cinematic dissolve, to re-emerge as an earlier-era dance band. The players are dressed in black tie and the guitarist now plays a violin. The drummer builds a backbeat, softly swishing his brushes on the skin of the traps. A muted trumpet accompanies him and plays in harmony with the violin's strains of a Viennese waltz. **Tra**-la-la. **Tra**-la-la. The house lights dim and a spotlight sweeps across the darkened dance floor to a table where a woman sits alone. She is wearing a simple black dress upon which, at the neck, glistens a single strand of pearls. A man appears, trim, with silver hair, and wearing a blue blazer. He leans toward her and offers his hand and, followed by the spotlight, they step onto the dance floor. They hold each other in a secure embrace, his right arm in the small of her back, the cuff of which is pinned neatly back onto the sleeve. And they dance, tracing a graceful symmetry, off into the night. Across the endless ocean.

Short Haul

"I remember the games of my childhood - the dark and golden park we peopled with gods; the limitless kingdom we made of this square mile, never thoroughly explored, never thoroughly charted…And when we grow old, what remains of that park, filled with the shadows of childhood, magical, freezing, burning?…what do we learn except that in this infinity we shall never again set foot, and it is into the game and not the park that we have lost the power to enter."

I was getting a haircut. A few years ago, on my way to attend Jack Cruickshank's funeral, I found a barber shop on Station Street and I was sitting in the barber's chair when the teen-aged girl walked past the open door. She wore a soccer jersey with the number 8 on the front.

The barber, Bailey, yelled, "Hey you!"

The girl turned back and leaned around the doorjamb. She had an inquiring grin. The number 8 slipped over her right breast.

Bailey said, "If you had bigger tits you'd be a 10."

Two of the three customers waiting in the chairs guffawed. The third man, the chunky truck driver, picked up a newspaper and fumbled in his shirt pocket for his glasses. The girl stuck out her tongue and disappeared around the corner.

"You oughta be more careful, Bailey," the customer with the hearing aid said, "old fart like you talking like that to that little piece of jailbait."

"Aw shit, Gus," Bailey replied, "she knows me. Right, Short Haul?"

"Yeah, Bailey," the truck driver replied, "wouldn't hurt to show a bit more respect, though." His eyes fixed on the barber, who had started working on my hair, and then turned to the newspaper. His face was like creased leather and had a few days' worth of grey stubble growth. He wore a black ball cap that said CAT on the front, work shirt, orange suspenders, loggers' denims, and heavy boots. He looked old to be driving a truck. He looked familiar.

He said, "Canucks won again last night."

"Ain't they a wonder," said the man with the hearing aid. "Reminds me of them Canadiens in the old days." He glanced up at the wall where there were pictures of ancient hockey players (some dead): Rocket Richard, Jean Beliveau - and Tim Horton, leaning over his stick in his blue and white Maple Leafs jersey. This was an old man's barber shop.

I whispered to Bailey, "Why do you call him that?" I should have known better.

"What? Short Haul? Well maybe we better ask him."

I wanted to disappear under the cutting cape draped from my neck. Before I could speak, Bailey said, "Hey Herv, this guy wants to know why they call you Short Haul." The truck driver looked at Bailey, then at me, expressionless.

"Ain't it got something to do with when you was young and handsome and you drove an 18-wheeler. Right? And then you got over the hill and ugly and they graduated you to a dump truck."

The other customers laughed and Bailey beamed, proud of his tongue.

The truck driver leaned forward and then back. His frozen face softened. He smiled. "If you say so, Bailey."

Herv. What had looked familiar to me now had a name. He got up and stepped outside and lit a cigarette. The girl in the number 8 jersey was back on the sidewalk with two other girls. He went over and spoke to her. She nodded and cocked her head sheepishly and looked up at him and grinned. She shrugged. They were a tableau framed by the borders of the barber shop window. Then he stepped away from her, into the sunlight at the edge of the sidewalk. That movement, the way his body turned, jogged my memory.

"What's his last name?" I said.

"Hell, I don't know his last name. He's just Short Haul Herv," Bailey looked out through the doorway, "Hey Herv, this guy…"

I cut him off as the truck driver came back in, the cigarette stuck between his lips. "You're Hervé Dumont, aren't you? You wouldn't remember me."

"Yep. Nope."

He looked back out through the door and then at the opposite wall. He sat down. I felt that Bailey and I had trapped him. I smiled and tried to catch his eye. "You wouldn't remember me because I'm a few years younger." There was now a hint of curiosity in his awkward gaze. "The last time I saw you, you were standing just down the street from here at the Craig Street corner with Rick McCabe and Larry Walters. Remember them?"

He was hesitant. "Yeah, I logged with them guys. But I don't remember that. That would've been long, long ago."

"It was in the early fifties," I said, "fifty years ago."

Bailey interrupted, "What was you saying about the Canucks, Short Haul? Where's that paper? What was the score last night?" No stranger was going to run the conversation in his shop. He snipped furiously around my ears.

The talk turned back to hockey and from then on I ceased to exist. Bailey, like a robot, clipped away at my hair as Herv read aloud the article about the Canucks and George and Gus (the one with the hearing aid) chipped in their commentary. Listening, I learned they were drinking buddies at the local Legion where they bet on the hockey games.

Herv didn't seem interested in being sucked back into that 50-year-old part of his life and, in a way, I could understand it. Rick and Larry were both dead. I sensed he'd buried some old memories along with them. That time when I had seen them on the street corner I was still a hairless kid and I was impressed with the big guys, particularly Herv. It was a sunny Saturday afternoon and they, in their loafers, chinos, and white T-shirts, were holding court after returning from a week in Reno. They bragged about all the money they lost gambling and spent on hookers. They were solid young loggers who worked in camps up the coast, made big money and threw it around when they came out. I knew Rick and Larry well. I knew Herv in another way.

Four years earlier, Hervé Dumont had played for the Toronto Maple Leafs during the NHL playoffs. They had called him up from the minors at the end of the Season and he had a few weeks of glory. The Leafs won the Stanley Cup that year and Hervé was a big part of it.

He was French, but not Quebec French. He came out of south Saskatchewan and he had some Indian blood. The papers made a thing of it. The Métis kid. Louis Riel and all that. I remember watching him in the news reels at the old Odeon theatre. He was built straight up and down with legs that pumped like pistons. He skated like a forward and hit like a defenceman. And he had moves and could shoot like he'd been playing in the League for years. He played right wing but they used him on defense as well. He was a sensation and the Toronto press couldn't get enough of him. Years later, watching Valery Kharlamov in the first Russia-Canada series, I thought I was seeing a Hervé Dumont clone.

That was it. Something happened in the off-season. Something to do with a young girl. The next time I saw him it was in person. Vancouver Island was a world away from the frozen ponds of a Saskatchewan winter and a whole universe away from the National Hockey League and its six eastern big-city teams. Herv had a sister in Duncan and I guess she was his refuge - as far away as he could get from the bloodhounds who wrote sports for the eastern newspapers. There was no hockey. Only a minor league team across the water in Vancouver. The nearest rink was 30 miles away in Nanaimo.

It rained a lot in the winter and the fields beside the lakes around Duncan would flood and for a short spell it got cold enough that we could skate on them. There were shinny games from early morning until well after dark.

On a clear night you could almost see well enough to play in the reflection of the moon and starlight on the ice. We built bonfires around the edge of the pond and set up crude goal posts. Silvery shadows glided and turned in the firelight. The *skiff-skiff* of metal blades whispered in the night. Sticks banged and clunked. There was the occasional *whack* of a slap shot. Herv Dumont was there, skating around us, through us, leaving a slipstream. He controlled the puck. It was impossible to poke it away from him, let alone move him off it.

One memorable night I stood in front of the goalie as Herv cruised in, braked hard on one blade and sprayed an arc of shaved ice in my face. He pirouetted to shoot - and the puck, rolling on edge, hopped over his stick. I flipped it forward and caught up with it, leaving him to recover from his surprise. I figured it was the first time he'd even noticed me. And he was chasing me, his skates grinding. I turned toward the edge of the pond and *wham!* His hip check propelled me head first across to the other side and into a bonfire. He followed me, hauled me out, and smothered the smouldering arm of my sweater with a handful of snow.

"Nice move, kid." He grinned.

I had second degree burns on my forearm and a sore leg but I was back out there the next night. I wore the bandage like a badge of honour. Now, as I sat opposite him, my right hand involuntarily crept across under the cape and I ran my fingers over the hard patch of rippled skin on my left arm.

I remember once thumbing through a Victoria newspaper when I was living somewhere else. I can't explain why or how I came across it. Uncanny, it just happened to be on a table in a doctor's, or dentist's, waiting room. There was a report of a spectacular traffic accident on a highway near Duncan. A loaded logging truck was descending a long decline when the brakes failed. The driver chose to steer the truck off the road to avoid crashing into a school bus that had stopped to let some children off. The truck rolled over and careened down an embankment. The photo was quite vivid. The truck's cab was crushed, upside down, and the logs were scattered, like pick-up sticks, into a ravine. The driver, strapped into a stretcher, was being winched up to the highway by a fire truck, guided and steadied by a crew of paramedics. The driver was Hervé Dumont.

I stared at that photo and reread the article. Then, carefully, I read it again, looking for a mention, even a hint, of who he once was. There was none.

And now, as I listened to these old guys in animated conversation, I thought about what professional athletes get away with these days. It was different back in the fifties and Herv's mistake could not be fixed. That few short weeks of glory was all there was. There is a record of it somewhere. On celluloid. In newspaper clippings. Even Herv, or one of his kids, may have kept a scrapbook. But I sensed that Herv had buried it - consigned the memory of it to an archive as a footnote in Hockey's history book. A memory perhaps only and occasionally conjured up by chance, by accident. By something like someone simply walking into a barber shop, sitting down in the chair, and looking across the room.

Time is hungry. It chews away at your world. Your folks pass on. Buddies get killed in the woods. Others drink themselves stupid. Still others just die. The wife pulls out for greener grass, supposedly somewhere. The kids grow up and leave for bigger cities, brighter lights. You never see your grandkids. Then you hit seventy and your world has shrunk into the smoky cab of your truck and the bar where you stop for a beer with the boys after work. You go home, fix yourself some supper, and fall asleep in front of the TV. Saturday night you're back at the local pub with the boys watching the hockey game on the big screen. The boys are in their 40s and 50s. They call you "Pop."

And once a month you go to the barbershop and, for the price of a haircut, you get to listen to the jerkoff proprietor's mindless insults.

I imagined that that was Herv's world. It was familiar enough, and I had the sense that he had a clear view of it. He could smile at Bailey's babble and appear to be content - as if in repose. And I imagined him having shucked the burden of those ancient memories and that there had been a transference. I, the stranger that sat facing him, had become the keeper of those memories.

"What's the damage, Bailey?"

"Twelve bucks." He removed the cape and I stood up as he brushed the loose hairs from my neck. "And you can tip me extra for introducing you to Short Haul." He winked.

Herv was watching me. I looked up at Tim Horton's picture. I said, "I remember you in the blue and white."

He blinked, as if he was trying to focus. It was between him and me. The others didn't know what I was talking about.

Rhymes with Love

When Sawyer returned to the west coast the woman who was living in his newly purchased house greeted him as he entered the kitchen. He was, momentarily, distracted by a newspaper on the table - the obituary prominent on the front page. Then he looked up. His furtive glance betrayed him.

"She didn't tell you I was Chinese?"

"No. Just your name. You don't sound Chinese."

"That's because I'm a banana." Her gaze was expressionless. Wary.

He grinned. He knew what she meant. Instead he said, "An edible woman?"

Her eyes burned two holes into him. Then she laughed, "That's a cute remark. I wouldn't have thought of it like that. Actually it's kind of dumb - cheesy. Anyway, I'm not a fan of Margaret Atwood."

"Yep, just a dumbass, cheesy remark."

"Dumb, for sure."

"Ok," he said, "now that we know that you're a banana and I'm dumb, what's next?"

She stood between him and the kitchen table, legs apart, hands on her hips. She shrugged. Then her shoulders sagged and she smiled. "I've made coffee." She gestured at the stove. "Would you like some?"

"Sure." He set the newspaper aside and sat down at the table. Then he stood up, walked over to the adjacent door and stepped out onto the patio, now awash in the late afternoon, early summer sunlight. He leaned on the railing, oblivious to the view, and tried to take stock. The fresh air felt good after the awkward encounter inside. There had been no sense of arrival, no chance for appraisal. Just the presence of this woman and all that that implied. He figured that the next three months would, at least, be interesting.

She came with the coffee. He watched her move toward him, effortless, gliding, her delicate, symmetrical features enclosed by long black hair, parted at the middle and flowing across her shoulders to her breasts. A white T-shirt draped over her nipples and into the cleft between her breasts. Her jeans fit snug enough to feature lithe, sensuous thighs. They stood at the railing and drank the coffee, Sawyer now more aware of the view.

"I work five days a week," she said, "shift work, including weekends. When I'm on day shift I eat at normal hours. I'll cook dinner for both of us on those days if you're interested. You supply the food. I've moved my stuff out of the fridge to the one in my suite. There's the basics left for you. Milk, eggs, butter, OJ. Bread in the bread box. You'll need to do a big shop." She looked at him as if trying to gauge his degree of domestication.

"There's no bed in the master bedroom. Annie. Annie Crook," she paused, noticing his enquiring glance, "Mrs. Mitcham, took it with her. I've set up one of the guest bedrooms and ensuite for you. Bedding, sheets, towels, so you'll get by until you have a chance to get settled. Just about as good as a four star hotel, eh?" She had relaxed enough so that now there was warmth in her smile. Sawyer almost forgot what she had just said.

"Annie Crook?"

"Yes. That's what some of the old-timers called her. It's short for her maiden name which, I believe, was Cruikshank. I gather she was a bit of a character. I wouldn't know. She was like a mother to me."

"Your mother?"

"She died when I was twelve."

She stepped away and disappeared into the house and then Sawyer heard the garage door open and then close again. It was nearly four pm and he assumed she had gone to work. They still hadn't introduced each other. They never did.

Back inside he sat down at the table, unfolded the newspaper, and read Tom Wade's obituary.

Thomas Wade, 1906 – 2001

> *"Tom Wade, the last living descendent of one of the original pioneer families that arrived from England in 1856, died yesterday at Nanaimo District Hospital. He was 95. Mr. Wade was predeceased by his wife Elizabeth, his brothers, George and William, his son Thomas, and his daughter Gally.*

The rest of the article touched on the history of the Wade family and Tom's involvement in the community, the Historical Society and his work in his early years on the Miners' Gas Committee. There was a brief reference to the devastation caused by explosions in the coal mines and the deadly odourless gas that killed the trapped miners without leaving a mark on them. Tom would have known about that, Sawyer mused. He certainly would.

Back from work after midnight and lying in bed, waiting for sleep, Lindsay could hear faint muffled sounds from the guest bedroom, which was above hers, as Sawyer unpacked his suitcases; footfalls, the closing of closet doors and dresser doors. Sleep didn't come as the awareness of a new reality sunk in. He had moved in. He was right there, right above her. And she was on her way out of a house she had considered home for ten years. She felt the grip of an old insecurity. And she was resentful.

When sleep finally came, it was interrupted by more noise from the bedroom above. This time it was the sounds of a nightmare. Sharp moans and cries. Instinctively she rushed up the stairs but she paused at the closed bedroom door, and now fully awake, realized that she best leave him be. Unintelligible sounds came through the door. She recognized just one word, a woman's name. She went back to bed.

When she arose she found him sitting, cradling a mug of coffee, on the deck in the morning sun. "Well," she said, "how did you sleep? Your first night?"

"Ok, I guess. Maybe a bit restless. Almost as good as a four-star hotel. How about you?"

"Fine. After I got back to sleep. After your hollering woke me. You were having a nightmare. Do you remember?" She watched embarrassment flicker across his face and, with that glimpse of his vulnerability, her wariness of him dissolved.

"No, I don't. It's been a while since that happened. So far as I know. You heard it?"

"My bed is directly below yours."

"I'm sorry. I'll fix that. I assume there's a Sleep Country around here."

"Yes. Who is Elaine?"

"Elaine?" His brow furrowed. "I don't know Elaine. Why?"

"That was the only clear word in your garble last night."

Sawyer bought the house sight unseen. The realtor's online presentation was persuasive but it was his conversations with the owner, Mrs. Mitcham, that sold him on it. He knew realtors and knew how reluctant they were to let an owner anywhere near a potential buyer. So this was unique. So unique that he found himself actually having to persuade her to let him have the house. The price was not negotiable. Later, when he had time to reflect, Sawyer wondered if he had succumbed to that childish urge to *really* want something that apparently you cannot have, simply for that reason. It didn't matter. As he wandered through the house on that first day he knew that he'd got lucky.

It faced south from a rocky promontory above Departure Bay, affording a spectacular 180-degree view of the harbour and the adjacent islands. The building was 25 years old - custom built in a contemporary west coast style. It had been on the market since Charlie, Mrs. Mitcham's husband, died five years earlier. The final two decades of a long and generally happy life with Charlie were embedded there and she, as was her nature, was not about to let just anyone have it. Her price was high and she refused to respond to lower offers and on two occasions took the house off the market when the prospective buyers actually met her price; because she "didn't like the cut of their jib." She went through several frustrated realtors.

When he was eighty a stroke had debilitated Charlie. Mrs. Mitcham found a competent professional, an ER nurse who worked part time at the hospital who would live in and help with Charlie, enabling him to live at home. After he died she decided, despite her affection for the place, that she didn't want to live there without him. She purchased a penthouse in a high-rise condominium in the Nanaimo harbour.

The nurse, Lindsay Lee, moved into a suite on the lower floor of the house (not a basement, as the slope of the property allowed for patio access and a fine view at one side). A roughed-in kitchenette was in an enclosed alcove. In addition to providing homecare for Charlie, Lindsay helped prepare and ate meals with the Mitchams and was paid commensurately, allowing for her room and board. She proved to be competent and compassionate and, as well, pleasant company. Annie

Mitcham, who was then 80 and childless, felt that she had been blessed with the gift of a thirties-something daughter.

After Charlie died, and Annie had moved to her penthouse, Lindsay stayed in the house for a nominal rent in return for looking after it. Much of the furniture remained as Annie had downsized and had purchased furniture that better fit with the new apartment. Five years later she sold the house to Sawyer after he was able to convince her that - as well as being a mature, responsible person and that his relocation to Nanaimo was, at age 61, his last move - he was duly appreciative of its location, craft, and design and, should he alter it, would at least try to preserve its essence. Lindsay Lee still had six months left on her lease. Sawyer agreed to honour it which meant that she would continue to live in the house for three months after Sawyer took possession and moved in. The lease would not be renewed.

The house was as Sawyer had imagined it. He felt comfortable and a bit elated as he wandered from room to room. Every room on the main floor, with the exception of the dining alcove and the bath-rooms, had vaulted ceilings. In the living room, which had the feel of a baronial manor with the fireplace prominent in the middle of one wall, the ridge beam was 18 feet above the floor which lent it a cavernous effect and was one of a few things that Sawyer would change. He figured decorative truss work would soften it.

Every room had a view, mostly south through spacious windows. The living room window was eight feet wide and rose 14 feet from the floor. There was clear wood trim - window and door casings, baseboards - throughout, providing a natural, satin-gloss accent to the whites and pastel blues and greens of the walls. The ceilings, supported by heavy fir beams, were tongue and groove cedar. The floors were hardwood, arbutus, which, Sawyer guessed, would have been milled on site.

Later, when Lindsay asked him how he liked it, she was taken by his quiet enthusiasm. She sensed none of the awkwardness of their initial conversation days earlier. "It's the light," he said. "All that glass brings the outside into the room which is critical during the fall and winter. In the spring and summer it's like you're living outside. You've probably noticed that the only doors are to the bedrooms and bathrooms (she hadn't). All the other rooms - this one (they were standing in the living room), the kitchen, family room, den, sun room - are all accessed through those wide entrance portals with their solid fir lintel beams. The space and light flow from room to room. It's called *interpenetration.* (Lindsay stifled a giggle). The architect knew what he was doing."

Lindsay, too, liked the house. She liked the grand, yet familiar, feel of it. It was her home. She had been happy there for ten years. It had become intrinsic to her life in a way that this new owner could not appreciate. Now as she looked around she saw it from a fresh perspective, through his eyes, and her heart sank, finally aware that the house was no longer 'hers' and in three months she would be gone. Adjusting, in the interim, to living with this stranger was not a priority. Focusing on an uncertain future was.

"What will you change?"

"Not much. More just maintenance. I'll put ceiling trusses in this room. And that's coming out." He pointed to the fireplace which had been converted from wood burning to natural gas. "There'll be a wood fire in it again. And I'll replace the gas furnace with a heat pump."

"You don't like gas?"

"No." He looked at her. "I guess you want to know why."

"Ok. Yes. I'm curious."

"Well, I built a house once. Without a basement. Just a crawl space. Three feet. I put a gas furnace in it. A horizontal one so it would fit. And one night gas leaked into the crawl space and the furnace pilot light ignited it. Boom!" He grinned.

"Really? Were you there? Were you hurt?"

"Yes and no. The whole house shook. Windows broke. It was like a small earthquake. It felt like the house lifted a few inches and then fell back which was not possible because it was anchored to the foundation. There was no fire, not even a lot of smoke."

She thought he might be having her on. Still she played along. "You're obviously not there now. What happened to it?"

"I gave it away, to a woman. She was living with me at the time."

The existing workshop, adjacent to the garage, was too small so Sawyer converted the garage to a temporary workshop and stocked it with a large planer, a table saw, mitre-saw, and assorted other tools and began fashioning the truss work for the living room ceiling from cedar beams he purchased from a local sawmill. This shattered the peace and quiet that Lindsay was accustomed to. Her car, as well as Sawyer's pick-up, now had to be parked outside. The screech and whine of the planer and the saws intruded on her daily rhythm such that she had to change her sleeping pattern. When on graveyard shift, instead of sleeping during the day, she now had to sleep after 4 pm when Sawyer, out of deference to her, stopped working with the machines.

Sawyer moved the living room furniture into the dining alcove (Mrs. Mitcham had taken the dining table and chairs) and, in the living room, he erected a platform ten feet above the floor, supported by scaffolding and accessed by a ladder. From there he would install the trusses that he fashioned in the garage workshop.

At first Lindsay, piqued by the disruption, avoided the project and was politely civil with Sawyer. But, as she had to walk past it daily to and from her car, her natural curiosity eventually got the better of her. One morning, as he was progressing along the edge of a beam with the router he found himself, at the end of the beam, looking at her belt buckle. He looked up to behold a gauze mask covering all but her eyes. Her hair, parted to one side, swept across her forehead, almost like bangs. It was flecked with fine sawdust.

Now, for the first time, Sawyer saw Lindsay's eyes, her dark almond eyes, separate and distinct from the rest of her face. Her curious eyes that straightened him up with the router still whirring and dangling from his right arm. Another women's eyes, nearly identical eyes, flashed at him - framed also by black hair, Dutch cut with straight bangs across her forehead. The jolt of the image startled him but if Lindsay noticed she would not have distinguished it from a presumed reaction to her unexpected presence.

She said, “What’s that?”

“A router.” He turned it off.

“No, that.” She indicated the beam. She stood in a settling cloud of sawdust amid little piles of shavings and butt ends of beams. The oily pungent cedar smell got in her nose.

“It’s a cross beam for a hammer truss.” He could see that this meant nothing to her. “The diagram is on my laptop. I’ll show it to you later.” He flicked the router on.

“Can I watch?”

“If you hang around here I’ll put you to work.”

She found it to be good work. Clean, creative, even sensuous. She liked the smell. She liked the feel, the heft of the beams and how the wood accepted, and seemed to respond to, the blades of the tools, surrendering to the design - to the form. She liked to run her fingertips along and across the sanded grain, to sense the tensile vibrancy of the fibre. Most days she showed up after work at the ER and spent whatever hours she could spare in her day helping Sawyer. She wore her long black hair tied into a bun with her pencil inserted into it, which Sawyer tried not to find provocative.

That afternoon she helped him raise the beam into place where he checked his measurement, marked it and then took it back to the shop for cutting. Lindsay was now, after three weeks living in the same house, in close quarters with Sawyer. As he immersed himself in the project, apparently indifferent to her, her awareness of him grew from that of a distant, though distracting, temporary presence in her life. He became real and vibrant. Flesh and bone. And, in her imagination, his hands and arms became sinewy extensions of the wood that he so carefully transformed.

Also, he smelled. A man smell that was a blend of odours, mainly sawdust and sweat. A variation on something Lindsay hadn't experienced in years. She didn't find it unpleasant. She said, "How often do you wash your work shirts?"

"Once in a while. I guess when they need them."

She gently grasped his shirtsleeve. "This one needs it."

When they were both 16 Sawyer nearly killed Lindsay's mother. They were driving to a high school basketball game in Parksville in Sawyer's car. Elaine was in the front seat beside him. Gally Wade and Dave Venturi were in the back seat. The car, a 1935 Ford sedan which Sawyer had purchased for $300 a week earlier, was struck by a freight train.

Gally was the instigator. She taunted him. "Cluck, cluck, cluck. Sawyer, chick, chick, chickee. Sawyer chickee shit."

"Shut your crooked mouth Gally. Big mouth."

Her eyes were set wide under slim, animated brows and separated by an upturned nose. The bridge was sprinkled with freckles and her mouth was slightly crooked - at least when she smiled. A wide, ready smile with glistening teeth. At one corner of her mouth her lips separated more than at the other, so it appeared as a crooked grin. She wasn't beautiful, but she wasn't plain. The energy that sparkled from those eyes and that mouth made her attractive. The rest of her was stunning. To Sawyer, she was the best looking cheerleader from the neck down.

The idea was that four of them - Gally and her date and Sawyer and someone - should all go in his car to the inter-high school basketball games at Parksville. This was because a school board trustee didn't like what she heard about the kids necking on the buses on basketball excursions (there were two buses; two boys' teams and two girls' teams, plus cheerleaders, managers, and coaches) so she segregated them.

"Come on Sawyer, let's drive there. Screw old bean-up-her-bum."

"You just want me to be the chauffer so you and Dave can make out in the back seat."

"Hey buddy, you're not as slow as you look." A crooked grin. "But you know what? I'll line you up with Elaine Wong so you won't be lonely."

The streetlights glowed through a light mist as they drove through the village. Sawyer didn't see the slow moving train as it entered a level crossing. He heard a bell clanging and he looked to see it a few feet away beside the front wheel of the diesel engine a second before impact. He couldn't tell whether he actually heard or felt the crunch of metal. The diesel engine drove directly into him on the driver's side and dragged the car down the track. The steering wheel shattered in his hands. Both passenger side doors burst open and everyone but Sawyer was thrown out.

They found Gally unconscious beside the track, inches from the train engine. Elaine landed right on the tracks in front of the engine. She and the two guys were shaken up - cut and bruised. Gally had a concussion and a broken leg. When Sawyer saw her he thought she was dead. They all caught hell, from just about everyone - parents, teachers, coaches. Sawyer and Dave were suspended for the rest of the basketball season. Gally's broken leg stopped her cheerleading. And Elaine's family suffered a perceived loss of face. She was forbidden to have any contact with Sawyer. As he recovered from the shock and realized that Gally would be all right, Sawyer was uncomfortable with the admiration, almost adulation, he felt from other students. He got a kick out of Gally. She wasn't so sheepish. To her, recognition for defying authority felt just fine.

Now, 45 years later, as Sawyer lay on his bed staring at the night, he was taken by how that memory could so quickly and so vividly be conjured up by the startling recognition of a woman's eyes. That it was still there. Back then Elaine had been just a convenient date. Instead, the incident served to bring him and Gally together for an intense and fatal sliver of their lives. Elaine's time came later. And now, as the result of a bizarre coincidence, he realized that that incident, and what happened a short time later, had left an indelible mark on him.

Sawyer was not, as Lindsay thought, indifferent to her. Initially, he admitted to himself, the attraction was physical, enhanced by her seeming lack of awareness of her sex appeal. She was graceful, without guile. But the unique circumstance of their relationship gave him pause. She had defined the space between them and he respected it - to the point of apparent disinterest. He seldom saw her wearing anything but her nursing attire or sweatshirts and jeans. He wondered why such an attractive, self-possessed woman had wrapped herself in a cocoon for so many years, house-sitting. Alone. No man. Fantasizing, he saw her waiting for him, poised and confident, eyes glistening, lips red, stunning in a sequined sheath and wearing spike heels.

Then, reality intruded and the image changed and he sensed her vulnerability now that he knew who she was. She didn't know 'who' he was and she didn't know what he knew. He felt it better to leave it that way. Until now, they had essentially remained strangers living under the same roof. He supposed that she had no idea of the feelings she aroused in him. He didn't know how he would handle that.

Lindsay held the collar brace in place. It was the final part to be fitted to complete the installation of the first truss. There were two wide holes, one in each end of the curved piece. Sawyer drilled a long screw into the bottom of each hole, attaching the brace to the main structure. Then he inserted cedar plugs into the holes and, with a razor sharp chisel, shaved the protruding ends of the plugs smooth and flush with surface of the wood. His stroke was quick and deft and sure and Lindsay marvelled at it as if he were a surgeon delicately tracing an incision with a scalpel. All that was missing was the blood.

They stood back and admired the intricate structure. The room was quiet, except for the soft rhythm of music from the sound system. "That'll give you an idea of how it will look when the rest of the trusses are in place."

"It's classic." She, in her mind's eye, saw the trusses, equally spaced and marching, serried, across the ceiling. The music tweaked her mood. "Who's singing?"

"The McGarrigle sisters."

"The *McGwho*?"

"McGarrigle. Folkies from Montreal. They're best known as backups; for people like Emmy Lou Harris and Linda Rondstadt. Old people."

They stood listening. Lindsay said, "It's…" She caught her breath. "It's beautiful. What is it?"

"Dinks Song."

"Dinks Song? Ha!"

"Not what you're thinking. Dink was the woman who sang it, who made it up. It's a lament."

"A lament?"

"Yeah, for lost love. You know, man leaves woman, woman grieves."

"How could someone with such an ugly name create music that beautiful?"

"She was an illiterate black woman that a man named John Lomax found living in a tent in a Texas work camp 100 years ago. The contractor had brought her and other women in to service the men, Negroes, who were building a levee. In exchange for a bottle of gin she sang her song for Lomax and he recorded it. She was pregnant and her man was gone."

Lindsay had been humming along with the song but suddenly she stopped. Her dreamy expression dissolved.

"What's wrong?"

"Nothing really." She turned away. "That's a good story. Too true."

"What do you…?"

She turned back to him. Her eyes seemed to plead. "My father did that. Walked out when I was an infant. Not typically Chinese is it? At least he waited until the baby was born. Me."

Dinks Song was ending. They descended from the platform. Sawyer went over to the stereo console and turned it off.

And so Sawyer, despite his best intentions, found that he was following the path of least resistance. He was in Lindsay's space, realizing that the hours spent working together with the wood was in itself a form of intimacy. They had begun preparing meals together. She washed his work clothes (and chided him with remarks about her Chinese laundry). She wanted no compensation for helping him. She was simply enjoying it. But he insisted, saying that otherwise he would have had to hire someone on a temporary basis. He started by tearing up her two remaining post-dated rent cheques. He planned something more for when she moved out.

In the evenings (when she was on day shift) they sat out on the deck and drank red wine and talked until the sun went down. He learned that her mother, Elaine, had breast cancer and died in San Francisco when she, Lindsay, was twelve. She then came to live with her grandparents in

Nanaimo where she finished high school. And she told him the little she knew about her father. When her mother was at UBC she met her father at a Chinese Varsity Club exchange with a university in San Francisco. It was a bad marriage and Elaine blamed herself. Lindsay said, "It was too quick. They really didn't know each other. That still doesn't excuse what he did. Mom married him on the rebound. Too soon after her relationship with a guy in Vancouver, a white guy, broke up."

That remark sent a dart straight into Sawyer.

One day while climbing the ladder, carrying the nail gun, Sawyer slipped and lost his balance, tipping the ladder. He, with the ladder, crashed to the floor. In that virtual moment on the way down he pressed the muzzle of the gun against his thigh and accidentally pulled the trigger. A three-inch spike shot deep into the flesh.

When he checked into the ER at the hospital, Lindsay was there. "Ohmigod! What's this?"

He lay, wired up, on the bed. "I shot myself." The head of the nail appeared to float in a crimson pool that saturated the denim.

"You shot yourself?"

"I slipped on the ladder and the gun went off." He pulled a pair of pliers from his pocket. "You could use these. I was going to do it myself but then I thought maybe I shouldn't. Maybe it was close to an artery."

She took the pliers and squeezed them. Her hand turned white. She tossed them onto the foot of the bed. With scissors she cut away the blood soaked denim around the nail head and then cut off the leg of his jeans. Then she helped him out of what remained of them. As she swabbed around the wound she muttered, "You slipped on the ladder. Alone in that house on a ladder with a nail gun." She shook her head. "You dummy."

"We've already established that, haven't we?"

"I'll get the doctor."

The doctor looked at the pliers and then selected a bright instrument that looked similar from a tray beside the bed. "How does it feel?"

"It's numb. Just throbs a bit."

A different nurse appeared. The doctor said, "I don't think it hit an artery. There'd be more blood. And there's no swelling."

He said to the nurse, “I’m going to pull it. Be ready to cauterize it if there is a lot of blood. Then I’ll put a stitch in it.”

There was not a lot of blood. The nurse disinfected the wound and bandaged it.

Sawyer said, “Where’s Lindsay?”

“She needed a break.” The doctor held the bloody nail between his thumb and his forefinger. Then he tossed it into a waste receptacle. He looked at Sawyer. “You must mean an awful lot to her,” he said.

About a year after Sawyer drove his car into the train, he and Gally Wade were dating and by April of the following year (their high school graduation year) they were inseparable. In essence, they had always been that way. They were born in the same year - 1939. They grew up together, virtually brother and sister. Gally had an older brother. Sawyer was an only child. There wasn’t anything that Gally wouldn’t tell Sawyer. She was openly cheerful. His buddy. He never considered dating her. As he watched her grow into a self-assured, almost brash young woman, not a classic beauty, but certainly pretty, he envied the guys who did.

Her body was classic - beautifully proportioned and the bumps, front and back, fired his libido.

"You're a good beer, Gally. Full bodied."

Sawyer grew more slowly and awkwardly, but by seventeen he had filled out. No longer skinny and knobbly, he retained a lean lank profile. He moved gracefully, deceptively lazily. This in contrast to his keen, alert eyes. He, six feet-three inches, played point guard on the senior boys' high school basketball team. Gally was a cheerleader. Both were bright students. She craved excitement. He was easily bored. This proved to be a volatile mixture.

Spring came early that year and one particularly warm evening, as they were driving up Comox Road (Sawyer had another $300 car, a '39 Chevy) past the cemetery, he said, "You ever go in there?"

"Nope. What for? It's a graveyard."

"There's a lot of history buried in there. Including your ancestors. Your great grandparents were some of the first settlers."

"Is that so? When did you get to be an authority on my family?"

"It's interesting. Not just your people. The whole place." He looked at her and made his eyeballs disappear into his eyelids. “It’s the ghoul in me.”

He persuaded her that it would be a neat place to sit and watch the sun go down. “Yeah,” she said, “it’ll be spooky. We’d better have a beer first.” So they stopped by the Occidental on Fitzwilliam Street, where Sawyer knew Cece, the waiter, who would serve them in a secluded corner of the room and pretend he didn’t know they were underage. Toward dusk they left with a six-pack and were sitting amongst the headstones in the Wade family plot in time to watch the setting sun.

The cemetery lay on high ground above the city. It had a grand view of the harbour and reminded Sawyer more of a park than a graveyard. “See that?” He pointed to a monument that stood on the crest of the smooth undulating lawn - a velvet-green blanket stitched with rows of grey headstones. “That’s the Jones plot. Some of my ancestors are buried there.”

“Like who? Your uncle who stabbed his wife in her boob with a cheese knife and then cut his own throat? Oh no! I’m sorry. I didn’t mean to say that.”

"It's Ok," he murmured. Then more clearly, "He's not there. And he was my father's uncle. Uncle Jeb. He's somewhere here in the cemetery. In an unmarked grave."

It was a Friday night in mid-April. Clear and mild. They sat on a blanket, their backs against the Wades' headstones. A full moon rose slowly in the eastern sky, spreading a silvery light across the cemetery. The grave markers trailed long shadows across the grass. The beer was starting to work.

"This is so peaceful," Gally said, "it's not even spooky."

"You disappointed?"

"No." She grinned. "You know Dinks Song?"

"Dinks Song?"

"Uh, hum. The first verse goes like this; *'If I had wings like Noah's Dove, I'd fly up the river to the one I love. Fare thee well, Oh Honey. Fare thee well.'*"

"Jesus, Gally," he teased, "when did you get so sentimental, like romantic?"

She turned and faced him. "Well, maybe you'd like the second verse better; *'I got a man, he's long and tall. Moves his body like a cannonball.'* That's you buddy." She slid her hand along his thigh and held it firm in his crotch. He removed it.

"Hey?"

"Not here. In a graveyard?"

"Why not? It'd be different. Right? It'd be a hoot!"

"Anyway I don't have…"

"Who cares? What is it you guys say? 'It's like having a bath with your socks on.' Well I want to feel *you* - not a sock." She stood up and wriggled out of her pants. Her thighs shimmered in the moonlight. His resistance melted.

She straddled him. She said, "Listen, you dummy. If you want to have a chance you've got to take a chance. All the girls want you. But I'm the one who's got you. I'm *invested* in you. And I'm going to get my money's worth." She reached down and unzipped him. They made love, silently, almost fully clothed. The early spring dew clung to them like sweat.

"Which verse do you like best, Gally?"

"The first one," and then, "do you love me Sawyer?"

He sat up. "I never thought about it. It's a given, isn't it?"

"I love you," she said.

Four weeks later, in early May, they went into the Furnace Portal mine.

In 1957, in Nanaimo, the last of the coal mines had been closed for several years. Most mines worked below sea level and were flooded after they were closed. A few were tunnelled into the rising ground toward Mount Benson. The miners could walk straight in instead of being lowered into the depths by cages. Some of the tunnels rose into the hillsides, others dipped. These were called slopes. When the mines were closed the entrances were sealed, often just by timbers and hoarding.

One of these slopes, the Furnace Portal, sealed years earlier and grown over by brush, was discovered by school kids near the end of Harewood road. They worked a hole in the barricade, and over time it was explored by boys who dared to crawl into and along the dank, black tunnel. An expedition in there gave a guy something to brag about. Sawyer had been in there. He didn't remember much about it except that it was cold and wet and scary.

Gally said, “Any girls ever been in it?”

“Not that I know of. Why?” Even though he knew why.

“Well… I could be the first, couldn’t I? I bet it’d even be spookier than that old graveyard.”

“No. No girls allowed.”

“Who made up that rule?”

“Me.”

“Well, time out buddy. Rule change coming.”

She kept at him and threatened to go in by herself so he gave in.

They wore rain clothes and each had a flashlight and a water flask. They walked up into the gradually sloping tunnel which was high enough so that they could stand erect. There were rotting timbers lying in the roadway and piles of rock and coal where the ceiling had given way. Gally was right. It was spooky - even more than Sawyer remembered. They heard water dripping and rocks falling in the darkness and they walked in rivulets that ran down the roadway between the rusted coal car rails. Timbers in the ceiling creaked. They got to a place where there had been a big cave-in and the debris went right up to the ceiling, except for a small space where someone had made an opening just wide enough for one person to get through.

Sawyer said, "This is far enough." But Gally wanted to keep going. Go up and through that hole to the other side. She was really grooving on the whole thing and he was starting to worry. She said, "I'm going in. You can wait here for me." So he went in first and then helped her through. But when she was coming down the pile of rock on the other side, she slipped and her foot caught and she turned her knee. And she hit her head and it was bleeding.

Gally held her handkerchief against the wound to slow the bleeding and then Sawyer tried to help her back up to the hole. But her leg wouldn't cooperate and he didn't think he could drag her up and through without hurting her some more. So he decided to go to get help. The last thing she said was to hurry because she was starting to feel faint. He left her sitting against the wall with a flashlight while he ran down and out of the mine and drove to the fire hall on Fitzwilliam Street.

The fire truck was back at the entrance within 30 minutes from the time that Sawyer had left Gally.

One of the firemen was older and had worked in the mines. He and Sawyer and another fireman went in with a stretcher. Gally looked like she was asleep. The older man knelt down and felt her pulse and then he put his hand up under her T-shirt and held it there and put his ear beside her mouth. He looked up at Sawyer and said, "She's gone son." He turned to the other fireman and said, "After all these years these fuckin' coal mines is still killin' people." Then he said, "We better get out of here fast. It's the goddam gas."

The headline read: **COAL MINE DEATH**

Two Kids go into Abandoned Mine. Only One Comes Out Alive.

The front page story in the Nanaimo Free Press described the events as Sawyer and the firemen related them to the RCMP, identifying both Sawyer and Gally as students at NDSS and members of prominent Nanaimo families. There was the usual background filler and an interview with a retired mining engineer about the danger of leakage of methane gas in abandoned mines. As well there was this; *"Police question Sawyer Jones about leaving Miss Wade to succumb to the deadly gas."* The fact that Sawyer, and virtually everyone else who had some responsibility for the safety of these derelict locations, was ignorant of the danger (some had never even heard of methane gas) was lost in the sensationalism of the tragedy. The weight of it all descended upon him.

After the inquest the doctor who performed the autopsy, who was a close friend of both families, and who testified that Gally died from asphyxiation, spoke to Sawyer privately. "Did you know that Gally had missed her period?" When Sawyer shook his head, the doctor continued, "She was pregnant. Barely but surely. I have not included this in my report. I think you've been beaten up enough by now. I will tell the Wades. I doubt that they will want to talk to anyone about it."

Now, half a century later, as he relaxed on the chaise lounge on the patio, wearing only boxer shorts to expose his wounded leg to the sunlight, Sawyer thought about Lindsay's reaction to his injury. She'd seen, every day at work, things far worse than a leg punctured by a nail. Yet she had been upset. Genuinely distressed. As if the injury was hurtful to her far more than to him. He'd spent most of his life trying to avoid that.

He couldn't recall the last time anyone had been upset *for* him. It had always seemed to be *because* of him.

The leg throbbed uncomfortably so Sawyer swallowed a Tylenol 3. The pain subsided and he dozed, drifting in and out of a half-sleep, half naked, bathed by the setting sun. Then the memories came.

Sawyer gets up, gets dressed and gets into his truck and drives downtown. It is late evening as he walks through the streets of Nanaimo. The sun, settling into a fringe of clouds on the western horizon casts the facades of the old buildings along Commercial Street into grotesque, shaded images. He passes the Newcastle, then the Globe and, at the intersection of Skinner Street and up a block, the Palace - each oozing windowyellow light and the sweetstale smell of spilt beer. One thing that hasn't changed. He remembers reading when he was young, that Nanaimo had more bars per capita than any other place in Canada. A hangover from the coal mining days. And there's the old Occidental up on Fitzwilliam. It goes back to the 1880s. The Oxy.

I saw Dave one night at the Oxy. In the back corner where there's a table half-hidden by the bar.

Slip Cece, the waiter, a blue bill and he'd forget you're underage. Drink all night on what he didn't keep for himself. I was thinking that with everyone pointing the finger at me, no one was missing Gally. Not Dave. He's sitting there, tears dripping down his face. Yeah, believe it. Cryinginhisbeer! You great big fucking cliché you. Dave.

The stores have closed. Vehicles nudge along Commercial Street. On the sidewalk, people move purposefully. Sawyer searches their faces, recognizes no one. He stops at Bastion Street in front of the building that used to be his family's hardware store. Now it is a large book emporium. Then along toward the Bastion past the red brick building, kitty corner, that was Wong's grocery, standing derelict - the windows, eyesblank, boarded up.

And Janet. Dear Janet. "I don't know how I can face the girls at I.O.D.E. again. You've ruined it for me with Betty Wade." Then, her face a mask of indignation, "This is Jeb Jones all over again!" That one stung. Old uncle Jeb had tried to kill Auntie Ethel. Stabbed her. Then he slit his own throat. Big headline in the paper. Mommy Janet didn't like headlines.

Goddam memories. Can't keep them out. Door's open now and they're pounding on through. The walls shake. There's my old man. Hardass Harry

Jones. With that bemused expression on his face. As if it was something that happened every day. As if he didn't give a damn.

He turns right at the Bastion and then down around the boat basin, the glass walls of the condo towers on Cameron Island now glaring in the sunlight. Annie Mitcham's. And beyond, the shore of Protection Island, where once stood creaking coal wharves and listing, sootshrouded colliers. Sawyer keeps moving.

I was in this fog. I was cold. Everything grey. No colours. Sound, voices, were muffled, far away. People, things, were blurred. Beyond my reach. I felt numb. Elaine yanked me out of it. Insisted I be her date to the Grad Ball. Defied her parents. I didn't want to go but couldn't say no. Given that. Almond eyes, browndeep. Saw my reflection there. Red lips, curving smile, soft symmetry. Teeth, like Gally's, glistening. "You were laundry, Sawyer. They hung you out on the line." Short, coalblack hair a wisp on my cheek. Faint scent of jasmine. "You didn't have a Chinaman's chance."

Up the hill to the museum. Sawyer gives the receptionist three dollars and enters a darkened room where, in the cone of a single overhead light, on a pedestal, is the Book of the Dead. He finds his grandfather; James Jones, 1931, Alexandra Number Five mine; fall of rock. He looks up the Wades. There are three of them, going back to the 1887 explosion in Number One mine; Gally's great-grandfather, one of 148 men killed that day. And then her grandfather, in 1912, in the same mine; explosion at the coal face. Finally, her uncle George, Tom's brother, 1926, Granby mine; crushed by coal car. And old Tom beat the curse and died in bed.

I went to see the Wades. To apologize. They just sat there saying nothing until I got up to leave and then Tom says, "Well, Sawyer, you tried to kill her once a couple of years ago. You managed it this time."

Toward the back of the book the last entry, number 657, in 1952, is in the middle of the page. Sawyer stands very still, alone in the dark room, and stares at the blank bottom half of that page. He fumbles in his pocket and finds a pen, holds it poised, and then he writes; **Gally Wade, Furnace Portal Mine, 1957**.

August came quickly. Sawyer (and Lindsay, when she could) were in the habit of eating supper on the patio at a heavy glass table under the canti-levered market umbrella even when it rained which was seldom. Most evenings were soft and sunwashed and the shadows lengthened as the days progressed.

Sawyer had become comfortable with the casual rhythm of his 'life' with Lindsay. Too comfortable considering the end of it loomed at the end of the month. The subject had not come up. He waited for some sign from her but she was non-committal. Still it was weeks away and not on his mind as he prepared to grill a salmon on the barbeque. He had anticipated this evening as it was the start of a week's vacation for Lindsay and he looked forward to seeing her more than usual.

She had defined the relationship - gradually, in reaction to his intrusion into her space, her living space, and they both had adjusted to their ongoing sharing of that space. They became the odd couple; living together, sharing meals, working together with the wood. Yet never consciously touching, seldom making eye contact. Physical contact was incidental - fitting a truss or washing the dishes. She gave the cues to the space between them which he welcomed as they were markers for his restraint.

Restraint. His initial visceral attraction to her had been tempered by the strangeness of their awkward arrangement as 'roomies' and by the age difference. But it was knowing that she was Elaine's daughter that sealed it. The implications of that on any relationship with Lindsay defied his imagination. Discovering that her beauty was intrinsic as well as superficial made it easier for him. He was able to elevate his regard for her - put her on a pedestal, so to speak.

Lindsay was able, subtly, to signal to him her willingness to be supportive, even to please, without being obsequious. She let him know, without words, that she was pleased that he was in her life. The wood was a clue. He had watched her as she traced her fingertips along the grain of a truss beam, almost as a caress, and he wondered if she transferred it to thoughts of him. He wondered if she could imagine that he could feel it.

With a sharp fillet knife, Sawyer severed the head then cut into the fish near the tail and with a few deft strokes sliced the red flesh along the backbone. He left the skin intact. He then turned what was left over and repeated this on the other side. He brushed the fillets with a butter-lemon based marinade and set them on the grill. As he sat down at the table and poured himself a glass of white wine, Lindsay called to say she'd started the rice and would be fixing the stir-fry in a few minutes.

He saw her standing in the shadow of the kitchen entrance and then emerge onto the patio to be enclosed, as if by a spotlight, in a slanting shaft of sunlight through the trees. She held an empty wine glass. He began to rise, wine bottle in hand, then stopped, half crouched, and sat back down. She stood there almost as an apparition. He pinched the bridge of his nose and looked again.

She wore a form-fitting white cotton shift imprinted with a cascade of bright tropical flowers that flowed from one breast across to her hip and then down the length of her thigh. She wore low-heeled, red, patent leather sandals. Her hair was pulled back and tied in a ponytail and a bright yellow hibiscus blossom was pinned above one ear. Her crimson lips lent lustre to her sun-bronzed complexion.

She smiled, "You look as if you've seen a ghost."

He started to say, 'I thought I had,' but instead, he managed, "What happened to the sweatshirt and jeans?"

"I thought I'd pretend for once." She batted her eyelashes too obviously.

He would never have imagined that Lindsay could do coy so well. Something was up. She appeared now as he had once fantasized. But by now he knew that she was more than someone who could simply be transformed by dressing her up. Still he was intrigued.

He poured wine into her glass. "What's the occasion?"

"My grad's 25th reunion is next Saturday. It's a dinner dance at NDSS. The theme is Hawaiian so I dug up this dress. It's been ten years since I last wore it. Seems it still fits. How do I look?"

"You look stunning."

"Thank you."

"But this is *this* Saturday."

"I thought I'd try it out on you."

"Be careful. I may be old but I still have some juice left."

"You don't say?" She cocked an eyebrow.

That set him back in his chair. This was a version of Lindsay that had existed only in his imagination - tucked safely away there. Until now.

"Who's the lucky guy?"

"There isn't one. I thought I'd just go to the dinner by myself - unless…"

Unless what? This was unfolding awfully fast but Sawyer was keeping up. Just then the aroma of the broiled salmon wafted across the patio. "How's the stir-fry coming?" he said.

"It's prepared. I just have to sauté it. Be a few minutes. The rice will be ready."

"Ok. The salmon is almost done."

They ate in silence. They watched, below them, the Vancouver ferry arrive at Departure Bay and then leave again. The fading light drew the darkness over them. Sawyer felt it closing in. Lindsay's 'unless' just hung there, refusing to budge.

Then she spoke. "I was going to ask you to be my date. Be my escort to the dinner and the dance."

"I gathered that."

"You've tried nicely to deflect it."

"Well you know me. Dummy. I wouldn't know what to say."

"It's no big deal. One evening out of your life. You don't go out much. Not at all, as far as I can tell."

"There's more to it than that. We both know that."

She looked away. Her light bronze cheeks turned pink.

He said, "We've made an awkward situation work, haven't we? Going out together, no matter how innocent, puts a crack in it, doesn't it? Right in front of the end of your time here."

Lindsay shrugged, looked deflated, which tugged at him. He added, "I guess we could consider it some sort of farewell gesture." Which was, he realized, as soon as he said it, a stupid remark. Still he blundered on. "You haven't talked about that. Do you know where you'll go?"

"If I have to, I'll live with a friend. Probably Sophie from work until I find a place."

"You haven't looked?"

"You know I haven't. I don't want to leave."

Somewhere in the shadows a tree frog croaked. Then a long silence.

Sawyer spoke. “You know, if you were ugly and an irritable shrew, there’d be no problem. I’d finish the kitchen in that suite and charge you an exorbitant rent and ignore you.”

“I’d settle for that. You could pretend I’m ugly and a shrew.”

“Ha! Fat chance. I’m not that dumb and anyway I don’t think that’s what you really want.”

“Well, if I’m not ugly, what am I? Don’t you, at least, find me attractive?”

Sawyer poured what was left of the wine into her glass. Then he stood up and went inside and came back with another bottle, opened it and filled his glass. He lifted the glass, and tipped it toward her. He said, “Here’s looking at you, kid,” in his best Humphrey Bogart. He sat down.

Lindsay reached across the table and touched his arm. “Answer me.”

He sat back and exhaled, almost inaudibly. “You are beautiful,” he said, “I’ve never known anyone as beautiful as you.”

No one had ever said anything like that to her. His words fell on her like a soft, warm rain. Her eyes misted then narrowed to suspicious slits. She felt that she had trapped him. She said, "You're not going to shut me up by saying that."

"I meant it." He felt relief rippling through him. "There's only one other woman who even came close."

Whether or not he meant it, Lindsay wasn't going to let the moment pass. "So what's the problem? You think I'm beautiful and I want to be with you."

"It's not that simple. It's complicated."

"What's complicated?'

Sawyer felt it all slipping away. It wasn't that simple. No way he could simplify it. Stupid to expect an easy way out. Either way she was going to hurt. And now he realized that so was he.

"Lindsay. Look at me. Do you want to know who that 'only one other woman' was?"

"Who?"

"Your mother."

Lindsay had anticipated a reaction when she stepped out onto the patio that evening. What she got, through the process, she wasn't sure. She wasn't even sure what she wanted, beyond convincing Sawyer that she should stay with him - and if that meant a visible change in her persona, so be it. But now, in the moment, it all seemed fuzzy. Blurred. What in the world did her mother have to do with any of this?

She looked at him. Incredulous. “My mother? How could you know my mother? She died thirty years ago.”

“I knew her before she died, before she got married.”

Now curious. “Is this another one of your stories?”

“Stories?”

“Yes. Like the time you blew up your house. And the one about that Dink woman’s song.”

He smiled. “Yes and no. This is more personal, and it’s long. Please listen because it’s the only way I can explain to you how I feel. Or at least try.”

He told her about Gally Wade and the train accident and how Elaine’s parents reacted. And he told her about the Furnace Portal mine and his long night of consequence. He told her about Gally’s father, Tom Wade and about Gally’s pregnancy and how it felt to be sharing a secret with someone who hated him.

"Back then, I was so absorbed with Gally's death that I didn't think much about the tiny life that died inside her. But to Tom and his wife Betty it was a big issue. It seemed to me that their image socially was more important than their loss of Gally. It was a sacred secret. I figured they hated me even more because I knew. It was then that I learned that grief has ugly wrinkles: like anger, resentment, even hatred. And for sure there has to be someone to blame. Tom was the last of them. I saw his obit the day I met you. I was, until now, the only one left to know about it. I haven't thought about it in years but right now I imagine her as a girl. Just a tiny fetus but potentially a bright, pretty young girl and, some day, an attractive woman. To the Wades she was just an embarrassment."

Sawyer stood and moved over to the railing, then turned and looked back at Lindsay. "Did you blame yourself for your mother's death?"

"Yes. It was hard. Raising me. Caring for me."

"What about your father?"

"Did I blame him? I guess. But I'd never even laid eyes on him - that I could remember. How do you think about a phantom, a sort of nebulous … *thing.* There was just a big hole where he should have been all those years before she died. You know, the single mom thing. No money. Other kids had dads." She shrugged. "No point in it is there? Just leaves you with an attitude about men."

"You can't trust them, can you? Specially the dummies." He grinned, awkwardly, realizing too late that that wasn't funny.

She gave him a quick look and then an obvious smile. "Really. I've tended to ignore them. Until now. I'm talking about the other guys. The charmers. The bad boys who girls seem to fall for. And it seems that any decent man I ever managed to meet was married. Anyway, I got over it."

Sawyer returned to the table and sat across from Lindsay. Darkness enveloped the patio and she lit a candle. Shadows wavered across her face in the candle glow. Her eyes burned. He said, "Maybe that's enough for now. Maybe we should sleep on it and start again in the morning."

"I'm not tired. I want to know how my mother gets into this." There was still a note of disbelief in her voice.

"Ok. We lived in an old, three-story Victorian house on the hill over on Hecate Street. It sort of rambled down the slope. My bedroom was on the lower floor and had its own entrance, like your suite here. After Gally died I hid in there. Went to school. Came home. Avoided my parents. Silent suppers. I stayed away from my friends - Dave, Sonny. Quit the basketball team. Some teachers tried to be supportive. Eventually they all, everyone, gave up on me. Except Elaine. Your mother. She was Gally's best friend. One Sunday she came to see me and we ended up walking around Westwood Lake and she got me talking. She understood that it wasn't just the guilt. That I *missed* Gally, probably more than anyone else. After that she came a few more times and then we would meet somewhere. Had to keep it from her parents and, I guess, the local gossips. We'd just go for walks - Newcastle Island, Jack Point, the Lake.

"When I started to come out of it I realized the chance she took. Defying her parents; and that she had no motive. She just cared. We graduated that year and I just scraped by. But I wanted nothing to do with the grad ceremonies. She insisted that I take her to the ball and I did. Then it was all out in the open. What she did, all through that black time, was the kindest thing that anyone has ever done for me. And now it couldn't be more surreal. I'm going to the grad ball again, after all these years, and my date is Elaine's daughter."

Lindsay started to cry. Sawyer kept on. "I went back to the Forestry Service camps that summer so I didn't see Elaine again until we were both at UBC in the fall and then only occasionally. Meet for coffee that sort of thing. She, as you know, was in Education and I was in Forestry so our paths seldom crossed.

"Then at the beginning of fourth year she called and invited me to a Chinese Varsity Club dance. After that we started dating and when she went home at Christmas she told her parents and there was hell to pay. It wasn't just me, although that was bad enough. It was the whole racial thing. They had put up with all the shit and degradation and learned how to survive and, in a sense, prevail. So they were very protective of her. I figured that they felt, with some justification, that a relationship with a notorious white guy was the last thing she needed. You lived with them. Did you get that impression?"

Lindsay nodded. "Yes. They were that way. But to me they were very old, ancient, and I didn't understand. They did their best and I loved them." She wiped her eyes, smearing the table napkin with mascara.

Sawyer said, "There's not much more. Do you want me stop?"

"No."

"I graduated that year but she needed another year in Education. She wanted to get married. Just take off after school ended in May. She'd thought it through. There was a shortage of teachers so she could easily get a job and finish her degree at summer school. And I had a job waiting for me with the Forest Service." Sawyer paused, like he was out of breath. Then, "I said no. *I* was that white guy in Vancouver. You know the rest. Except why."

"Yes. Why?"

"I don't know. I thought about it, agonized about it but everything just seemed like an excuse. I still don't know. But sometimes I think it had something to do with Gally Wade. What happened to her and how it had affected me and I guess I just wasn't ready for more unpleasantness, even blame, if something went wrong. Elaine's parents were one thing. But this was the early sixties and mixed marriages weren't common like they are now. I guess I was, like her parents, wary. I chickened out. Gally would not have been proud of me. I was in love with Elaine but I didn't know how deep, how profound, it was until later, when I heard that she got married. I've never gotten over it but I managed to put in on a back burner until that day I first laid eyes on you. That morning something flickered in me and since then it's all flared up like a strange dream. Not a nightmare. A dream.

"It's so hard to sort it out. Like if I'd stayed and married your mother you wouldn't exist. I wouldn't be saying this to you right now. I can't seem to come to terms with that. It's like I've been given an exotic gift that I don't deserve. That's just part of it. Part of trying to look at you and not see her. Part of wondering if you, when you look at me, are not seeing a man you want to be your father. Part of despising myself when I realize that I want my dead lover's daughter in my bed. Heavy stuff. Too heavy.

"You, from the inside out, are so much like Elaine it's uncanny. Then I have to remind myself that when I knew her she was only half the age you are now. Somehow there's been a transference. In my muddled brain you've become your mother's mother. I've been living with a ghost since day one. Now you know. You think you could handle that?"

"Yes… no." Lindsay wiped her eyes. "I don't know. I'm overwhelmed."

"You say you'd settle for being my tenant. We could even pretend that it's so you'd be here to help me finish the truss work. That's cute. Even if you are serious we both know what comes next. We're already half way there."

Lindsay nodded and half smiled; as if some pleasant thought had intruded into the heavy going.

"And then what? Does that sort it all out? Or is it the start of a long decline? I'm healthy but I'm your mother's age. She and I were born on the same day in 1939 - in the same hospital. This has been so fine. Having you here with me. Wouldn't it be better to call it a day and cherish the memory?"

"No! I don't want to be a memory."

Lindsay rose from her chair and disappeared into the house. She went downstairs and changed her clothes. Sawyer heard the car door slam and the car leave the driveway. She found herself driving downtown, on her way to Annie Mitcham's condo, thinking about what to say to her and then hearing the response in her head. No-nonsense Annie. Lindsay turned the car around.

You could speculate until the end of time about what might have been. But this much Lindsay knew for certain; by some bizarre, cosmic, twist of fate she and Sawyer were put together in that house. And now there was love there. And the chances of something like that ever happening are near zero. Only a fool would let that get away without a fight. She wasn't a fool. She decided that Sawyer was just hiding behind his fears and it was not only him who had received the gift. She was not about to give it up.

Lindsay came to him after midnight. She found him lying fully clothed on the bed. Moonlight streamed through the clerestory window. She sat on the bed.

"Listen Sawyer," she said, "I listened to you. Now you listen to me."

"I'll listen so long as you promise to go back downstairs when you're done."

"This is what I promise. I'm not leaving. Ever. I'm here for the duration. If you want me out, you'll have to get a court order. I'm not my mother. I'm me. *The most beautiful woman you have ever known.* The past is past. I'm not going to let you make another mistake. You got lucky Sawyer. You got me. I'm going to make you love me."

She leaned over to him, cupped his face in her hands, and kissed him. Hard. Then she got up and went back downstairs.

Later, after the moon has passed, Sawyer dreams as he sleeps in the darkened room. In his dream he is, as dusk falls, walking up Fitzwilliam Street. To the west a bright star - he reckons Venus - sparkles. He stops in at the Occidental and Cece the waiter sells him a six-pack. He continues on up to Pine Street, turns right and when he gets to the cemetery, crosses over it to Gally's grave. He finds her there sitting on her headstone, sylph-like in the moonlight, smiling her crooked smile. He sits down beside her and offers her a beer. They watch the big, orange, August moon rise with Mars dangling beneath it like a tiny, shiny pendant.

"What was it again, Gally? The guy was long and tall, moved his body like a cannon ball? No. That's the second verse. What about the first? Yeah. Something about a dove. Rhymes with love."

So distant, yet seeming so close, almost as if he could reach out and touch it.

"Yes, that's it. I got lucky, Gally. I have a chance."

The Shed

Angie was in her sewing room when I got home from the hospital. "How is he?" she asked.

"He's cheerful. Got tubes and wires sticking out all over him. His grip was firm. Strong as I ever remember it."

The late afternoon September sunlight flooded the room and burnished her hair, now a faded auburn, highlighted with streaks of grey. A partially finished quilt lay on the table. Others, bright patterned patchworks, lined the walls of the room.

"How was he with you?" She sat in profile within the bright frame of the window so that the light cast soft shadows across her face. Her look was curious, concerned. It was a look she had patented. The look that melted me a long time ago. And, in the play of light and dark on her still exquisite face, I caught a flicker of the quiet determination that had once sustained us. Something that, as the years had passed, I realized I had taken for granted.

"Fine. Amazing, actually, considering. He said, 'Hey where've you been?'"

"And you said?"

"Oh, I mumbled something about looking for him. Finally tracked him down. I was nervous."

"I can imagine," she said, "after all those years of silence." There was a note of bitterness.

"I told him I was surprised he let me in. He just said, 'there's no time for that anymore, is there?' He's still skookum, at least what I could see of his upper body. Face is a crumple of creases and there's that scar."

"Has he got his own room?"

"Yes. A typical, bleak hospital room. Only his is even worse. Institutional green walls. Draw down blinds. No curtains. A compact stereo system in one corner. No flowers, no photos, no pictures. Nothing personal. Only a calendar on the wall. A calendar? What the hell for?"

Angie picked up the quilt. “I’ll be finished this tonight. I was going to put it in the Fall Fair but I think I’d rather give it to him. At least it will brighten up the room.”

“You sure?”

“Yes, I’m sure.”

She had felt as guilty as I did after the breakup. But Dan’s attitude and some things he did then changed that. She got angry. I guess I never quite got over it. No time for anger now either.

“Oh, yes, I almost forgot. The faller called. Said he’d be here this afternoon.”

I showed the faller the tree. Behind, in the bush, obscured by cedars and alders that had grown up around it over the years, lurked the shed.

“How’s your buddy?” he said.

“Not good. How much?”

“Let’s say one-fifty.” The faller adjusted his spurs, picked up a small chainsaw and headed for the tree, his climbing gear jangling. He looked up the length of the tree. “Reckon we all gotta kick the bucket one day.”

He was a little man. He scrambled up the trunk, hoisting the belt and the safety rope in lagged spurts. The chainsaw hung from his waist. When he reached the first limb he, with one hand holding the saw, severed it and sent it crashing down. He continued this way toward the top, leaving a mounting pile of limbs on the ground. The tree, an old dryland fir, was dying. The top 20 feet was a lifeless snag - the tip a sharp point. One quick cut and the snag carved a lazy arc into the sky as it descended point down and impaled the roof of the shed. I watched the stabbed shed quiver.

"Holy shit!" the faller shouted, "I didn't see that there. Goddam! I ain't never done that before. Shit! There goes my profit. In thirty years I never done anything like that."

I unfolded the quilt on the bed. It was a patchwork done in fall tones, browns and beiges, interspersed with bright reds and yellows. It was rich and warm - crafted with care and meticulous attention to detail.

"Angie thought you might like something to brighten up this place."

Dan ran his coarse fingers over it and pulled it up to his neck and across his shoulders. He closed his eyes and said, "Tell her thanks."

A nurse came in with a pill and a paper cup of water. "Here Danny boy, one in each hand, that way you keep them to yourself." She winked at me. Dan was single but I'd heard that he had at least two children. Two different mothers. They probably would have their own kids by now. Grandpa Dan. There was no sign of them in the room. No pictures. No crayon drawings. I found an old photo of Dan's retriever, Cruiser. A goofy lab with his tongue hanging down his jowl. I had it blown up and I stuck it on the wall. And I brought in a framed print of the Cowichan River by E.J. Hughes and hung it up. It was of a spot where we used to fish for steelhead. These, along with the quilt, helped warm up the room.

"Remember that old shack?" Dan said.

"Yeah, that shack."

"Whatever happened to it?"

"Still got it."

"No shit! Wonder it's still standing. How long ago was it? When we built it."

"Forty-five years."

"Jesus. That long. You haven't changed much. Just look forty-five years older." He grinned.

"Well, I'd always recognize you. That clamshell smile on the side of your face."

"Mark of distinction. How's Angie?" He caressed the quilt with the palm of his hand.

"She's okay. Getting old, like us. Doesn't look it though. At least to me." I told him about the faller.

"What the hell! What kind of piss-assed amateur would do that?"

"He's a professional. Remember Wally Weeks?"

"That little weasel! I taught him better than that. Jesus!"

"He doesn't log anymore. Has a tree removal business now."

"Goddam, I liked that shack." His eyes darted all around the room. Face flushed and animated. He sat up and stretched the IV tube stuck in his arm. I caught flashes of the man I once knew. I was reminded of what I had liked about him. What had taken me a few years, upon reflection, to figure out. He was all there. Including the scabs and the raw spots. There were no secrets. He was refreshing, not complicated. He was the guy that when you sat with him at a table in a bar with a couple of beers, that's all there was, all there needed to be, between you. There was no empty space.

"Take it easy, buddy," I said, "it's just a shack. Years ago, when I was building the house, I moved it off the beach. Strapped cables around it and had the excavator pick it up with the bucket and walk it up to the back of the property. I use it as a storage shed. The roof's rotten. Needs new shingles. I'm thinking of burning it."

He slumped back onto the pillow. His eyelids drooped. The pill was taking hold.

"Sure liked that shack," he murmured.

While he slept my thoughts drifted back to that time. Dan and I built it on my property on the shore on Mill Bay, not far from the estuary beside a little creek. It was sturdy for a shack. Two-by-four walls on a platform of two-by-eight joists. One window and a low-pitched roof that hung over the porch. Room inside for two bunk beds, a table and chairs and an iron wood-stove with a stovepipe chimney that angled out through one wall. There was no insulation. We kept the stove burning through the cold fall nights. In the late fall we hunted ducks on the mudflats in the estuary and hung them from the porch to season. We would sit out on gloomy November afternoons and watch the southeasters ruffle the bay up white and drink beer and laugh a lot. With his Buck knife, Dan carved the profile of a mallard in flight into the door. Underneath he inscribed:

Dan McBride and Mark Mitcham
Deadeyes

There was a dark morning late in November in 1963. I awoke to the banging of firewood going into the stove and the clang of the cast-iron door. I dozed and then felt Dan's hand on my shoulder. He gave it a hard shake.

"Wake up, college boy. Ducks are waiting."

We'd been in the shack all week. This was our last day. "We've got enough ducks. Give 'em a break."

"No way." He rolled me out of the bunk onto the floor. "You make the coffee. I'm gonna fry some bacon. Want to be out there before daybreak. Shoot a few quackers. Then I'll take you into town and introduce you to my new girl."

"New girl? What girl? I don't recall an old one."

"Wait'll you see her."

Dawn crept up Saanich inlet and nudged away the blackness over the tidal flats. We slogged through the muck, across the rivulets from Shawnigan creek, eyes on the emerging horizon. Two ducks rose from the gloom near the water and streaked into the grey lit sky. Dan was behind me.

I heard a muffled *whumpf* and turned to see the mud flat erupt. Dan had stumbled into a pothole. As he pitched forward the shotgun barrel stabbed into the mud and he, bracing himself, must have pulled the trigger. The blast spattered mud and shards of clamshells all over him. A piece of shell sliced his face open. On the way to the hospital I examined the shotgun. The barrel looked like a twisted banana peel.

"Why the fuck didn't you have the safety on?"

"Didn't want to miss a mallard." Dan grinned through a film of mud and blood. "They're quick, you know."

"Well, from now on, you go first. I'll walk behind you."

Angie was waiting at emergency. Dan introduced us and assured her that he was alright. She appeared to be calm, almost serene, but there was concern in her alert eyes, in the way she anticipated him, ready to respond.

"Just a little gash, my dear. Give me that, what you call it, distinctive European look."

One look at her was enough.

"Where'd you find her?" I asked him later.

"I dug her up."

Well, I thought, you struck gold.

There is a picture of Dan McBride in the foyer of the Forest Museum in Duncan. It is blown up to life size and it is the first image you see coming in. He is standing, legs braced apart, on the large, prone trunk of a cedar tree. One hand holds a double-bladed axe. The other rests on his hip, elbow cocked at right angles. His hard hat is perched back from his forehead, revealing a cheerful face that mugs out at you from the photo. A face rugged in intensity, beaming, full of itself. His figure, oozing a swagger, fills the frame. His grin is inviting, yet you get the feeling that you should ask permission to enter. The picture is in colour, in contrast to most of the others, which are black and white - those in Wilmer Gold's legendary portfolio of logging in the Cowichan Valley, taken in the twenties and thirties.

Dan's picture is dated 1963. It was taken just after he had felled that massive cedar with a chainsaw and just before he had limbed it with that axe. He strode along the carcass of that tree, his footing firm in his caulk boots, like he was the drum major in a pipe band, the axe rising and falling in a rhythmic arc - a deadly baton that relentlessly severed limb after limb. I know this. I took the picture. We were both very young then.

I teased him about being a relic. Already in a museum. In a sense this was true. He was among the last of the real loggers, who could do every job in the bush, from falling to high rigging, before mechanized specialization. In the sixties self-propelled steel towers were replacing spar trees. High riggers became extinct.

There are women who are attracted to men like Dan. Men who live on the edge and have a reckless smell to them. (Now, as I've learned from my law practice, they're more apt to be found in a suit and tie, running a high-powered business.) These women tend, at first, to overlook the faults. Then they try to correct them. Some succeed, but they end up with a different man. Most don't.

Angela Wilson came from as different a background from Dan as was possible in a small community. About a hundred years ago, retired British expatriates began migrating to the eastern, more bucolic, side of the valley; colonels and generals and colonial administrators from India, and others from England, some with titles. These were her people. She grew up as Angela Beaumont-Wilson.

Her folks sent her to a private school in Victoria. She dropped the Beaumont when she went to university. Dan quit school when he was fifteen to follow his Irish immigrant father into the bush. They met after she came back to teach Home Ec. at the high school. By this time Dan had his own log hauling business.

They made a sharp couple. Dan was a big man, slab shouldered but lanky with a flat belly. Good looking in a weather-worn way. She was tall and lithe. Her long auburn hair, parted at the side, flowed across her forehead. Wide-set, curious eyes. Friendly mouth. Dancing, in heels, she was at eye level with me.

I didn't have a steady girl. We, Dan and I, double dated. Most often I had a different girl. A couple of times Angie lined me up. My feelings were scrambled. I didn't know if I was envious of Dan or jealous of her moving in on our friendship. As winter came on I realized that it was Angie who was having to fit in. As much as he cared for her, Dan wasn't about to give up most of what he was used to and what he was used to, what he enjoyed, often included me. As if two sides of the triangle were bowed out. Pressure from the top down.

Winter passed this way. One Saturday night in May there was a party in Lake Cowichan. Dan had driven up early to see a customer. I hadn't planned to go, but he talked me into bringing Angie to meet him there. It was the first time I'd been alone with her. I was surprised to see a book under her arm.

"Am I that boring?" I said, nodding to the book. It was *Sons and Lovers* by D. H. Lawrence.

"No." She blushed. "I just thought if I was going to sit around and wait for Dan, it's not fair to expect you to entertain me." Her voice was strained. The words deliberate.

I started the car and turned out onto the highway. "I've read it," I said, "I think it's his best."

"Really? You've read it?"

"Yes and the other two. I read *Lady Chatterley's Lover* first. Naturally, because it was banned."

She smiled. "I liked it too. I've only just started this." She tapped the cover of the book, which lay between us on the car seat.

"Seems," I said, "that his stories are concerned, at least partly, with the choices women make. You notice that?"

"No."

"Have you heard the story about his ashes? Lawrence, I mean."

"No?" Her voice rose an octave.

It was like something had dropped onto my lap, something furry and warm. I could have tossed it out the car window. As I talked, I became aware that I wanted to impress her. From her reaction I sensed she knew that.

I told her about when I was bumming around after dropping out of college and discovered the shrine on a remote bush ranch in the pine hills above Taos, New Mexico. And that the ashes were mixed into a crude concrete block at the base of the altar.

"You're joking!"

"Surprised me too. When I saw it. You don't believe me, so I'll shut up."

"Okay, I believe you."

"You sure. You sound bored."

"Tell me!"

"Three women, two lovers and his widow, Frieda, fought over what to do with them. Frieda threw them in a wheelbarrow full of wet concrete. That settled it."

"Now I'm not sure, again, that I believe you. His ashes in concrete in a wheelbarrow. Sounds like something Dan would dream up."

"Two of the women had titles. Frieda was a Prussian Baroness. Lady Brett, was the daughter of a British Earl. The third, Mabel Dodge Luhan was a New York socialite. And he was the son of an English coal miner - like me. Except mine was Scottish. And I'm his grandson."

"Think you could handle three fancy women?" The imp was in her voice now.

"Not likely. I'd be happy with just one good one."

Dan showed up late. He'd been in the Riverside beer parlour with the customer and he'd had a few. Then he decided to have a few more. So Angie and I danced and talked. On the dance floor, with my hand resting lightly on her hip, I found myself drifting in close. I ended up driving them both home - Angie in the front seat with me and Dan passed out in the back. When I let her out she said, "Thanks for the story. Whether it's true or not it sure beats talking about logging, hunting, and fishing."

"You could look it up. There's plenty of books on Lawrence. Biographies. There's a lot more to it. Like what was he doing way out in the bush in New Mexico in the first place? How did he get hooked up with those women and why was he buried originally in France?"

"I'll wait. I want to hear it from you."

I decided to go back to school. Looking back at it now, it seems bizarre. So many of my important decisions have been generated by confusion or desperation. The situation was too complicated. I had to get away. In three years logging, I'd saved enough money for another year at UBC. It seemed to be the easiest solution. Getting an education was not a priority. It turned out to be one of the smartest things I've done. One year turned out to be three. I ended up with a law degree partly financed by my uncle who was a prominent lawyer in Nanaimo. I articled with him until I worked off my debt.

That winter Angie wrote to me:

"I don't know what I'm going to do about Dan. He's been so moody. The woods are closed because of snow and he's at loose ends. He wants me to move in with him, but I put him off, which just made his disposition worse. Last month he spent a whole week by himself at the shack. Except for one night when I stayed there. I plucked and cleaned a duck that he shot a few days earlier, which we ate. He drank too much beer and then fell asleep. He farted all night long. Nearly stunk me out of the place. Around midnight the fire burned out and I nearly froze to death. It didn't seem to bother him. He just kept snoring and farting until about four. Then he got up and started a new fire. And that outhouse! Ugh! Is this what you guys call fun? He says he misses you. I get the feeling that I'm to blame for that. By the way, Mitch, I miss you too."

When I finished the school year and came home in May things were different. There was a lot of shouting and some shoving. The incident that sticks hardest with me is Dan at my door with his Winchester lever action 30-30 dangling at the end of one arm. He shoved past me into the kitchen and sat down. He pumped a cartridge out of the rifle, set them both on the table and then produced a pair of pliers from his hip pocket. He looked at me with blank eyes.

"Watch this."

I watched as he gripped the lead nose of the bullet with the pliers and separated it from the powder-filled brass shell.

"Now watch this." He put the lead between his teeth and bit down hard. He removed it, examined the teeth-marks, and then tossed it back into his mouth. He swallowed it.

"I had to make a decision," he said, "one of two options. The other was you got this." He held up the shell between his thumb and forefinger.

That was it. The way Dan put paid to his best friend and the girl he loved. That was forty years ago, but it is as if it was yesterday. I remember, after he left, trying to feel something other than cold and numb. Dan had a tendency for dramatic gestures and I can chuckle about it now. But it wasn't funny at the time.

That September, Angie and I got married. It was a quiet ceremony. I didn't have a best man. Dan moved away, up-island, to the Comox Valley and our paths seldom crossed. One night, years later, I walked into a bar and Dan was there. He'd had a few but not enough to make him miss his mark. He gave me a hard thump in the middle of my forehead. I got up with a raised fist but the pain seemed to be somewhere else inside me. I turned and walked away. That was the last time I saw him. I didn't tell Angie about it. Dan was gone from our lives. Talking about him was painful. Memories were suppressed. He remained simply as a shadow. Until now.

The late autumn sunlight slanted through the leafless branches of the oak tree outside the window. It cast grotesque shadows across the walls of Dan's room.

"How long I been in here?"

"Nearly three months. I took down the calendar."

"I never noticed. How long you been coming here?"

"Soon as I heard."

"From day one?"

"Almost."

"Yeah. Come to think of it. Yours is one of the few faces I see. Thanks, buddy."

I'd noticed that. An Anglican priest for an hour once a week. The lady who had done his house keeping. In the old days Dan had plenty of friends. And there were those families he spawned. No sign of them now. No point asking about them. The nurses helped me fill the gap. They liked Dan. He was jovial with them, kidding, sometimes a fumbling fondle with his good hand. The one that wasn't attached to the arm that was attached to intravenous tube.

There was an exception. One morning I walked in to find an elderly woman sitting talking to Dan. He said, "This here's Cassie," and to her, "meet my long lost buddy, Mark."

She looked to be in her eighties but her alert eyes and her erect composure implied a younger woman. She was wearing a Toronto Blue Jays baseball cap. She looked at me and then at Dan. "I always figured him to be indestructible." Her voice quavered.

I gave Dan a 'who is she?' look. He just smiled and carried on with the amiable conversation that I had interrupted. I sat down and listened and an old image crept back into my memory. It was a photo I'd seen in the paper years ago. Dan and this woman, this Cassie, were in the picture. Then I recalled the whole story.

Cassandra Jackson. *Cassie.* She was a retired Sociology professor at UVIC. She had a PhD. And she was the oldest demonstrator arrested at the Clayoquot back in 1993 when environmentalists blockaded roads in an attempt to stop the logging.

Dan had a show on one of the side hills in there and sure enough he was the big bull logger at the standoff. When Dan pulled up at the barricade with his crew in the crummy they were met by a couple of hundred protesters and about half as many Mounties. That was when Cassie Jackson flopped down in the mud in front of Dan's crummy. He got out, scooped her up and, as she screamed expletives, sat her down on a stump at the side of the road. Then, when she ran out of breath, he planted a juicy kiss right on her lips. That photo made the front page.

Cassie got the longest sentence - one month. It would have been shorter if the judge hadn't added on an extra week for contempt of court after she told him he was paranoid. And it would have been jail time had not Dan McBride *just happened* to be in the court room.

Turning on the charm, Dan allowed as to how impressed he'd been that a woman with her credentials had the courage to risk her life and her freedom for her convictions. Cassie stayed out of jail, had to wear an electronic collar on her ankle, and promise to stay away from the Clayoquot. The press ate it up. It was great story. The logger and the lady.

She rose and I walked with her to the elevator. She said, "We hadn't talked for some time, so I just learned about this yesterday." A rueful smile. "Funny isn't it? How you can find the damnedest people in the damnedest places." She hitched up her tote bag, straightened her ball cap, and stepped into the elevator.

The nurse wheeled in the lunch tray. I took the cover off the plate and announced, "Pork chops today, my friend." I cut them up into chunks, impaled one on a fork, and fed it into Dan's mouth. "This'll give you an idea about where you're at. You could feed yourself when they let you in."

"No shit."

He chewed slowly, methodically. Good appetite still, but the skin drooped off his arms and his face sagged. Deep eye sockets. He was being eaten.

"That's enough," Dan said.

"You bet. There's nothing left anyway."

"You know, memory's a funny thing."

"Yeah?"

"Yeah. Like I buried you. After the shock of it. Made you disappear. Oh, I know, the odd time I saw you the old rage flared up but I doused it.

Then I smashed my head in that car accident. Drunk. You know about that?"

"I heard about it."

"Fractured my skull. Nearly died. Best thing that happened to me. Quit drinking. Saved my life."

"I wanted to visit you that time but I wasn't sure I'd be welcome."

"You should've. I discovered I could tolerate thinking about you. Like I said, memory's funny. What do you think?"

"I don't know. Maybe it has something to do with time."

"But it was different with Angie."

Dan's gaze was fixed on me. I turned away and looked at the Hughes painting. I pictured Dan and me standing in the river, rods extended, the current pressing against the tops of our hip-waders.

"I didn't want to lose her memory. Nursed it. Kept it working in my mind. Don't know whether that was what made me half-crazy. Or was it the other way round? Might of kept me from going right over the edge. Had these weird ideas too.

What you call them? Fantasies? Used to dream up situations where me and Ange would be together doing things like in the old days. Actually dreamt them sometimes in my sleep. Reckon it don't happen often. Guy loses his girl and his best friend all in the same go round. All in the same package. Could call it the old lump of coal at Christmas.

"Spent a lot of time at that big house on Lakes road where she lived with her Mom. She stayed there for a few years after the old lady died. Hell, you know that. Wanted her to move in with me. Get married. Reckon she must've been waiting for you to come back from university. Sure as hell didn't know it at the time. Could be wrong."

He spoke quietly but his words thundered in my ears. I felt the weight on my shoulders and my chest tighten and the pain rise from my gut. I wanted Dan to stop and then suddenly his voice trailed off. His head slumped back onto the pillow, eyes closed. His breathing was short wheezes.

I sat listening to the silence, broken only by the harsh sound of Dan's breathing. I must have dozed in my chair. I was startled by Dan's voice again.

"Ange? Is that you?"

It was as if a ghost had spoken. The words seemed disembodied. I shivered.

"No Danny, she's not here. It's me, buddy. Mark."

"Oh, yeah. Where am I? This the hospital?" His eyebrows dipped, knotted together in concentration.

"Yes. But Angie isn't here. Just you and me."

"Condemned man," he whispered, "gets one last request."

"You want to see her?"

He nodded.

Angie was in with him for about half an hour. I waited in the lounge and then she was standing before me. She was like she was the first time, when I took Dan to emergency. That controlled calm that masked her concern. But this time those alert eyes were fixed on me.

"Did he know you?"

"Yes. He was quite lucid." She anticipated the obvious question. "It was fine. It wasn't hard. It was, actually - good." She smiled. "He said he had one more request."

"Yes?"

"Don't burn the shack."

T*ap, tap, bang*! *Tap, tap, bang*! The nails were sharp. One tap with the hammer to start, another tap to secure the nail and then a solid bang to drive it home. Two nails to a shingle. I finished the first course and snapped a chalk-line for the next one. Angie laid the shingles out in a row along the line. They were set six inches to the weather. *Tap, tap, bang*! The hammering made a reassuring rhythm. The rows of shingles moved slowly up the roof of the shed.

The shingles made a pleasing pattern. Warm contrasting shades of woody rusts, yellows and browns, they varied in width and were set apart in narrow channels. The knots were irregular and dark, almost black. Dan gasped for air and gurgled it out. Short, rapid, tortured gasps that pounded against the walls of the room and rippled the quilt that covered his swollen belly and heaving chest. His eyes clamped shut, his lips mouthing through the final, grotesque nightmare as he fought the crab clawing at his lungs.

I cut open a bundle of shingles and reached into my pouch and grabbed a fistful of nails. They were prickly against my palm. I squeezed my fist tight and felt the warm, soothing liquid ooze through my fingers. It dripped onto the bright shingles. Angie placed one, seeing it now streaked red.

"Mark!"

Behind my eyes I heard Dan gasping. Angie took the hammer. She bound my hand with her handkerchief. "It's over now," she said.

Annie Crook

"They are not dark by race, but dark with coal dust. The shadow of forests, immeasurably older than man, has stained their skin."

ONE: ANNIE

Now she is an old woman. But, at age 90, she still strides purposefully with the aid of a walking stick as she navigates through the cemetery. As if she owns it. She knows a lot of people here, all the relatives and others (some friends, some not) she has outlived, including her mother and her mother's two husbands. The first, Alec Cruickshank, was her father. All three are buried in the same grave.

Annie is still striking. An unweathered face framed by swept-back, gently coifed, silver hair that wisps in the breeze and glistens in the glow of the late-September sunlight. Her clear-eyed demeanour betrays no grief. Instead it is a sign to those departed souls, should they be aware, that Annie Crook does not often come here and when she does they'd best pay attention.

Propelled by her cane she cruises along the rows of markers, pausing here and there to speak down at one or another to deliver a lecture or finish a long festering argument, punctuating it with repeated jabs of her stick into the yielding green turf.

Yet, as she progresses, the thought begins to nag: why is she here? Really. On her way she'd stopped to buy a single red rose which she, now silent, places on her husband's grave. She doesn't do this often. She doesn't feel the need to visit him. And, anyway, she figures she'll soon join him. There's space on the headstone for her name beside his.

It was something else. Something that happened in the night. Had she been awake? Or was it a dream? She couldn't remember. But in the morning, she'd found herself driving up Comox road to the Nanaimo cemetery. Her soliloquies to the unresponsive dead weren't part of the plan either - just an opportunity to get a few things off her chest, some of which had been there for decades.

Annie's odyssey among the headstones ends at her mother's grave. At first glance she doesn't recognize the marker. Then she remembers that one of her nephews (she thinks it was Jack Cruickshank) had arranged for it. She had contributed to the cost. This is the first time she has seen it.

Her father became the grave's first occupant in 1931, marked by a slab of concrete with his surname stencilled into it. Nothing else. No first name, no birth date, no death date, no inscription. A pauper's grave. Her mother, Nellie, remarried a longshoreman from Seattle and lived there until he retired. They moved back to Nanaimo and when he died his ashes were buried alongside Alec's remains in the same grave. A long time passed and then, when she was 92, it was Nellie's turn. Her ashes were inserted into the cool earth to join with her two husbands. Still the stark concrete marker remained. CRUIKSHANK.

Seeing its replacement, a handsome block of granite engraved with the names and relevant dates of all three of her parents, Annie wavers. "Steady," she whispers and, with both hands, she drives her cane into the earth. Her gaze is riveted to the finely hewn inscriptions and she is struck by the intimation of identity - her identity - no longer obscured in the anonymity of a crude piece of concrete. Now her night-time discomfort gathers form. It no longer is a vague spectre. She now knows what brought her here.

Annie lingers in the warmth of the mid-morning sun and then, as she steps away, she glances back to observe her shadow move across the face of the headstone. Like an eclipse.

TWO: ALEC, THE NIGHT BEFORE

Annie sits up in bed and waits and watches as dusk falls and the harbour darkens. She switches on the bedside lamp, opens her book, and reads herself to sleep. Later, in the depth of the night, while she sleeps, her father switches the lamp off.

She awakens feeling the chill of air wafting across the room. She'd anticipated that the heat of the day would yield to the night cooling so she had closed and locked the balcony door. She is sure she had. But there is no doubt that it is open. The sheer curtain ripples in the breeze and the dull reflection of the harbour lights slices through the gap. She tries to switch on the bedside lamp and knocks it onto the floor. As she reaches down to resurrect it she smells smoke. Now, fighting panic, she straightens up and looks back toward the open door where the embered end of a cigarette glows - a red pinprick in the murky half-light. It casts a faint aura upon the smoker hunkered down against the wall.

Annie gropes around on the bedside table for her cell phone and remembers that she left it in the kitchen. All she can see is the illuminated digital clock. It is 12:01 – midnight. She remains silent in the bed, not even suppressing a scream, eyes riveted on the intruder crouching across the room. And then, in the thrall of surprise, fear and confusion, Annie recognizes something in the smoke smell that seeps deep into a crypt of her memory. When she was a child she washed her father's work clothes on which, immersed in the grime from the coal pits, was a distinctive odour of what she recognized as tobacco smoke blended with what she learned to be the acrid smell of sweat-soaked coal dust. Determined scrubbing never rid the clothes of this but she was at least able to soften it so that it was hardly noticeable. It was her father's smell. Interred, long ago, into the graveyard of her memory, that smell is now in her bedroom.

"Dad?"

"Aye, Annie." The ember glows brighter as her father sucks on the cigarette.

"You…?"

"None other."

"You're dead!"

"I am that, Annie."

"Am I dreaming?"

"Maybe. Maybe not. Either way, you're talking to a ghost."

"Very funny!" Fear gives way to curiosity. Then she is angry. She raises her book to throw it but then lets her hand fall back, still clutching the book. Her mind rages between wonder and disbelief.

"Still have a temper, I see," he chuckles.

"I got it from you."

Annie shivers. She draws the bedspread around her and sits silently watching, barely able to discern the outline of the now equally silent form across the room. The film of cigarette smoke hovering in the air is starting to annoy her. She considers telling her father (his ghost?) to butt out but it occurs to her that telling a ghost to stop smoking seems somehow absurd. And, anyway, the burning cigarette ember is her only point of reference for the sound of his voice.

"Still sleep with the lamp lit, girl?"

"No." She feels her face flush. She'd stopped leaving a light on when she married Charlie. "Why?"

"I doused it for you. Like I used to."

"You *doused* it? Like you used to? What in hell are you talking about?"

"I'd snuff the flame." His voice is calm, as if to settle her. "Before I went to work. While you were still asleep. It worried me. You wouldn't remember. It would've been a long time ago."

"What? You worried? About me?"

"About you. About us all. Baffling, isn't it?"

"I'll say! And it *was* a long, long time ago. In another life."

"Not for me," he whispers, "it's the only one I remember. I've lost track of time. It stops when you die."

His cigarette has burned down and he pinches it out and tucks the butt into the cuff of his pant leg. He strikes a match and raises it, in cupped hands, to the replacement stuck between his lips. The flare from the match illuminates his face and Annie sees him, sees his crushed, disfigured face exactly as she remembers it on that morning when she and her mother went to the morgue to identify him. Her anger fades. She tries to speak but she chokes on the words.

"Dad…"

"What is it, Annie?"

She tries again. "Do you know what day it is?"

"I don't even know what year it is."

"It's oh-one. Two thousand and one. And it is September. September twentieth."

"Aye, so it is. My anniversary. Dead seventy years today. Quite a coincidence, isn't it?"

"Yes, it is, seeing that it's when you decided to drop by and haunt me."

"Is that so unusual?" He pauses. "There's plenty of ways to be haunted and most folks are, I reckon. In their minds. Mistakes. Bad memories. Baggage they carry around."

"Not I. My bad memories got buried in your grave. And then I walked away from it."

"Maybe you should pay it a visit. Just for the sake of it. You're the last of us that knew anybody in there." Annie is about to speak to that but her father continues. "Been meaning to look you up over the years. Maybe talk about some unfinished business. Just that the time never seemed to be right. Ain't never a right time is there?

"But the other day, young Jackie came with the cemetery crew and they installed that new headstone. That roused me, so to speak, though it wasn't the first time. That was when they put Mac Hardy in with me. Must've been back in the fifties. I didn't much mind. There was room, being that it was only his ashes. And he was a good man. Nell was lucky to find him.

"Then, after another long spell, in comes Nellie. And all those years and an extra husband gone between us. I wondered if she'd remember me. She did. I thought about looking you up then. But the time wasn't right. Too much grief and such. Now, of course, time's running out. How old are you, Annie? If I'm dead seventy years then you're ninety. Yep? The last of us. There's just the grandkids and their kids and none of them care - 'cept maybe young Jackie. And, in my mind, I'm still in the world, not finally dead. I won't be until there's nary a memory of me. Until the last soul who knew me, who still remembered me, is dead. That's you, Annie. You'll take me with you to your grave. It won't be over 'til then."

Annie sits in her bed in the dark listening to her father, his ghost - mesmerized. Yet, like background noise, a thought nags, 'Is it a relief? Being dead?' To her life was a statement, and death was simply the period, a pencil's dot, at the end of it. Beyond that there was nothing. Death was not mysterious. It was simply an abstraction. Until now. Until her dead father appeared in the night. She wants him to shut up.

"You say you buried your bad memories into my grave. But you know what day it is today. You haven't forgotten that. Maybe I reminded you. Then again maybe you've been fooling yourself."

"You bet!" Her voice rises. "You've reminded me. Isn't it's a wonderful cliché? A coal miner's daughter. Growing up in a dead-end coal camp. Literally, for all the men it killed. My father one of them. I hated that place. Hated everything about it. The pit works. The hideous black slag heaps. The soot and the grime-stained miner's cabins."

The words do not ejaculate but flow evenly in a controlled eruption. "I hated everything about it. The drudgery. Dirt poor. Literally. I cringed at wearing underpants made from flour sacks and cardboard for the soles of my shoes. Being bound with everyone else there like slaves to the mine owners. I hated what it represented. No future. Just brutal work and maimed or dead men. It was a shame, what it was doing to my mother and to you. And…I hated you."

"No doubt. The horse would've been enough."

"It would have been. But it wasn't. I hated you for getting yourself killed. For leaving us with nothing. Nothing but a hardscrabble patch of dirt with a mortgage that rendered it worthless. Nada."

"Looks as if you managed to get over it."

"Yes. I *managed.* It took a while. Why?"

"Because, if you hadn't, I reckon that gutful of bile would've choked you soon enough. You wouldn't be sitting there talking to me."

"And if you weren't here talking to me, it wouldn't be…like a…"

"Funny, isn't it? How two people can look at the same thing and see the opposite in it. Must have something to do with what you expect."

"How so?"

"Well…" There is a shrug in his voice. "Put it this way. The ground was always shifting. You had to keep moving just to stay even with it. We, me and Nell, we were in that army of ants that marched helter-skelter across the face of it, never owning nothing but the clothes we wore, and stopping here and there to burrow down into it. Getting ahold of that patch of dirt was a step up. It was solid ground. You were raised on solid ground, Annie. There's a lot in that that doesn't meet the eye, no matter what you think. Solid ground. There's no shame in that."

Annie does not reply. They sit silently facing each other in the darkened room, father and daughter, a few feet, a grave, and seventy years separate. Alec pinches out his cigarette and speaks. "I'm gone now, Annie. Your day's coming. I'll watch for you."

"Wait!" Annie croaks, but he's not there. She leans down to retrieve the fallen lamp and discovers that it is back, standing upright, on the bedside table. She switches it on and examines the space by the balcony door where her father's ghost had been seconds earlier, seeing only that the door is now closed and locked. She looks at the digital clock. It reads 12:01 – unchanged. She thinks it must have stopped but, as she watches, it ticks over to 12:02. Overwhelmed, she slumps down into the bed, a jumble of thoughts and images rattling inside her head, and tries to sleep with the light on.

But sleep won't come. Her scattered thoughts gradually coalesce around one dominant image. That ground. Five acres of cleared land in Alexandra, a mining camp six miles south of Nanaimo. It sloped from Gomerich road down to marshland that surrounded a small lake - Beck Lake. The rambling, ramshackle, house overlooked the property from a corner near the road. On it her father kept animals; a cow, pigs, chickens and two horses, and her mother grew vegetables in a large garden on the rich bottom-land soil. Sustaining ground to weather the vagaries of a coal miner's existence.

Annie and her four siblings had their chores which included care of the animals. She got the horses, two pit ponies that the Company gave to her father just to get rid of them. Rube (short for Rhubarb) was a gentle old swayback mare well past her usefulness in the pits. Newt, a robust bay gelding, was found to be too ornery and difficult to handle underground. Her father figured, even if he wasn't a dray horse, he was strong enough to pull a plough. He didn't want Rube but she was part of the deal. If he wanted Newt, he'd have to take her too.

Everyone was wary of Newt. He'd bite and kick. And he was dangerous in his stall. He'd try to crush you against the sideboards with his rump. Everyone except Annie. She could control him, even ride him, which she did, in high school and after she went to work. When she found the time.

Now, after more than 70 years, Annie remembers sitting with her mother on the back porch, watching her father wrestling with the plough and flailing at Newt with a long knotted rope as they carved neat furrows through the loam of the bottom-land. It would be on a Sunday in the spring in preparation for planting potatoes and corn. At the end of the day he would unhitch the plough and give the horse to Annie and she'd take him to the stable, remove the harness, comb him down, feed him and settle him for the night. A rare good memory, as were almost all to do with that horse. But one.

Annie is ready for sleep now. As she drifts away her mind rests on one of those brief and desperately few instances when she caught an unguarded image of her father, with the ploughing done and him, his shirt sweatdrenched and the sweat in his eyebrows dripping into his eyes and trickling across his face, almost like tears, if she could imagine that, handing her the reins, looking at her. The trace of a smile. A wisp of exhilaration.

This was his ground. A space within which he had some control. A separate place of order where he sequestered his family from the chaos outside.

THREE: THE MORNING AFTER

Before deciding to go to the cemetery that morning Annie took her coffee and sat out on the balcony in her kimono. The seaplane traffic hadn't yet started and the harbour was quiet. Pleasure boats lay slumbering at anchor between the islands. She felt the warmth of the sun rising over Gabriola. Looking north she could see, on the bluff above Departure Bay, the house that she and Charlie built after they retired - a handsome dwelling in a prime location with a southern exposure and a fine view of the islands and the harbour. Now, she realized, it was 25 years old and, like her, showing its age. And was it, like her, a place where you talked to a ghost in the dark? Charlie's ghost? She felt bewildered and numb from her experience in the night. Was it a dream or had she been hallucinating? Was she starting to believe in ghosts?

That was their second house. One of only two they'd ever lived in. They built the first, a stylish Craftsman bungalow that featured two eyelid dormers and a large front porch with distinctive posts and railings, in the Townsite in 1939 when Charlie's law practice had set down roots. The house looked out at the neighbourhood with a somnolent, satisfied smile. More than just a house. Outwardly, to them and to whomever else who would notice, it was a statement. What two kids could achieve if they were able to kick themselves free of the coal camps. And, within, it was their baby. Charlie had wanted a family but Annie said no. To punctuate it she had her tubes tied. Yet, for such a positive event, the birth of the house was not without complications.

Annie embedded her aspirations in Charlie. Working to enable his success as a lawyer would enhance life for both of them. This was understood. Their marriage was a partnership with deeper meaning than what marriage ordinarily would imply. So that, while he found part time work, it was her regular job as a stenographer that made the difference. That put him through law school - no mean feat during the Depression. There was no time or space for tension beyond what the work and schooling itself imposed. That came later with the inevitable confrontation of wills.

Initially, and on the surface, the partnership ran smoothly. Annie qualified as a legal stenographer and the office of Charles Mitcham, Barrister and Solicitor, consisted of the two of them and part-time help when needed. But as the practice grew and became more demanding and Charlie more detached, Annie began to feel less like a partner and more like an employee. Charlie sensed this in her mood swings and her increasing tendency to interfere in matters that involved lawyering, not administration.

So their decision to build could have been considered a necessary distraction. But it was time anyway. They had lived in apartments far too long. They designed the house themselves and then contracted with a builder. Annie plunged into it and, like a genuine clerk-of-the-works, managed every detail. Charlie generally agreed with her choices; cabinetry, wall colours, fixtures and the like - except for the flooring. Annie wanted red oak hardwood throughout the house. Charlie also wanted wood but, instead, edge grain fir (he had a client who ran a lumber business). He was insistent and one afternoon, while they were at the site, arguing about it, a truckload of edge grain fir arrived.

Furious at being presented with a *fait accompli*, Annie demanded that Charlie send it back. He turned away from her and calmly instructed the truckers to unload the flooring. Annie watched, speechless, as the truck backed up to the open front door. Then she looked for something, any object, handy and solid enough, to throw at Charlie. Instead she found, leaning against a wall, a length of 3/8-inch rebar and, wielding it with both hands, she swung and bent it across Charlie's shoulders. He went down like he'd been pole-axed. And Annie, reacting as if she had actually struck herself, fainted. Meanwhile, in the living room, the truckers methodically continued stacking the load of edge grain fir.

Charlie, his right arm numb and dangling, roused Annie and together, with him steering with his good arm and her shifting gears, they drove home where she took a sedative and went to bed for the rest of the day. He called a taxi and continued on to the hospital where x-rays revealed a broken collar bone.

Down through the years they avoided mention of this incident. But two things, important things, resulted from it. Charlie volunteered that September, after war broke out, and was rejected because of his injury. And its impact served, as well, to take a whack out of Annie (as she slept that afternoon her father's agonized visage loomed in her dreams). What was left of her belligerence became redirected - mainly toward anyone she encountered whom she considered to be a fool.

FOUR: THE NEXT NIGHT, SIRENS

A siren. Annie stirs then rises from the bed and gropes her way in the dark to the balcony door and steps outside. She didn't notice sirens much until after Charlie died. They lived in a quiet neighbourhood then. Not like here in the condominium, by the boat basin downtown. Maybe it's being alone. Or because of the proximity. Whatever.

Now she hears them; police cars, fire alarms, ambulances. Maybe a fire somewhere in the north end of town. The mournful cadence of this one undulates across the harbour and she sees red lights flashing along Stewart Avenue. The sirens have become not simply irritants in the night that disturb her sleep. They conjure up the wail of the sirens of her childhood - that pierced the busy quiet of her elementary school classroom in Alexandra. And men running toward the mine entrance. The quiet would suddenly become a voluntary silence - a stillness so profound as to drown out the siren's shriek. Every head in the room would turn to the windows, eyes cast at the profile of the mine workings. Now, as then, her throat constricts and her breath stills. Then it would stop and the teachers would send her and her classmates home.

The night is quiet now. The alarm has passed and somewhere out there men and women are attending the emergency. She wonders if there has been a tragedy. If someone has died. So this is what happens. This is how you wait for death. A cranky old woman alone in the darkness haunted by a ghost and uninvited memories. Is this why you went to the graveyard?

Annie is up with the sunrise and, as if as an antidote to the sirens in the night, immerses herself in memories of her life with Charlie. She pulls back the curtains and sunlight floods the great room, illuminating pleasurable objects and mementoes. She sits in the breakfast nook, savouring her morning coffee, and surveys the room; the Galle and Daum glass vases collected during their many trips to Europe - in Paris, Nancy, and Prague - and displayed securely in an antique Art Nouveau glass cabinet; the sterling silver tea service (bought at auction) at the centre of the large rosewood dining table where places are continually set for two; the series of Japanese woodblock prints, purchased in Tokyo, that hang on the wall above the sideboard; the Persian rugs. All these, the accumulation and enjoyment of them and many other things, she associates with a place and a time. A moment of pleasure with Charlie.

Shelves above the carved rosewood writing desk in the far corner (her personal space) display photos, ornaments and recognitions, including plaques proclaiming gratitude and honours from the IODE, the Rotary Club, the United Way, and other charities. As well, there are trophies; Annie, years ago, won the Golf Club's Senior Woman's championship three years running. In recognition of a long, satisfactory, even satisfied, life.

In the den Annie has recreated Charlie's study, albeit in tighter dimensions than his lair in the big house, as if in tribute to his memory. A shrine? Perhaps. But is this not better than wallowing in grief? She enters the room and sits at his desk, facing a glass wall beyond which, across the harbour, loom Protection and Gabriola Islands. She is in her comfort zone, surrounded by the essence of Charlie; the glass-encased bookshelves, the overstuffed leather sofa and chair, a wall smothered with memorabilia, including Charlie's degree from the Vancouver School of Law, his QC, his Commodore's cap from the yacht club, a large photo of their sailboat, Crystal Sea, other pictures of good times with friends, cruising and skiing. On the desk, beside the gold, inscribed, pen and pencil set stands a framed photo of Zlata, their golden retriever, her head tilted, eyes fixed expectantly forward with a stick of driftwood gripped between her jaws. Annie has even draped Charlie's ancient, worn, Harris Tweed sports jacket over the back of the chair. Sitting there she imagines she can smell him.

Such nostalgia. And irony, considering Annie's generally no-nonsense attitude to life. She hadn't anticipated that it would be so sustaining in her widow years. For that matter she hadn't even considered what life would be like without Charlie. But does his memory really warrant this reverence? Was he really a saint? Obviously, in her eyes. And now that she is very old what else is there? Life with her husband diluted, if not erased, the bitterness of her childhood. That alone is worth a lot.

Of course it wasn't always an idyllic stroll down lover's lane. There were barren stretches. 62 years of marriage is a long time, and Annie's impetuous nature tested it on occasion. Perhaps that was a part of her that appealed to Charlie. Their experience out in the open, or behind closed doors, was never dull. And to her he was so steady, so certain, so unperturbed. He encouraged her exuberance, was patient with her moods. They were partners, in the broadest sense. She felt secure in that.

Occasionally she wonders if it would have been different with children? She couldn't imagine. But she did think about how it would feel, at this stage, in her solitude, to have grandchildren to hover over, even spoil. She'd witnessed the raising of their children by one of her siblings and her close friends and sensed that she'd missed a certain love which was different than the devotion and, as well, the visceral experience that she'd shared with Charlie - one that implied a special kind of intimacy that only a mother would know. And she'd witnessed the tribulations and heartaches that come with raising children.

She thinks about her own childhood. She shared a closeness with her brothers, Steven and Stewart. There was no rivalry, instead simple trust. Those were good memories set otherwise against the reality of poverty and tension. Her twin sisters, Emily and Evelyn, were an afterthought, born ten years after Annie, and were at a vulnerable age when Alec died and their world fell apart. Only a miracle, in the person of Mac Hardy, saved them. He married Nell and took her and the girls to Seattle. Annie seldom saw her sisters after that. And when Mac and Nell moved back to Nanaimo, the girls were grown up and gone. They predeceased Annie. She lost contact with their children.

When she thinks about it, Annie marvels at how her parents coped. Hers was a family under constant pressure that was eventually torn apart. Maybe that was why she'd had her tubes tied. Or maybe it was because she was just selfish. She didn't know. Still, now alone with her memories, she has no regrets. And she thanks Charlie, who had wanted children, for deferring to her.

So it was not a surprise when she found that she preferred her solitude. At this stage in her life being sociable was too often a chore. Time seemed now to flow like an old movie in reverse - in a steady stream of flashbacks. There wasn't much to look forward to. TV. The British mysteries. Andre Rieu in concert. A glass of wine on the balcony when the weather was good. The solitude.

All the interesting people she had known were gone. It was hard to find new ones. Her stiff leg had kiboshed golf and the women at the IODE, all younger, were too deferential which she found to be patronizing. She still volunteered at the food bank, where she found the casual social atmosphere to be complementary enough to her otherwise solitary life. The only person she looked forward to seeing was a young woman, Lindsay Lee, who was less than half Annie's age. She, a nurse, had been hired by Annie to help with Charlie after his stroke. She lived with them in the big house and she and Annie became close.

And there was the yacht club. She and Charlie had been active members. The club was a focus of their social life and she continued with it after he died until she began to feel that she'd outgrown it as well. The tipping point was an incident with Arnold Hammond, a widower who had made an awkward (and absurdly comical) pass at Annie after Charlie died. One evening, as Annie was animatedly enjoying a drink and conversation with two companions at a table near the projection lounge, Arnold approached her and demanded that she tone it down. He couldn't hear the movie.

Annie replied, "Really Arnold, if you can't hear that's your problem. Sorry to disappoint you."

"You're not sorry!"

"No, I'm not! I suggest that you go back and sit down and turn up your hearing aid. And if that doesn't work then drop dead!"

Which Arnold did. He sat with his eyes closed and his head nestled back into the overstuffed leather chair long after the movie ended. Thinking he was asleep the bar staff left him alone until closing time. Annie didn't attend his funeral. And that evening was the last time she set foot in the Nanaimo yacht club.

With the shift in her mood from nostalgia to reflection Annie's reverie dissolves and her gaze is drawn from the room and across the harbour to Gallows Point. There a group of tourists is listening to a speaker (presumably a guide) who stands upon the concrete cap of the old Protection Island mine shaft. He, no doubt, is talking about the fetid tunnels under the harbour that leaked seawater from the ceilings and soaked the miners working below. And the elevator cable that broke dropping 16 men down the shaft to their deaths. And the ship full of gelignite that was blown onto the shore in a storm and exploded, levelling the mine buildings, including the head frame, and shattering windows on the buildings on the other side of the harbor. Right where Annie is now sitting.

The rebuilt head frame stood for another 33 years until, one autumn night shortly after the end of the war, it again burned down, this time on purpose. It was the last of the mine workings still standing in Nanaimo. Annie remembers taking her mother down to Newcastle Avenue where crowds lining the foreshore extended across the bridge and into downtown. She remembers the skeleton of the head frame etched eerily against the horizon in the creeping dusk and bathed in a golden aura by the glow from the harvest moon hanging directly above. She remembers the flames rising, crackling, from the base, and the seven story structure becoming a small volcano spewing sparks, ash, and smoke into the clear night air.

And she remembers the siren! The shock of it pierced the festive murmuring of the crowd. It shattered Annie's intense focus on the conflagration across the harbour. The crowd fell silent.

Then, in realization of the intent of the siren's wail, a cheer, muted at first, rose from the crowd across the river. It echoed along the foreshore and Annie and Nellie joined in as it reached a crescendo, accompanied by the Silver Cornet band playing 'So Long It's Been Good to Know You.'

FIVE: NELLIE (REFLECTIONS)

A sturdy woman, physically and emotionally, Nellie Rankin instinctively knew that survival meant a partnership with a man equally strong and committed. She was born in a wagon in a Colorado coal camp and then, for 18 years, drifted with her family up and down the eastern slopes of the Rocky Mountains as her father followed work in the mines. In 1903, during a strike in the southern Colorado coalfields, they were living in a company house (owned by the Rockefellers) and were evicted.

As they squatted on their belongings at the railway station in Trinidad, Nellie saw Alec Cruikshank and his brother John approach across the crowded platform. She knew them only by sight and that they had worked with her father underground. Alec spoke to her father. "Jimmy, we're bound for Canada. What about you?"

"I'm waitin' for the agent. Says there's work at a new mine down in Gallup."

"Don't count on it Jimmy. It'll end up another show like this one here. You'll never get settled in this country. We heard there's a place up there where life's better for the likes of us. A man can own land up there." He spoke with a soft brogue.

"Where's that?" her father asked, eyes downcast.

"Place called Nanaimo. On the coast. They're looking for diggers. We'll give it a shot. Can't be any worse than this corner of hell. You coming?"

Jimmy Rankin spoke inaudibly into his chest. Then he looked up at Alec.

"You're coming. That's what I hear you mumbling. Get up off your butt, mate." He turned to Nellie's mother and grinned. "It's in British Columbia, Mrs. Rankin. They speak our language up there. You wait here with the wee ones while I take Jimmy with me to get the tickets. There's a train leaving for the coast this afternoon."

Nellie watched him disappear into the milling crowd. "We sat there, lost, wondering 'where next?' And he just walked up and took charge. I still don't know why he even cared. But I remember him standing there, coiled like a spring, and so cocksure of himself. And that was enough for me. The train took us to San Francisco where we boarded a steamer for Victoria and then the E and N to Nanaimo. I tried, and mostly succeeded, not to let Alec Cruikshank out of my sight the whole way. We were married later that year."

Nellie came to understand, through the years, that that confidence masked something deeper. Something that, to her, was rooted at the bottom of that black hole that he descended into every day of the week except Sunday. He never acknowledged it but she sensed it and she knew he would never let it beat him. And so there was a tension in Alec that was vital to him. That which was, she realized, so attractive to her that first day on the railway platform in Trinidad. She remembered someone saying that one of the things that separated coal miners from most other men was that they had come to terms with fear. That rang true. But it was always ragged for him. Nellie knew that.

"We never spoke about it. It just lived with you. Like an unwelcome guest. You couldn't do anything about it. You kind of got ornery about it, and then you got to laugh. You always tried to be good-humoured. Like the bright face, you know.

But every time he walked out that door to go to the mine I wondered if he was coming back. One day he didn't."

During that journey from Trinidad to Nanaimo, Nellie discovered more about Alec that deepened her attraction to him. He had a presence, a refinement, which set him apart from most other coal miners, though he did not display it. "One thing was the way he talked. He was direct, no nonsense and his grammar was correct. He didn't drop his "gs" like most of the men around him although you didn't notice it at first because it got lost in that Scottish burr of his. He'd gotten a decent education but I never found out where or how. Where he came from children went to work in the pits when they were as young as eleven. They grew up almost illiterate. And then over here the other immigrants came - Finns, Italians, Slavs, Belgians, Chinese, hardly able to speak a word of English. So a man who could speak well tended to stand out. I was lucky that way too. My father couldn't read or write but my mother could. When I was growing up, moving from camp to camp, education was spotty. Some camps didn't even have schools. My mother, Anne, read to me almost before I could talk. I came to love books and reading. She taught me numbers too. The three R's. For all the agony we went through, we made it understood that our kids had to finish high school."

Alec Cruickshank's "presence" wasn't "pretence." There was no room for that underground. He was looked up to. He naturally became a union organizer. Above ground he was involved in the community and served a term as the chair of the local school board. As well he represented Alexandra on the council of the Nanaimo branch of the

Forester's Lodge which, with other like organizations, provided crucial support to the social fabric of the logging and mining communities.

SIX: NELLIE (EXTENSION)

In Alexandra life *was* better for them. At least above ground. They owned their own home and there was enough land, five acres, to graze animals and keep a large garden, something unheard of in the American mining camps. No more evictions from company houses. Nellie's parents rented a small house, also in Alexandra. As long as they lived she kept them close to her and when her father died she took her mother in. Underground? As Alec would say, "A coal mine is a coal mine, wherever. The same digging and the same danger."

"That first winter we lived in a tent and Alec started building the house in the spring. There was just the two of us. It took us years to finish but we could live in it after the first year. Then, one night, the scabs came and burnt it down. We had three kids by then - Steven, who was five, Stewart, three, and Annie, still just a baby.

"Alec worked here in Alexandra at first and then over in Extension in Dunsmuir's Number Two mine. He'd walk there and back over the hump. An hour each way. After I'd wash him down, he'd eat and then go straight to bed. Every day, six days a week. He never saw daylight in the winter.

"Then the mine blew up. We heard it and felt it over here. It's only three miles. Shook the house. Alec was home that day. He'd cut his hand with the axe the night before and he went to Ladysmith on the train to get it stitched up. It was his right hand and it was swollen so he stayed home. First day of work he'd missed in years.

"There were several coal mines in Extension so we didn't know which one it was. When he got there Alec found that it was the Number Two mine. His shift. They were all killed. 32 men. He knew every one of them. There would have been 33 bodies if he had gone to work that day. He stayed and helped recover and identify them. He was there all day.

"He came back all in, face white as a ghost. First and only time I recall him coming home from a coal mine not looking like a nigger. He told me the recovery went well once the gas had cleared. Seeing their faces, like they were having a quick snooze, was the hard part. The only bloody one was Milos, the Greek. He must have been close to the blast and it threw him way along the tunnel. The others ran, trying to stay ahead of the gas, the afterdamp, but it caught them. They just lay there, Alec said, like life-size rag dolls without the colourful clothes and not a mark on them."

The Extension mine remained closed and Alec found work in another mine in Alexandra. He and Nell kept working on the house during mine shutdowns and on days off. Then, three years later, the miners went on strike. It lasted two years and 1913 was the worst year. That summer the miners rioted throughout the coalfields - in Ladysmith, Alexandra, Extension, Nanaimo and as far north as Cumberland. In August there was a gunfight in Extension. The strikers trapped some scabs in a mine site compound and the two sides traded gunfire all day. The government declared martial law and sent in the militia to break it up.

"I was thankful for our little farm and miners' strike pay. That kept the wolf from the door, but not the scabs. And we had time to finish the house for all the good that did. Still it was a bleak time. We couldn't win for losing. But Alec didn't lose his cock-eyed sense of humour. He cut a picture of Jimmy Dunsmuir out of the newspaper and tacked it to the wall. We threw darts at it."

SEVEN: NELLIE (THE SCAB'S EAR)

"We could hear the shooting in Extension. Alec went over there with his deer rifle and was gone all day. He came back stone-faced and not talking and I kept my mouth shut. Just damned relieved to have him home. It's hard to see a man ground down and grown old before his time, particularly if he is your man. One night after dark we heard a mob coming along the road. Alec figured they were scabs and sure enough they were. We roused the children and hid in the stable. Alec had the rifle. We couldn't see much but from the sound of it they ransacked the house and set fire to it. Then one of them came over to the stable. We saw his profile in the entranceway set against the flames from the burning house yonder. Alec shot him. He yelped and lurched away out of sight. Alec fired two more rounds into the darkness. The shock of something like that must concentrate your brain because I still, after all this time, have such a clear picture of it in my memory. Then the scabs were gone and it was quiet except for the roaring and crackling of the burning house. I held the boys tight. Steven was holding Annie. I can still see their faces shining in the firelight. See the terror in their eyes.

"By morning the house was a pile of ash and there was no sign of the scabs. Only the dried bloodstain on the hard-packed dirt in front of the stable entrance. The Starichs, up the road, took us in. Pete Starich went over to Camp where he learned that the bullet had torn the scab's left ear off. Alec came that close to killing him. Pete said that people over there watched our house burn. They told him it lit up the whole valley. Like a beacon.

"We waited for someone to show up, from the constabulary or the army. But no one ever did. The strike lasted another year until the war broke out which caused peace to break out here. The miners, the ones who didn't join the army, went back to work. You could say that the strike, the two long years of it, was a waste. That Dunsmuir and the other owners won. For sure they kept the union out. And the piece-work system didn't change. But working conditions did. The coal mines gradually became safer. And Alec and I started to rebuild our house."

They had help. One morning, as Alec and Nellie sifted through the still-warm remains of their dwelling, three men aboard a horse-drawn hay wagon pulled up to the front gate. The driver spoke to Alec and he opened the gate to let them in. With heavy tools they immediately set to knocking over the chimney that, like a defiant witness, stood stark amid the rubble. They set the bricks aside against the stable wall and heaved the carcass of the cast iron kitchen stove and other incinerated metal and ceramic objects into the wagon.

The men were strikers and they belonged, like Alec, to the Foresters Lodge. The activity attracted more volunteers, neighbours and others from Camp, and by late afternoon they had hauled several wagon loads of debris away leaving Alec and Nell to contemplate the bare, charred, patch of earth where their house once stood. Then, in the days following, wagon loads of building materials began arriving - bags of cement, mortar, lumber, nails, shingles - such that Alec had to request that they stop. He hadn't even had time to draw up a plan.

"We got the old tent out of the stable and put it up. The well still worked and we still had the cow, the pigs and chickens and the vegetable garden. So we got by. We were grateful to accept the free labour but Alec insisted on paying for the materials. He kept a tab with someone at the Foresters.

We were into the new house before winter but it wasn't until the strike ended and Alec went back to work that he started to pay back.

"Charity? I guess you could call it that. It's a word that Alec would choke on. I look at it differently and I reckon he would too. If he admitted it. Coal families are a clannish lot. It isn't as if it's one big family and too often it isn't happy. But there's something that sticks us together. You could say that coal dust is the glue. Or, if you think you're smart, you could say it's the beer. The way some of the men drink it. To me the beer time is something else. It's 'stop time' from what they leave underground: the dark, the dirt, and the danger.

"I doubt the men think about it much - until there's a crisis. Which is often enough. But for the women it's a way of life. A shared feeling that binds us. A vague sense of dread that lasts through the day until he comes home alive and in one piece. And there's that evening ritual that no other woman but a coal miner's wife performs when she scrubs him clean of his workday grime. A coal miner's world is separate. That's a fact and it would be even if the rest of the world didn't look down on us. Which it does. So we stick together. It's our charity, our way of life. The best we can do."

There was something else. During the strike, well into its second year, there had been no shortage of incidents in which strikers, individually and in groups, had shown exceptional courage. They had been jailed, shot, burnt out, and impoverished. Still, against this background, the 'scab's ear' incident stood out. It ignited the imagination of not only the strikers but the general public as well. The Nanaimo newspapers wrote about it with an accompanying photograph of the injured strikebreaker, a bandage plastered onto one side of his head, leaving the hospital under police escort. This was a story of a man alone in the dark with his family, confronted by a violent gang of drunks that had put the torch to his home. He fought back and drove away the tormentors. It came at a time when the strikers, having endured a bitter year, were desperate. It provided an enormous boost to their morale. Alec Cruikshank, unintentionally, had become legendary.

EIGHT: STEWART

After Charlie died, and after the intensity and focus of dealing with the details of his absence, when Annie surveyed the deserted landscape, she found the only one of her siblings still standing was Stewart. The others, like most of her friends, were dead. Annie was duly aware of the attrition as time wore on, but then there was always Charlie. And then he was gone and then it was the cumulative effect of it that hit her. As if the neatly braided strands of her long, satisfied, self-absorbed life were suddenly fraying and starting to unravel.

This was not unique and Annie knew it. She had had the good fortune, or misfortune, to have outlived them all. And she knew that she was blessed to still have the memories engendered by that good life. She was simply old. So now after a long life of engagement, there was solitude. Was that so bad? The memories resided there, surrounding her when she sat alone in Charlie's carefully recreated study with a smile in her mind and the taste of tear salt seeping down around her mouth and onto her tongue. And then there were those other, those banished, memories that sneaked in, disguised in nostalgia, wafted on the breath-sweetened smell of the cigarette smoke exhaled by her father's ghost. She had to deal with those.

Stewart was the quieter and more reflective brother. One beating was all that was necessary to instil a basic rule: that he keep a measured space between him and his father's temper. One wet and windy January night, when it was his week to keep the coal scuttle full, he forgot to shut the coal shed door. By morning there was a pile of soggy coal. He had often witnessed his brother's punishment and, vicariously, he had shared Steven's suffering. That afternoon he endured two dreadful hours as he waited for his father to come home from the mine. He actually felt relieved when the proceedings commenced. He was seven years old.

Alec sent him to cut a branch from a willow bush down beside the lake. It wasn't thick enough. The second one was and it inflicted enough pain to make him howl - something, it later occurred to him, that he'd never heard from Steven for whom the beatings seemed simply to be a fixture in his brother's life.

Now he was 88, two years older than Annie. He had been a hard-rock miner, eventually becoming a manager of one of the mines, and then retiring as the company's senior executive. He lived alone in a small town in the East Kootenays, waiting to die. He had outlived his wife and one of his two sons. Annie visited him there in his home on a rise that faced toward the western ramparts of the Rocky Mountains. They sat beside a window that framed a view of jagged snow-streaked peaks bathed in the glow of the afternoon sun.

He said, "I wanted to get as far away from him as I could. First I went to Cassiar, up near the Yukon border. Then, after a few more stops, I ended up here. I would have kept on moving as long as I could find work. And then he died. Didn't anticipate that. I guess that settled me. He was gone. This was far enough."

"Did you ever go back to Alexandra?"

"No. But I sent money. You know. Like we all did. To help with Nell. And again after Mac Hardy died. What's it like there now?"

"I can't say," Annie replied, "I've never been back. Even though it's only 10 minutes down the road."

"You know, I got so I never thought about him much. I was hard on my boys. Strict. Punished them. But I didn't beat them. Never laid a hand on them. There's other ways. Rob, the eldest, he eventually had enough. Walked out of here when he was 16. We never saw him again."

Annie nodded. Rob was dead.

"He kept in touch. The phone'd ring in the middle of the night. The odd letter. It was hard, 'specially on Win. I know it softened me up. I took it easier on his brother. But one day, when we were butting heads over something, don't recall exactly what, he, Jackie, he yells at me, 'Why don't you ever touch me? Why are you so goddam cold?'

"Cold? I'll tell you, that stopped me. Cold. That was one time when I thought about my father. Our father. Alec. Took a while to get him out of my head. I couldn't remember him ever laying a hand on me, in anger or otherwise. Not even when he beat me with that stick. And here was my son, calling me on it. It dawned on me that, even if I didn't know it, my father's shadow was all over me. That there was no escaping him."

His voice fell to a whisper and his eyes flickered in the fading light. "It's an awful shame. I loved my sons. I got to thinking that maybe I wouldn't let myself get close to them because I was scared of the pain I'd feel if I lost them. I just don't know. Maybe that's it." He paused. "One thing I do know: cruelty can be careless. The trick is to recognize it. I don't believe I did any better raising my sons than my father did."

"Do you think you could have loved him?"

"No. I didn't know how. And anyway he wouldn't have let me. He didn't know either. Who knows how he was raised. But I think you loved him Annie. Even if you won't admit it. And I know Stevie did. For all the sass back and mischief he gave and all the retribution he got, he still not only looked up to him, he cared for him. You could see that at the funeral. As bright as he was I don't think he ever understood the problem."

"The problem?"

"Yeah. He shook up the old man. Threatened his sense of order - without even trying. Just by being Stevie."

They sat silently as the light continued to fade and Stewart slipped in and out, his head propped on a pillow pinned to the back of the armchair. The reflection of the sunlight off the snowy mountain flanks burnished one side of his face. The other side lurked in a colourless, pewter sheen. Annie, watching his eyelids twitch and his lips quiver, wondered about the pain and what part of it was worse, the guilt or the sorrow.

NINE: STEVEN

Irrepressible Steven. Inquisitive, intelligent, energetic. All words Annie would use, if asked, to describe him. He was handsome too. And muscular and lithe. He smiled easily, even with his eyes. Annie loved him. So did the twins. Especially Stewart. Their big brother. He was always into something - including trouble.

Annie remembered the time, the last time, that her father beat Steven. He was maybe fifteen and her father told him to do something, fetch something, she didn't remember what. Stevie didn't respond quickly enough. Or he might have said the wrong thing.

Slap! An open hand to the back of his head. "Do it now!"

"Alright. I will."

Again, slap! "You're not quick enough. Get moving!"

Alec had slipped on a wet spot on the linoleum floor. (Now, Annie remembered, he'd told Steven to get a mop.) Steven rose slowly, eyes welling, and stepped toward his father. "N..no. No more," he stammered.

"Smack!" He reeled back, his mouth bloody. Then he lunged forward and caught the arm that was raised to hit again. Clutching in a desperate embrace, his blood staining his father's only white dress shirt, he sobbed, "No more. Please Dad, please don't. I won't let you do this any more."

And Annie remembered this - more clearly than anything else; Steven's face buried in his father's shoulder and the hand, the striking hand, slowly moving across and over and above the small of her brother's back where, for a few graceful seconds, it paused and cradled the back of his head.

She didn't realize it then but as time passed, she discovered that the incident signified a change - what she perceived to be a gradual shift in the lay of the land. In her remembering her mother appears (she must not have been in the room at the beginning) and, at the sink, she washes Steven's lacerated lip and swabs it with disinfectant. Then she turns to her husband who has removed his bloodied shirt and is handing it to her. "You heard him Alec. No more. He's had enough. And so have I. I've stuck with you this long, but it's not forever. Not if something doesn't change."

Her father did change. Not that his anger evaporated. But it was no longer wreaked upon his sons. Instead it bore deeper into him and continued to torture him in other ways.

TEN: THE COAL MINER

The last time Annie saw Steven he was in uniform. During the war. He stayed with her and Charlie in their bungalow in the Townsite. And Nellie was there, the only occasion in that house that all three bedrooms were in use at the same time.

He was an officer, a Lieutenant Colonel in the Canadian Scottish Regiment. Slim, yet robust with chiselled features and a Clark Gable moustache. Cheerful and confident and going off to war. Annie blinked at the realization that this man, so striking in his uniform, his kilt and colours, really was her brother. Her big brother. The real thing. Not just a body dressed up in a soldier's costume arrived to impress and entertain. Looking and being as the man she'd imagine he'd become during all those years away; in the sincerity of his embrace, in the way he gently touched his fingertips to his mother's cheek as he kissed her forehead. In the steadiness of his gaze. Her brother.

And Nellie. The letters and photographs. Her archive of her eldest son. His scholarship, his degree in Civil Engineering from Queens University. His marriage and his children, his military career. His success. A record of a boy grown to a man. All this so important. So necessary to be kept in anticipation of the day when she, at last, would see him, touch him, again.

She sat beside him on the sofa, her hand in his while, with the other hand, she absently smoothed the fold in her dress. She looked straight ahead, her eyes moist, her faced bathed in a light that seemed, to Annie, to emanate, that was not a reflection. Steven had come home. Nellie felt the warmth of his hand in hers drain away the shock of it. As it was with Annie, this was real. A lifetime of struggle, heartache and hope was now distilled into this indelible moment. She would need more time to fully absorb its impact. To allow pride to smother disbelief. To let love defeat anxiety, knowing Steven would be gone again, this time to be in harm's way.

Later, after Charlie, and then Nellie, had gone to bed, Annie sat with Steven by the fireplace. They drank red wine as if in an unspoken toast to the occasion.

"You know," he said, "I trusted him."

"You did? Our father?

"Yes."

Annie's eyes widened. They reflected the flames from the fireplace.

"Even though he beat you?"

"He was constant. I knew what to expect from him. He didn't frighten me like he did Stewie."

"That was obvious. Nothing frightened you."

"Yeah? Not so. A lot of things scared me. Just too stubborn to show it."

Annie smiled, "You were fun. A fresh breeze in that suffocating little place."

"I never told you much about that summer I worked underground. When I was 16. That was scary, at least at first."

"No. But I remember you coming home so black I hardly recognized you. Two white eyes and a red mouth. You looked like a ragged Al Jolson. And then, because Dad was in the tub in the kitchen, Stewart had to wash you down outside by the well pump. We weren't supposed to watch but I peeked anyway. What a hoot! Stewie hated it. Good thing it was summer. I still can see you standing there, bare butt to the breeze."

They both laughed and Annie said, "You sure owed your brother. He helped you wash yourself every day, six days a week, all summer."

"Well that was one time the old man surprised me. I thought I knew him but now I figure you never really know someone, maybe not even yourself. For sure, not him. Anyway, after I got used to the routine and started to think about it - and I had a lot of time to think about it down there.

Hacking at a coal face is pretty mindless - I realized that he'd set me up. It showed me his subtle side."

"He didn't want you, or Stewart, to work in the pits."

"Right! You knew that too?"

"I probably realized it at about the same time you did, even though I was just 13. Seeing you come home filthy and exhausted every night wasn't the image that any of us had for you. Especially Mom. Those small hopes that she had for us were really focused on you. She wanted us, at least, to finish school. To graduate. And I started to notice other things. The way Dad spoke. He didn't sound like a coal miner. His grammar was correct. I don't think he was chair of the school board because he enjoyed giving up his precious free time."

"Well, I guess that I, by then, having grown taller and heavier than him, he decided he couldn't bully me so he finessed me. He got me the job underground and made it rough enough so that, after one summer, I'd never want to go back. I still can't describe my reaction when the light went on."

"Why did you want to be a coal miner anyway?"

"I don't know. I think sometimes you never know the real reason for an important decision. I've thought about it and I guess it was just that I was a restless kid going through my changes. I don't have to tell you that things, most of the time, were pretty bleak. Both of them did their best but it was an exercise in survival. Barely money enough for food, clothing and a roof over our heads. No running water, no electricity. Outdoor privy. Angry father. Constant tension. But all of that is just an excuse. I could have stuck it out. And, after I got a taste of the coal pit, I did."

Annie nodded. She had had similar feelings and then her horse died.

"I wanted out. Freedom? What a joke! Freedom in a coal mine? Makes me think about that line in a song about owing your soul to the company store. And every kid I knew, my buddies, they all went into the mines after grade eight. And, as you know, if you did want to graduate you had to take the train every day to Ladysmith to finish. That expense, on top of the extra fee that rural students had to pay, made it seem awfully remote that I'd be going anywhere, given the financial condition of the Cruikshank family."

"You were going to tell me about working underground."

Steven smiled. "Well, my experience was different. That's the point. He wanted to make it unpleasant right off the top. Most green kids start work above ground, sorting coal on the picking tables or tending the pit ponies. That kind of work. Eventually they end up digging coal. But not me. He took me straight to the equipment room where we got our gear, including headlamps. He grabbed a handful of tags and then we're in the railcar with a dozen or so more half-awake bodies and zip, down the slope we go. He had some authority down there. He was a fire boss."

"You mean the miner who sets the charges to blow up the coal?"

"Yes. I'll tell you about that in a minute. Anyway, because he's got some pull I go directly down into the dark where a pick and shovel are waiting for me. I could tell that this was unusual from the reaction of some of the men, who had safety concerns. I had no ticket, no experience. They shut up when they found out that I was Alec Cruickshank's son. Still, I got the dirtiest jobs.

"At first, it's spooky down there. Dark tunnels in a hazy yellow light and guys trudging along the tracks followed by their shadows on the walls. I kept looking back. Didn't want to let the slope car out of my sight. But after a couple of turns, right then left, or maybe the other way round, I lost my bearings. Then I just concentrated on keeping up to the old man.

"We came to a room, called a stall, where at least one wall was shiny black coal. Three miners with long hand drills, they're called breast augers because the driller pushes his chest against a steel plate to put pressure on the drill, were boring holes in the coal face. When they're done Alec steps up with his flask of gun powder and fills the holes, tamping them tight with a wooden rod. Then he attaches the fuses and lights them with his cigarette and we all duck around the nearest corner.

"*Whump*! *Whump*! *Whump*! Everything shook. Like an earthquake. The face shattered into a million chunks of coal. The dust and smoke stung my eyes and got in my nose. I stood there stunned until I discovered a shovel in my hand. Then we went at the pile of rubble, filling little rail cars that conveniently appeared from out of the grimy haze. Alec hung his tags on them and a mule towed them away. The cars kept coming and we spent the rest of the morning shovelling in that room.

"After lunch, Alec told me he had a special job for me. I found myself digging coal out of a narrow seam so tight I couldn't even kneel in it. I spent the whole afternoon lying on my side hacking at it with a pick. Come quitting time I could hardly walk to the slope. A seam like that is called a pinch because it gradually narrows down to nothing. Generally, it's better quality coal and that's supposed to make the agony of getting it out worth it. I wonder.

"So that was my first day. There were a lot more like it but I got used to it. Just enough to keep me going through to September. Then I told my father I was going back to school. He tried but he couldn't suppress the hint of a grin and a softening of those hard eyes. I took that as a rare sign of approval."

Steven stayed through the weekend. On Saturday night they took Nellie out for dinner at the Plaza and then went over to the Pygmy where a 12-piece band was playing big band music. Once, before they were married, Annie and Charlie won $100 in a 24-hour dance marathon at the Pygmy. This night they danced again to *In the Mood*, *Stardust* and other nostalgic tunes. They all danced with Nellie, even Annie.

In the morning Steven took his mother to Alexandra in Charlie's car. When they returned he told Annie that the old house was still standing but looking decrepit. He figured the bank had just let it go after repossessing it 10 years earlier. He said it looked as if squatters were living in it. The porch sagged and a board was nailed across a missing step and a piece of cardboard was taped over a broken window. Smoke rose from the chimney. He said Nellie cried so they didn't linger. He said that, from the look of it, two coal mines were still in operation although, it being Sunday, they were shut down. Annie had a few casual questions. The school, Taylor's store. But that was the sum of her interest in the place.

Steven left that evening to join his Regiment. He was then shipped to England. In 1944, on D Day, he went ashore at Juno Beach with the Canadian Third Division. He got as far inland as Caen where, for him, the war ended. He is buried further up the road in the Canadian cemetery at Beny-sur-Mer. Steven had two children, a girl and a boy, who never knew their father. Their mother remarried after the war. Annie didn't know if she was still alive. She knew very little of the children except that they were now grandparents and that they lived somewhere in Ontario.

ELEVEN: NEWT

When Annie graduated from high school she got a job as a sales clerk in the cosmetics department at Spencers in Nanaimo. She rented a room on Albert Street where she lived five days each week. The store closed on Wednesdays and Sundays so she came home on the evening train on Tuesdays and Saturdays - more out of a sense of duty than preference because she was enjoying her freedom and the notion of self-sufficiency. Still, especially in the early days, she looked forward to seeing her mother and the twins (Steven and Stewart were gone). She shared in the household chores and she gave part of her paycheque to her father. She did this faithfully for two years.

As well, she looked forward to the few hours of leisure that she was granted, often taken up riding Newt, the horse that was now necessarily, but not happily, in her father's care.

One golden September morning, a Wednesday, Annie, after helping Nell pick beans for canning, crossed through the apple trees and, entering the stable, was greeted with its familiar, bracing, mélange of odours - pungent manure, astringent urine, sweet hay. Newt's stall needed mucking out. She would do that when they returned.

The hackamore hung from a nail on one of the stall posts. Beside it hung a three-foot length of heavy plough chain. Annie, while whispering to the horse and stroking his neck with one hand, took the hackamore in the other hand and slipped it over his snout and secured it across his brow and behind his ears. The other horse, Rhubarb the mare, dozed in the adjacent stall, upright on all four legs.

Annie shucked her boots and, with her left foot set on the edge of a board in the stall cribbing, she boosted herself up and flung her right leg over Newt's bare back. She caressed his flanks with her bare heels. She held the reins firm and even to prevent his head from turning as she coaxed him, backed him, out of the stall. The Newt horse, familiar with this and alert to its message of freedom from the plough, co-operated. Horse and rider then passed under the lintel of the stable door with Annie leaning forward against Newt's neck as they emerged into the sun-dappled orchard.

She felt the rush of rippling horseflesh between her legs as she turned him, now at a canter, north along Gomerich road.

Newt wasn't a heavy-hooved draft horse but Alec used him as one. Though well past his prime he was still sleek and spirited, despite the gelding. Annie imagined him as her racehorse. She preferred to call him Prince instead of the name he bore as a result of her father's lop-sided sense of humour. To her he pranced and danced and he raced with the wind.

They continued out on to Scotchtown road and down across the E and N tracks into Camp, past the hotel and the church to the school where young children were gathered in the school-yard. To the north the tipple of the Number Five Mine hissed and clunked. Coal rumbled down into the waiting railcars below. "Look, there's Annie Crook," one of the children cried, and they all poured out of the school-yard and crowded round the horse. "Mind his hind end," Annie warned, "he kicks."

She turned Newt back on to the railway tracks where he burst into a full gallop along the edge of Beck Lake with Annie leaning forward, clinging to his neck, reins loose, giving him his head. Her long black hair streamed behind her and the slip-stream teased tears from the corners of her eyes. They crossed the marsh at the end of the lake, the horse now in a lather but still strong. She slowed him to a walk up to the stable where she rubbed him down with a wet towel. She mucked out the stall and layered the floor with fresh straw before she put him away to feed. The last thing she heard as she left the stable was the sound of Newt snuffling in the feed trough. She glanced back to see his profile above the stall cribbing. That was the last time Annie Crook saw her horse alive. That was on Wednesday, September 9, 1931.

As she crossed the yard from the stable to the house Annie noticed a pile of chopped firewood waiting to be stored and stacked. That had been Stewart's chore until he went away and before him, Steven's. It was left now for their father to do. As well as tend the animals (including Newt) and plough and sow the field, and all the other chores once done by her and her brothers.

Steven. Gone now six years. And Stewart. And now her - although she came home from Nanaimo regularly and helped out. Still the sight of the woodpile gave her an ominous chill, something that she could trace back to the time, when she was about 12 and her big brother, Steven, told her he was going to quit school and get a job in the mines. That was when she began to feel uneasy, when she began to develop an attitude toward the place - the coal camp, its flimsy impermanence and her place and that of her family as part of it. A place with no future. Now, at age 20, she could feel the gradual wearing-away. The mines were dying. Her father talked about shrinking markets as coal was replaced by oil. He was 51 and no longer able work six days a week in the pits and keep up with the demands of the property. Nellie had the twins to help her but they were still young children. The focus of their life here had been, and still was, survival.

With the exception of the transient, single miners who lived in the hotel and the rooming houses on Minto street, Alexandra was a tight, settled community of supportive families whose lives centred around, and were controlled by, the six coal mines. The Blacktrack Mines. In her imagination Annie saw it as a verdant cove, unscarred by festering wounds - the deep holes in the earth, the huge humps of black waste and the soot-grimed chimneys spewing black smoke. Instead she saw a green and golden landscape, scattered with farms and cottages wisping smoke from fireplace chimneys. That sustained her in her dark moments until she graduated and it was time for her to leave.

When Annie arrived home the following Saturday evening, the hay had been scythed and stooked. A crew of neighbours would come by in the morning to load it onto wagons, one of them pulled by Newt, which she would drive. Her father would keep what he needed and sell the rest. That evening she found him to be irritable, more so than usual.

"What's bothering him?" she asked her mother.

"Last week, Thursday? Yes. One of his crew was killed. Roy Gilmour."

"How?"

"Apparently a pit pony bolted and dragged a coal car over him. I don't know much of the details. He won't talk about it."

"Roy Gilmour. He was a beer buddy?"

"Yes. And, naturally, he feels responsible. Even if it was the stupid horse."

Early the next morning Annie awoke to a screeching wail that reverberated through the house. But it came from outside. Half asleep she thought it was a siren from one of the mines. But it was too close and it sounded human. Then it subsided into a choked sort of whinny. Newt!

In seconds she was out of bed, down the stairs, and across the yard to the stable door where she encountered her father coming out.

"What?" she stammered, seeing his blood-spattered face and the reddish gore on his shirt and hands.

He grasped her shoulder. "Don't go in there!"

She slapped is arm away and ran to the stall where she found the horse lying on his side on blood-drenched straw, a hind leg reflexively kicking at the cribbing. One side of his forehead was crushed and the eye dangled from a thin thread of pink flesh, leaving a pool of blood in the socket. The length of plough chain that had hung from the post beside the hackamore, now stained crimson, lay, serpentine, on the floor.

Annie tried to lift Newt's head but succeeded only in smearing her arms and her nightgown with his blood. Gasping and sobbing she ran back out of the stable, this time passing her father as he went in carrying his rifle.

"You vile, evil, monster!" she screamed after him.

She heard the "crack" from the gun as she stumbled into the house where Nellie was waiting to embrace her.

"Why?" Annie moaned.

"He said the horse was trying to kill him. Using his rump to crush him against the cribbing. He said he had to use the chain to make him stop."

"He didn't have to beat him to death!" She tore away from her mother, clattered up the stairs, got dressed and was gone on the noon train to Nanaimo.

TWELVE: ALEC

Annie didn't return to be at home the following Wednesday. Instead she spent most of the day wandering around Nanaimo. She ended up on the beach at Departure Bay sifting sand through her fingers and toes and watching children playing in the water. When she went back to her room she found that the landlady had prepared supper for her but she had no appetite. She lay on her bed, fully clothed, and slept through the night.

Saturday evening she returned to Alexandra to find the hay gone and a mound of freshly dug earth at the lower northeast corner of the stubble field. Nellie told her that the neighbours who had come to haul the hay didn't need to be persuaded to help dispose of Newt. No one wanted a dead horse stinking up the countryside. To avoid seeing her father she walked over to Camp and by the time she got back he was in bed. In the morning she was relieved to learn that he had gone to work.

"A new tunnel needs to be propped and lagged," Nellie said, "it's best done when the mine is down. He and Pete Starich took the job."

Annie found a shovel, selected two boards from a pile behind the stable and fashioned a rough cross which she and her mother took down to place on Newt's grave. As she dug it in she straightened up to the wail of a siren. She looked across the valley at the Number 5 tipple and then she looked at her mother and saw her go pale. "Is anyone else working the pits today?"

"I don't know. I don't think so."

The two women, bound together by their sense of dread, hurried up to the house. "I can't help it and I hate myself for it," Nellie said, "but I hope it's Pete." They opened the gate and began their journey on over to the mine.

There were no other men working that day. A silent crowd parted for them as they approached the pithead and they found Pete Starich, tear-stained and barely coherent, slumped against a coal car at the slope entrance. He was talking to some men dressed in safety gear. Something about "a niggerhead* that fell out of the ceiling." Inside the coal car, his body covered by a canvas sheet, lay Alec Cruikshank.

*An outcropping of coal embedded in the ceiling of a tunnel (common vernacular in coal mines of that era).

THIRTEEN: ALEXANDRA

The white Eldorado convertible turns off the highway at Minetown Road and humps across the railway tracks at Scotchtown Road as if it has eyes of its own. Annie marvels at how well she remembers the way. But that's all that is familiar. The mine workings, the towering smokestacks, the loading sheds, the tipples, are gone. One slag heap remains and even it, after 70 years, is disguised by a mantel of vegetation, including tall fir trees. She slows the car as if to somehow allow time for her to adjust to the revelation of this now strikingly beautiful little valley draped in a panoply of variegated greens and golds which, to the west, slopes gently down to the marshland that borders Beck Lake.

A scattering of older houses, some of which are renovated miners' cabins, are all that is left of Camp. Time has healed the place and then passed it by. It is now as she, as a young woman, had imagined it when she blotted from her mind the degradation of the coalfields.

And there on the western slope, still intact and gleaming in the late August sunlight are the five-acre properties that descend from Gomerich Road to the marshes and the lake. Annie can see the land upon which she was raised but she doesn't recognize the house. She drives toward it, stops the car on the narrow road in front and gets out, leaning on her cane. The front door of the house opens and a walking stick emerges, followed by a man with receding white hair and wizened features. He lopes toward her, a roll-your-own cigarette jammed into the corner of his mouth. He gapes at her and then at the Cadillac. Until now the incongruity of a 90-year-old, stiff-legged, woman driving a luxury car on an isolated country road hadn't occurred to her.

"Nice ve-hicle," the man says. "Don't see the like of it 'round here much." He looks at her quizzically.

"I just stopped for a minute," she says. "I lived here once."

"Not in this house, you didn't," says the man. "When I come here after the war there was nothin' here 'ceptin' that stable yonder. I built this house. That was 50 years ago." The cigarette remains secure in the corner of his mouth.

"No," Annie replies, "our house was very different. It was probably burned or torn down." She looks at the stable. She doesn't remember it being so small. Now, forlorn and sagging, it squats among some scraggly apple trees, the corrugated metal roof rusted deep red, almost black in places, and the wooden, weathered, grey walls rotting from the bottom up.

"You use it?"

"Naw, not now. It's just full of junk." Then he grins, as if something has occurred to him. He sucks on the cigarette and the tip burns a bright crimson. "Found an old hand plough in it. Came with the place. Kept forgettin' to give it to a museum. Buried under a pile of my junk now." He waits for a response but Annie keeps quiet. A breeze rises up from the lake below and she turns to feel it on her face. Across the valley the slag heap looms. Her gaze follows vehicle tracks down to the northeast corner of the property where a deer fence encloses a vegetable garden.

"How's the hay this year?"

"Good. Got one crop off in June. This one," he waves his arm across the claim, "we'll cut next week. Contract to a fella down the road. Keeps horses."

Annie looks at the stable and then looks down the slope to the garden. He, puzzled, runs his fingertips across the hood of the car. "Good place for a garden," she says.

"Yep. Good soil down there. Bottom-land."

"Yes," she says. "Good soil."

The Night Tony Shot the Lights Out

I was drifting in that kind of murky space. Somewhere between being asleep and awake and feeling all enclosed. Safe. Hidden in the fog. Where no one or nothing could get at me. It was a good, numb feeling, like I was outside of time. The crows put a stop to that. *Crawk! Crawk! Crawk!*

Goddam crows. Couple dozen of them, up in the big maple by the river bank. Right at the crack of daylight. They kept it up while I got into my jeans and a T-shirt, brewed some coffee, and went out and sat in the sand by the shore, cradling the warm mug in both hands. Dawn broken shadows retreated across the face of the river. A tree frog - a tiny, shiny green creature - made a great big, dark green noise. I heard shale moving on the bank and looked to see an alligator lizard peeking out.

He'd be waiting for the sun to hit him and stir up his juices.

The river slows here - to take a breather and slip into the back-eddy that curls around and brushes against this strip of sand. You can hear it of an August morning, murmuring, burbling, talking to you. It's as if time, like the river, has stopped and turned so now it's flowing upstream.

My father built this shack back in the 30s. Set it up on pilings to keep it out of harm's way when the river rose in the winter. He shot ducks in the fall and fished steelhead in the winter. Taught me to hunt and fish. Me and his big, black Labrador dog, Sal. I live in it now. After I came home from overseas I moved in with Mom, into my old bedroom above the restaurant in Cowichan Bay. That was a couple of years ago. 1946. But my hollering in my sleep upset her so I moved up here to this shack. When I can afford it I'll fix it up. Add on. Make a proper house out of it.

It's on a morning like this I can feel my old dad here. In my mind's eye, see him standing out there in his hip waders, shotgun in the crook of his arm, heavy set with his legs astraddle to anchor him against the current as it tugs in ripples around him. See him shrouded in the mist that drifts like smoke across the water and is lit up by the glow of the morning.

If bullets were visible they'd look like the pair of mallards that streaked upriver just below the treetop horizon on the opposite bank. And there's my ghostlike old man. With a flick of his arm he raises the gun and swings the muzzle in a wide arc across the sky and *wham, wham!* As the birds crash into the water and the dog splashes out into the current after them he turns toward the shore. The triumphant look on his face fades. Because I'm not there.

Yeah, it's on mornings like this. I feel the sun rise warm across my back and watch a line-up of mergansers, six of them, paddle in and, one by one, nestle themselves into the sand at the river's edge. All I wanted to do was sit and absorb the morning. Be with my menagerie and the ghost of my old man. But I had to get a move on. There was business to attend to in town - because of some monkey business the night before.

I never figured on having to adjust to coming home. But my time over there - that being the mother of all adjustments - tended to skew the way I looked at things, even familiar things. I had to work at straightening it out. Get the lay of the land all over again. There really hadn't been much change. Duncan, the valley, the people, were all pretty much the same. Almost as if the place had been put in mothballs for the previous six years, which made it a bit unreal for me. I had to resist the urge to touch things, hold them, just to make sure. I found myself shaking hands and holding the other person's arm with my left hand, not wanting to let go. Once I climbed a big cedar tree down by the river and sat on a limb and talked to it. Had a real serious one-way conversation. But it's the river that talks to me. When I get to dwelling on what's missing.

For sure, there'd been a change. But it was me. After two years I was starting to feel I belonged here again. Not like other guys I knew who were still fighting the war. This morning I was headed for a rendezvous with two of them.

As I drove down Gibbins Road, like I'd done maybe a thousand times before, my hillbilly neighbour Virgil Buck waved from the front porch of the shack where he lives with his wife. The nine Buck boys sleep in the bunkhouse next door. It's about three miles from my place to town and it's rural all the way. Small acreages. Stump ranches. Some cows, the odd horse. Lots of chickens. I passed by the yellow stucco house that John Starich built and then the Schmidt homestead. Billy Schmidt was in my outfit in Italy. Got killed crossing the Lamone River. I tooled along, all the time rummaging around in my head, trying to sort the events of the night before. I had a dull headache and my eyes felt sticky. The sunrise over Mount Tzouhalem glared. No sunglasses. Hank Williams was singing on the truck radio about a lonesome whippoorwill. As I passed Laura's house, I noticed her porch light was still on. That took me back a bit - to before I went away.

Porky Cochrane was waiting for me at the police station. His real name is Porter but everyone calls him Porky, which is apt. He's the sergeant and he runs the detachment. Been the local cop as far back as I can remember. He'd been up all night writing his report and making an inventory of the damage and he was grumpy. His desk was littered with paper that surrounded an ashtray full of cigarette butts and a chipped coffee mug that looked like he'd been chewing on it. The room smelled of cigarette smoke and Porky's stale sweat. I pretended I didn't notice.

The Duncan detachment is a three-man show - Porky, two constables, and two vehicles. He and his wife, Nora, live in an apartment in the building. There isn't a lot of crime in the valley. People don't even lock their doors at night. Generally, Porky and his boys look bored. So when Tony put on his little show last night, it was the most excitement they'd seen for a long time, probably ever. As I was observing the proceedings, I could see poor old Pork was confused and didn't actually know what to do. I sensed he was grateful when I came up with my idea.

"Here's the list," he said, "and you better make damsure that crazy English bastard checks off every one of them. He's gotta talk to the people involved and pay each bill for the damage."

That crazy English bastard is Tony Ashworth-Beever who came home from the Italian campaign paralyzed from the waist down and a little bit loopy to boot. Last night he did some damage to downtown Duncan with a shotgun.

"I'll make sure," I said, figuring I'd have to do most of the leg work. Tony not being capable or inclined to talk to anyone on the phone.

I could hear the battle raging inside Porky's head because it kept spilling out of his mouth. "Lookit all this goddam paper. I been at this all fuckin' night. Just on account of that little shit-head gets drunk and thinks he's Dead-eye Dick. What's he doin' gettin' shitfaced in the Zoo for chrissake? Why wasn't he home sittin' in front of the fire in that big country house of his? Where he belongs. Jerkin off or doin' whatever he does for amusement 'stead of goin' mesachie all over town." He glanced up at me accusingly and then cleared a space in the pile of paper on his desk and stared at it.

"This ain't nothing compared to what I gotta do if I have to bring him in." He started muttering about trials and lawyers and witnesses and cursing snot-nosed Englishmen and stupid Indians. He looked at me with an expression that seemed to be half pleading and half threatening. "But I will, Crook. Don't think I don't know where he is. I know ever' shit- brindled square inch of that reserve, includin' Samson's hidin' places. He's got four weeks from tomorrow to get everything fixed. If not, I'm goin' out there with the wagon and he's comin' back here. In there." Porky jerked his thumb behind him where I could see the iron bars of the one small cell in the building.

"Listen to me Crook. There ain't many guys I'd do this for and I ain't comfortable with it even for you. If it wasn't for you that little cripple'd be danglin' his useless legs over that cell bunk right now. I got no sympathy for him. War hero or no."

But Porky really wasn't doing this for me. The basic notion that was driving him beyond his coffee hyped, sleep deprived state was the dread of actually having to arrest Tony. The war hero bit was a clue. This valley produced a bumper crop of them in both wars. One, who didn't come back, won the Victoria Cross. So here Porky was having to deal with two live ones with their own share of medals, including the Military Cross. In his mind Sam, the Indian, he could handle if he had to. Tony, with his background, was a whole other matter.

Still, Porky could give vent to the braver half of his head. As I left I heard him hollering at me down the hallway, "Jesus, whatinhell's got into you, Crook? These here're growed up men. They can face the music. Don't need you to be lookin' out for them. Like you was their jeezly fuckin' father or somethin'. For chrissake!" The old Pork always did have a way with words.

You turn off Trunk Road onto the reserve between Abel Joe's and Clarence Point's. There's a dirt track that winds around humps and through gullies that gets you down to the river near the Black Bridge. The one for the railway. The Indians, I should say the Department, used to lease the land for a golf course. That was back before the Depression. Now there's a few houses on it, some barely better than shacks. Most of the natives live upriver in a settlement clustered around the White Bridge.

That's where the Big House is. Down river there's a network of trails and dirt roads that take you through reserve country all the way to the estuary at Cowichan Bay. In the old days the salmon runs up the river were the main source of food for the tribes. They trapped the fish in weirs made from sticks. Still eat a lot of salmon but the weirs are gone. Now they spear them.

The morning was warming up and my head started to clear. On the way to Sam's place, I could see the leaves of the cottonwoods that lined the riverbank twinkling in the breeze. The river was low and the water that clear blue-green that made me feel like I wanted to just forget all about poor fucked-up Tony and jump in and have a swim. I could see the bridge, a black skeleton sharp against the blue sky, and remembered how I used to dive off of it when I was a kid.

Sam's cabin sits high on the riverbank. Rustic, just a couple of rooms with a wood stove for heat. Heavy cedar shakes on the roof and vertical board and battens on the outside walls, grey and weathered. The porch stretches across the whole front of the place. As I drove in, I spotted Tony sitting in a chair on the porch squinting at the sunlight and clutching a tin cup. Sam was leaning in the doorway behind him. His frame just about filled the opening. He's my height. Six feet, but he's sturdier. Big upper body like a slab. Flat belly. Arms like a gorilla. No hips. I always figure his Levis are going to fall down. His hair was close cropped. He wore moccasins.

I knew him in high school. He was one of the handful of Indian kids that managed to stay out of the residential schools. He was actually sent to one but he ran away. I heard they were rough places. Sammy, he never talked about it, except to say that it was like being in jail. His parents had died in the flu epidemic in 1919, the year he was born. He was raised by his aunt, a lady I used to visit when I was a kid. She knitted a couple of Cowichan sweaters for me out of thick lamb's wool. We, Sam and I, graduated from high school together and a couple years later we wound up in the same unit in the army.

"Hey Sammy, whatcha got there?" I said as I got out of the truck.

"You know what I got, Crook. I got the Captain. He's been sittin' here orderin' me around. Seems he can't understand the mess he's in."

Tony sat still in the chair. His withered legs hung from the knee joints, limp in his trousers. He looked his normal grin, which sometimes wasn't a grin at all because the stiff side of his face distorted his mouth. His head slumped to one side. I saw a purple lump above his bad eye. He ignored me.

"Sounds kinda quiet to me," I said.

"Yeah. He must've run out of breath."

"What happened here, Sammy?" I touched the forehead above my left eye.

"I had to sock him. Wouldn't let go of the shotgun."

"I say," Tony yelped, raising his head and looking at me, "this ignorant heathen has me captive here in his shack on this godforsaken Indian reserve. And he struck me. That's a court-martial."

"Oops, he's got his breath back," said Sam.

"These are your orders, Sergeant Cruickshank." His good eye fixed on me, snakelike. "Dispatch me immediately to my own comfortable abode."

"That I'm planning to do, Captain." I figured I might as well humour him. We'd played this little military rank charade regularly since we came home after the war. "But first you'd best have a look at this." I held out Porky's list.

"What?"

"It's the list of damages. You remember what you did last night?"

"No. What did I do?"

"Well, not much. You only shot up half of downtown Duncan. And with my shotgun."

"No. Really. Humph. Spot of bother. Eh what?"

"Yeah Captain," Sam said, "just a little spot of fuckin' bother. Nothing like having a couple of suckers like Crook and me to bail you out. Right? Captain Anthony fuckin' Ashworth hyphen Beever."

I looked up at Sam. His broad face was blank, except for a small curl of a smile. It wasn't a sneer. "You want to read it, Captain." I held the list in front of him. He slumped back in the chair and his head dropped forward. He was exhausted. I figured I'd best get him home or his transportation might end up being an ambulance.

I started to read it to him and then thought better of it. I folded the paper and tucked it into his shirt pocket. "It's all there, Captain. Just six little items. I'll explain this to you later when you've had some rest. In the meantime, you can think about it. All of this has to be fixed. You've got four weeks. If not, your comfortable abode is going to be that little room behind bars down at the police station."

Sam's smile disappeared. Like that possibility was more troubling to him than it was to Tony, who was still not able to grasp the situation.

It was Sam's idea. We were going to use up a nice bright August Saturday by taking his new canoe for a paddle down the estuary and out into Cowichan Bay. He'd just finished making it and he was keen to try it out. I felt a bit flushed. It's not often an Indian invites a white man to 'pull canoe,' as they say. He kept the canoe in a shed on the estuary and as we drove out there he said, "Let's go get Tony. Let's take him too." That caught me up. I didn't think it was such a great idea, but Sam seemed sure.

"Where'll you put him?"

"Oh, he can sit in the back and watch for sea monsters while you and me paddle."

"Is the canoe big enough?"

"Yeah. Just."

"You know you're asking for it, Sam. He's not the same person now. He'll treat you like shit. He has treated you like shit."

"I can handle it."

Tony's home is one of those big Tudor-style houses on acreage out on Quamichan Lake. He lives there with his old mother, a handy man, and a maid that looks after them. His father had the place built. I got to know Tony when I was growing up. I worked after school and on week-ends on some of the big properties around the lake, including his family's place. Mowing lawns, tending gardens, that sort of thing. That was where the English bigwigs lived. Most of them had come here to retire and they had some money. They bought lakefront properties and built big houses. A lot of them were retired British military men; majors, colonels, even a brigadier general.

His father had been a colonel in the British Army in India. One of those so-called Anglo-Indians that settled here in the valley. That amused me, these people referring to themselves as Indians. Not many of them had ever met a real one. Not the Canadian variety anyway. Tony was just born when the first war broke out and his old man went straight off to fight. He didn't come back. I'd see Tony during the summers when he was home from private school and sometimes he'd help me with the gardening. He was my age but a few inches shorter - wiry and strong for his size. We were from different worlds but I didn't envy him. I felt sorry for him, getting sent away to boarding school. That was something I would've hated. And I had a father.

Tony wheeled himself out onto the verandah and cocked his good eye at me, then at Sam. "Should I consider this an honour? Since when do I receive unannounced visitors? Fishermen - and one a savage to boot!"

"Listen Tony," Sam said, "we thought you'd like to go for a canoe ride."

"Canoe ride? What canoe? Whose canoe?"

"Mine. I just finished it."

"Your canoe, Corporal? Yes, Corporal White. Samson White, if I'm not mistaken." He turned to me. "Don't you find it somewhat ironic, Sergeant Cruikshank, that this red-skinned native Indian should have the name White?"

Before I could think of a reply, Sam said, "No stranger'n some wise-ass little white twerp havin' the name Anthony Ashworth hymen Beever."

"That's *Captain* Ashworth-Beever, Corporal. And it's with a *hyphen*. A hymen is part of the female anatomy."

I waited for Sam's retort but he just shrugged and said, "Let's get going."

We put Tony's wheelchair in the box of the pickup. I secured it with a piece of rope that I threaded through its wheels and tied to cleats I had welded to the floor. Sam carried Tony and together we hoisted him up into the chair and buckled him in with one of his belts. He sat facing backward with his back to the wall of the cab. We went to the river.

The shed where Sam keeps his canoe is where the river fans out into three channels, through mud flats that are exposed at low tide, before it hits Cowichan Bay. Most of the other canoes there are ten-man racing canoes, long and narrow. Some with Indian designs painted on them. I've seen races and always wondered how they can hold ten guys without sinking because they sit so low in the water. Maybe just six, eight inches of freeboard.

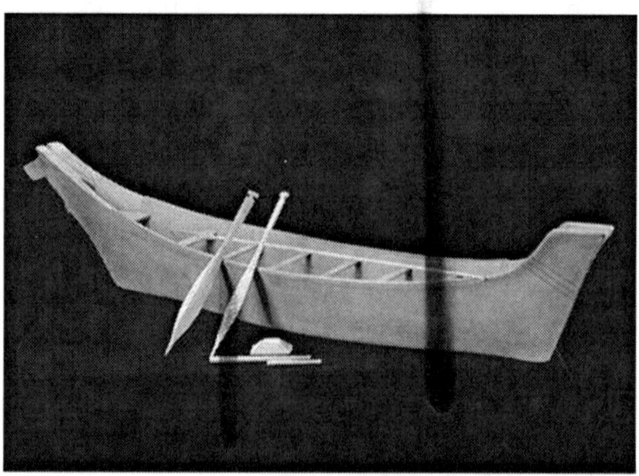

Sam used a chain saw to hollow out his canoe from a solid cedar log and also to shape it rough on the outside. Then he used an adze to chip, chip it to its final shape so it looked like a canoe. Then he did a lot of planing and sanding. It turned out to be a sweet little craft. Looked just like, actually better, than the old traditional made canoes which had been burned hollow. He even stained and varnished it. We carried it out to the river bank. He looked proud. At least as proud as that blank face of his would allow. Mostly he was like a sphinx.

Tony said, "I say, where are you going to place me in that foolish little toy?"

"Well," Sam said, "Crook and me's gonna paddle. You can sit in the back and be that little guy who grunts at us. Whatcha call him. The cock?"

"You must be talking about real rowing, Corporal, in sculls. That chap is the cox. Short for coxswain. Cox. Got that?"

"Cocksucker."

I sensed that Sam was getting tired of Tony's ranting. There was nothing much more to do but just wait and watch to see what would happen next and hope Tony would mellow a bit.

We made a seat using a piece of split cedar for support and a folded blanket as a base in the back of the canoe where we installed Tony. Sam and I climbed in and we paddled down the river.

The tide was up and we passed a flock of trumpeter swans cruising along the shore. There was a light chop on the bay and the waves slap-slapped against the side of the canoe. Sammy and I got some rhythm going as he murmured, "Pull, pull." The little hollow log, with points at each end, sliced across the surface of the bay. I looked back at Tony. His hair was wind-blown and he was gazing all around with that one good eye. He had what I would judge a contented look; as contented as that twisted face would allow. In front, Sammy was stroking his paddle and looking around while keeping an eye on the wharves at the village across the bay. Mt. Tzouhalem stood straight up out of the water on our left. I stopped paddling. All three of us were looking at the same things but I figured that we weren't seeing the same things. The way something looks to one person is apt to look a whole lot different to another.

The late afternoon sun had moved west up the valley but it was still a bright angle on the bay. The ruffling surface sparkled. Around noon on a day like today the sun is straight up overhead, suspended like a floodlight. The light is hard and flat and almost white. Objects lose their features because the light comes directly down and shadows are confined. They are like dark holes where things hide from the sun. Like my father's face under that wide brimmed felt hat he wore on the water on hot days.

Things appear to be one way in a certain light and then they change when the light changes. Depends on where the sun is in the sky. The light is softer at sunup and at sundown. And in winter, when the sun sits low to the south and the sky is clear because of a stiff westerly that blows down the valley and brushes up the surface of the bay, making the sea run with whitecaps. The light from that low-lying sun in the clear air slants into the valley and makes the heaving sea a deep blue. And Tzouhalem is fresh and green rising up out of the blue bay and the firs and hemlocks look like they were etched into each other and against the granite bluffs. It's as if the angle of the light drew shadows all around them. You could count every tree. And the sky is a lighter, clear, blue above the mountain. It's easier to sort things out in a light like that.

Sam turned to me and I put my paddle back in the water and started stroking. Presently we pulled into Peck's wharf in front of the Anchor Café. We'd been on the water less than an hour. As we walked up the wharf to the café, Tony cradled in Sam's arms, I could see the commercial fish boats at the government wharf, where my boat was moored.

The Anchor Café smelled of fish and hot grease. Fluorescent lights made the linoleum floor shine. The windows, which stretched across the whole front of the room, looked out on a panorama of the bay and the mountain. On the walls were pictures of fish boats and photos of grinning guys in Indian sweaters holding up big Spring salmon. Knick-knacks here and there. Dried starfish, glass Japanese net floats. There were a couple of guys sitting at the counter and people sitting at tables scattered around. Bud Holland and his wife at one of them. Looked like everyone was eating fish and chips.

"This place stinks," said Tony.

"Listen Tony," I said, "we brought you here because you like fish and chips. And you haven't seen Agnes for a while. She'll be glad to see you."

Agnes is my mother. She owns the Anchor and she cooks. Terry, the waitress, took our orders and then went and told Agnes we were there. We were at a table by the window and we propped Tony up in the chair so he could see the view. She came out in her worn apron and gave me and Sam hugs and then she gushed all over Tony. I was worried that he'd repeat his remark about the smell of fish but he just tilted up his head and gave her a big twisted grin and lapped it all up.

"Are you ok, Jackie?" she said, pushing a wisp of hair away from her eye and tucking it behind her ear.

"I'm fine, Mom, how about you?"

"Bearing up," she said.

That was the right answer. I knew she had her moments.

Through the window, to the east, I could see Godiva bobbing at her berth. My old man's fish boat. She's a two-man Petersen troller. She's mine now and I still fish her. Take her up the coast during the season. Namu, Bella Bella. Mid-coastal country. One man can fish her but it's rough work. In a good run, hauling heavy fish in with the gurdy, clubbing them, one after another, can test a man.

There was just the three of us back then, during the Depression. It was a rough time but we had it better than most. Dad owned Godiva outright. No payments. I worked with him when I was in high school and we built this place. We lived in an apartment above the restaurant. After I graduated I went fishing with him during the summer openings and the rest of the time we helped Mom with the restaurant. Gradually, each year, things got better. Dad and I were close, but he was a quiet man. Never talked much. There were some things between us that were just understood. Me leaving university and going off to war wasn't one of them.

Now there's just Agnes. I watched her as she stood and gabbed with Tony, smiling and gently teasing him. Said he was a handsome devil. She's still a good looking woman. And young enough. Not quite 50. She'd be an attraction to a man. Plenty of them come in here, decent guys mostly. Single for one reason or another. But she's not interested. Says she's satisfied with keeping up the business and having me around. She's got a well of memories to draw on. The heart's memories that keep true to you. Don't play tricks like the ones in your head. She's loyal to my father's memory and she seems to be at peace with that.

I'd gotten into the habit, on Saturdays, of having my supper late at the Anchor and then helping Agnes close up. Scrub the grills with pumice, clean the deep fryers. Then we'd go upstairs and she'd make us tea or I'd have a beer. She closed the place on Sundays and, if it was a nice day, we'd take Godiva out. Go somewhere, up through the narrows, and anchor in a cove. She'd bring a picnic lunch. So this night Mom would have to manage on her own. I planned to see her on Sunday.

After we left the Anchor, and paddled the canoe back to the shed, Sam had said to Tony, "Crook and me, we're gonna go to the Zoo, Captain. We'll take you home first."

"The Zoo?"

"Yeah, you know, the beer parlour downtown. The Tzouhalem."

"Beer parlour? Can't say I do. Never been there."

"It's not your kind of place, Captain. We'll take you home."

"Humph! Never been there. Should have a look."

Tony had mellowed out since we picked him up. He was quiet and he had stopped harassing Sam. What the hell. A canoe ride and fish and chips for supper. Better than sitting in that big dark room of his, stuck in that wheelchair.

"You sure, Tony?" I said, "it's a pretty rough place."

"Yeah," Sam said, "just a bunch of drunks and Injuns. Drunk Injuns. Lotsa fights."

That was it. No way Tony was going home. He had to see the Zoo.

I wasn't keen on an evening in a beer parlour but this was turning out to be Sammy's day so I went along with it. For sure I figured it was better that we take Tony home.

It was a typical Saturday night in the Tzouhalem Hotel beer parlour. The place was full. We got the last table. Yellowish light, murky haze of cigarette smoke. That stale, sweet, blended cigarette and spilt beer smell. Tables crowded into the room holding up a sea of glasses, full of yellow beer. Guys yelling, laughing, arguing. Getting up and staggering to the can or out the door. Waiters zipping between tables with large trays loaded with glasses of beer.

The Tzouhalem is named after the mountain that got its name from the wild Indian chief that lived up there in a cave with his 40 wives. He was a hero for his revenge raids on the Haida but then he got to be a menace to the local tribes. Started killing the chiefs and taking their wives. They banished him to the mountain. He had a head as big as a black bear's and a heart as small as a salmon's. So the legend goes.

We wheeled Tony in and pushed him up tight against the table. One of the waiters came by with a tray full of beers.

"Three rounds, Lou."

He dropped nine foaming glasses on the table and we each grabbed one and inhaled. I leaned back, cradled my glass in both hands, and felt the cool liquid slip, sparkling, down my throat. I looked at Tony. He was well into his second beer. That one eye of his gleamed as it darted around the room. Sam sat up against the wall looking at Tony. Grinning.

"Stop staring at me, you simple savage."

"Sorry Captain," Sam said. He kept staring and grinning.

I got to thinking about Tony and that rancid stew bubbling away in the back of his head. How hard it must be. Knowing what he used to be. Tough, rugged little bugger. Not just his body, his head too. Coming from his background and having to adjust to the idea that the one person who cared about him most was this simple savage. Except Sam wasn't simple. Not by a long shot. The savage part? Well, I don't know. The way I saw him in operation in Italy, there just might be some truth in that. We drank the last of our beers and ordered another round.

"Listen, Captain," Sam said, "here's one for you. You heard about the Injun who comes into the beer parlour with a bucket of horseshit, a pistol, and a pussy cat? He puts the bucket on the floor and then he orders a beer. Takes a gulp and then he picks up the pistol and fires a couple rounds into the bucket. Then he pokes his finger up the cat's ass and the cat screeches and runs around the place with the Injun chasing it. The waiter comes over and says 'What the hell you think you're doing'? The Injun says, 'I want to be like white man. Drink beer, shoot the shit, and chase pussy.'"

"Is that supposed to be funny, Corporal?"

Sam grinned at him.

"He doesn't get it Sammy," I said. "It's a dumb joke anyway."

Then Tony had to go to the can.

"Where is it?"

"Over there," Sam pointed to a door in the corner. "I'll take you."

"You will not."

"You think you can stick handle through that mess of tables by yourself in that chariot?"

"Certainly."

Off he went into the smoky haze. We sat and watched as he veered to miss a waiter, ricocheted off the bar, and thumped into a table full of beer, knocking the glasses over like ten pins. Sam and I jumped up and got to him just as he raised his arm to take a swing at the poor bastard in the red baseball cap who was sitting there. I figured he was probably wondering where the one-eyed guided missile came from.

Sammy scooped him up and took him to the can and I ordered and paid for more beer for redcap and got him settled down. By this time, the whole place was in its normal Saturday night uproar. No one even noticed our little problem. Except one table. Or, actually, two tables.

The room looked to be half full of young loggers out of the camps. Caycuse and Nitinat. In town to whoop-it-up after a couple weeks hauling cable around the bush. I knew a few of the other half. Local guys, some of them loggers. Salty Salstrom and two of the James boys were at one table. B.O. Pitts, a bullbucker from Hillcrest, was sitting in a corner by himself. Weren't any other vets. They'd be drinking in the more respectable joints; the Commercial across the tracks, or the Legion.

Lots of loud talking and hollering across the room. The odd ruckus. I saw the bartender, Charlie Butt, pick up the phone. Probably calling Porky Cochrane to bring around the paddy wagon. There were some Indians. A couple of tables. They were pretty drunk, but quiet. No trouble.

I would have preferred to have been somewhere else. I guess I'd had my fill of beer parlours, although for a glimpse of the rougher side of valley life you couldn't beat the Zoo. Great entertainment. But I'd seen enough of that. Recognized myself in those young bucks. But that was ten years ago. This wasn't my idea of a Saturday night anymore. Laughing it up in a stale, smoky, beer-smelling room just didn't cut it. I thought about Laura.

I went and sat down and waited for Sam and Tony. That's when I noticed the young punks next to me. There were six of them at two tables, pushed together. I'd never seen them before. I guessed they were from out of town, probably Nanaimo. They sure as hell weren't loggers. They looked to be well into it, hunkered over their beers and making sly glances in my direction. Then the nearest one, tall and skinny, he stood up and leaned toward me. He was wearing a fancy striped shirt and those drape pants, shit catchers I think they call them. He had slicked back hair, duck-tailed and bucked off at the back of his neck.

He says to me, "Wassamatter with you pop? You got nothin' better to do? Drink with a one-eye cripple and a fuckin' bowanarrow?"

“Never mind, sonny,” I said. The other five, I noticed they wore the same kind of clothes, were watching. One had this drooping gold chain hanging from his belt to his pocket.

“Doncha know Injuns ain’t supposed to be in here?” said gold chain.

“Neither are pukey little under-aged punks like you.”

Sam came across the room, pushing Tony in his wheelchair. The skinny kid sat down.

“What’s this, Crook?”

“Nothing Sam. Just some jerk-off kids.” They were still looking at us, all turned toward us.

I guess, Tony, he sensed the situation. Even after four beers. He turned and fixed that evil eye of his straight on gold chain, who seemed to have the most belligerent look about him.

“I gather you young whelps are intending provocation.”

“Huh?”

“He means,” Sam said, “that you are greasy, mouthy, little pricks. You should have more respect for your elders.”

Uh oh. I looked around for Lou, our waiter.

The skinny one stood up.

Sam stood up and extended one finger. He put it firmly on Skinny's chest and pushed. The kid fell back off balance and sat down on the floor.

Crack! Tinkle. Gold chain was holding the jagged stub of a beer glass. My stomach tightened, like a fist clenching. I looked for the bartender and the waiters. They were busy at the entrance door trying to keep a couple of prize fighters that they'd ejected earlier, now with their arms around each other, from coming back into the pub.

That was when Sam put his knife on the table.

It just appeared in his hand. With his other hand, he pushed aside the beer glasses and put it down on the beer-spattered table. The blade gleamed in the yellow light. He was still grinning, stark white teeth, like he had been all evening. But there was nothing funny about that grin. His eyes, which were always hard to see under his heavy brow, had all but disappeared. Just glints, flickering.

I remembered the feeling. Like a cold numbness building across my forehead and slipping down into my eyes. I'd only felt it once before. Nothing, not even the tension of some of the tight situations we got into in Italy, felt like that. It came up out of the smoke and noise of the bar. But it was another bar, years ago, in a small village in England.

We were in the Plough, a pub in the country south of London. I was standing at the bar. The room was full of soldiers, all from our division. I remember hearing a commotion in the corner of the room. I looked and I saw Sam. He was jerking this soldier's tie. He held it up close right against his neck, leading him across the room, jerking the tie. The soldier kind of dug in straight-legged, like a stubborn mule. Sam just kept jerking and pulling, heading for the door. The soldier's eyes were bugging out. His hand went into his pocket and then the knife, a switch blade, sliced across Sam's forearm. And then I saw a knife, a Bowie knife, in Sam's good hand, just before it slipped, slick as an instant, in under the soldier's arm pit. The soldier slumped sideways with Sam still clutching his tie with one hand and that knife dripping red in the other. I remember all this.

In that long space as we stared across at the juvenile delinquents and waited for something to happen, I thought about the time when Sam went to jail. The time when Tony was whole and his body was strong and his head was straight and he was in his glory. The time when Sammy tried to hang himself.

I went to visit Sam in the detention centre at camp headquarters. It had been a week before they let me see him. They actually let me into the cell with him. There was no visiting area. An MP watched us the whole time.

He looked the shits. His face was sort of pinched and his eyes had all but disappeared. The strangest thing was his skin. His face was so pale he looked like a white man. An awful sorry-looking white man. He had a bandage on his left arm where he'd been sliced. The charges were a whole long list. Causing a disturbance, carrying a concealed weapon, attempted murder. He was looking at 10 years minimum in a military prison back in Canada.

"How long I been in here, Crook? I lost track."

"Only a week, Sam."

"Jesus, it seems like a year. I can't stay in this cage, Crook. I can't."

I had no idea when the court martial would be. For Sam, waiting for it would be bad enough. But thinking about another 10 years after that? Well I figured that wasn't even on his mind. He was trying to deal with the here and now. The adjutant told me he was depressed. He wouldn't eat. There was a lawyer who'd seen him only once.

Each time I visited him he looked worse. He paced back and forth like a caged animal. He would grip the bars, eyes darting. No focus. He wouldn't talk. Then one day he wasn't there. He'd made a noose out of a shirt sleeve and jumped off a chair. He was asleep when I saw him in the hospital. His neck was bruised. I remember thinking, *Is this what it's all about? Sending us over here for this?* I went looking for Tony.

The clerk said, "Captain Ashworth-Beever will see these men now, Sergeant. You can wait here."

The MP stood up, hesitated, looked at Sam and me and then sat down. We proceeded into Tony's office, which was at one end of Company C barracks.

I hadn't seen Tony much since we got to England nearly a year earlier. He looked spiffy. Ginger moustache. Neat-fitting tunic. Starched shirt, tie. New red Captain's pips on his shoulders. Sitting there, ramrod, behind the desk. We saluted and he waved at the chairs in front of the desk. We sat down.

He looked at Sam and said, "Private White, I understand that you are a Duncan boy, like me."

Sam sat. Silent. I nudged him.

"Yes Sir," he said.

"What tribe Private? ClemClemaluts? Quamichan?"

Sam's head perked up. "Somenos, Sir."

"Good soldiers, the Somenos. My father had a few of them with him in the Great War." Then Tony said, "I also understand that you have created a problem for yourself."

"Yes Sir."

"Would you care to tell me about it?"

"Well I, I,"

Tony looked at me. “Maybe Sergeant Cruickshank here could help explain it.”

Sam looked at me.

“Yes, Captain,” I said, “Private White was drinking down at the Plough one night and this soldier insulted him. Called him a dirty redskin. Said he wouldn’t be allowed in a bar back home.”

“Is that all?”

We were going over old ground here because I’d told Tony all this before when I first saw him about Sam. I guessed this time it was for Sam’s benefit so he knew that Tony knew.

“No Sir. There’s more. Private White ignored the soldier. I think his name is Kemp. But then Kemp started in on the women.”

“What women?”

“There were two English girls sitting with Private White and his friends. Kemp called them whores and sluts.” I went on and re-described the action all over again and Tony kept nodding as if it was all new to him.

"So this man was defending a woman's honour and then defending himself. Self-defense. Right Sergeant?"

"Right, Sir."

"Do you agree, Private?"

Sam sat there in a stupor. Like he hadn't heard a word.

"Do. You. Agree. Private?"

I kicked Sam.

"What? Yessir. I agree. Yessir."

"I should tell you something, Private White. I have been known at times to be quite Machiavellian. Do you know what that means?"

"No Sir."

"It means that I can be a sneaky, back-stabbing sonofabitch if I have to."

Sam straightened up.

"And," Tony said, "it so happens that in your case, Private, I have. Enough said. Right Sergeant Cruikshank?"

I kept quiet. I didn't think he wanted a response. I thought I could hear troops outside on the parade ground. Marching feet. A dim sound of music. The Colonel Bogie. Maybe it was just in my head. It was a good sound.

Tony said, "There is talk we'll be moving soon. I must consolidate my company. Be prepared, as the Boy Scouts say."

He paused.

"Sergeant Cruikshank, you have been reassigned to my company. Company C. You will report to Sergeant Major Perrin in the morning."

He turned to Sam. "Private White. You have also been assigned to Company C. You must settle your affairs with the adjutant general first. When you are ready, report to Sergeant Major Perrin."

Tony picked up his swagger stick and rapped it hard on the desk.

"Corporal Grierson," he hollered, "send in the MP."

The MP appeared and Tony handed him a package.

"Escort Private White back to the detention centre. You are to deliver this dossier to the adjutant. It contains documents signed by the brigadier general authorizing the release of Private White into my custody."

"That is all, gentlemen." He nodded to us and a smile flickered across his mouth.

We stood up, saluted and followed the MP out of the room.

"What's happening, Crook?"

"You're free, Sammy," I said, "you're free."

I managed to catch our waiter's eye and waved him over.

"More beer boys?"

"No. Lou, don't you think these kids are underage?"

"Look old enough to me, Jack."

"Did you check their ID?"

"No."

Then he noticed the knife on the table. He turned to the greasers and said, "OK guys, you got driver's licenses?"

But by now the six of them were heading for the door. Then Lou turned back to us, head thrown back, kind of indignant. "Where'd that knife come from? Knives aren't allowed in here."

Sam picked it up and it disappeared behind his back.

"OK. Now you want beer?"

We ordered a round and killed about another half hour. It was getting near closing time. The place had settled down. The fighters were either passed out or thrown out. Everyone else seemed to be numb.

I was feeling no pain and Sam looked quite relaxed. But Tony, he looked different. That evil eye of his was fixed on me even more like a spotlight and his face was twisted up more than normal. I figured we'd better get going.

My truck was parked across the street and as we wheeled Tony over, I saw the six zootsuiters standing on the corner under a street light. As we were tying Tony down in the box of the truck Sam said, "They're headed this way, Crook."

"Ignore them, Sam."

"Fuck no!"

The next thing I know he's got my Parker twelve-gauge off the rack in the back of the cab with the barrels broken and he's shoving shells in them.

"Sam, put that away!"

He gave the gun to Tony, sitting up there in his wheelchair throne.

"Stand guard, Captain."

Oh shit. We've got to get out of here. I was still kneeling in the box, securing one end of the rope to a cleat.

Blam!

The blast was right in my ear and I fell sideways and saw the shattered pieces of the street light bouncing on the sidewalk. The tough guys had disappeared. And Tony, for Christ sake, was reloading.

Sammy grabbed the gun and yanked it. But Tony wouldn't let go. The little bugger still had strong arms and shoulders. He whipped it around and whacked Sammy upside his head.

"The Jerries are coming, Corporal. Blasted Nazis."

I clean forgot about tying the wheelchair down. Sam and I jumped into the cab and we took off down Station Street. By now it was after midnight and there was no one around.

Blam! Blam!

I heard crashing glass, "What the fuck's he doing, Sam."

"He just shot out Westwell's window and the front door of the Greenhaven."

"How many shells he got?"

"There was a whole box. Twelve."

Blam! Again.

"What was that?" We were now at the end of Station Street.

"The neon sign on the Odeon."

I pulled over and was going to get out and try to get the gun away from Tony. Try to reason with him. Tell him the war's over. But out of the side view mirror, I saw the police car scream by across the intersection and disappear down Craig Street. I figured we'd best keep moving.

I turned the other way, onto Government Street and headed east toward the Reserve.

Blam!

"Another street light. He must think they're Stuka dive-bombers."

As we crossed the tracks and headed up the hill on Trunk Road, I heard the siren and saw the red light flashing in the side mirror. Next I heard a bang, clang, and watched in the rear view mirror as the wheelchair with Tony in it, shotgun cradled across the arms, rolled back down the hill. He was aimed straight for the oncoming black and white.

I pulled over and watched the police car swerve to miss Tony. The wheelchair just kept rolling across the tracks and then toward the gate to the fairgrounds beside the old armoury. We heard another blast as Tony blew the lock off the gate. Then he disappeared into the fairgrounds.

Inside was just a wide patch of bare ground. There was a full August moon above, so the whole place was lit with a flat white light. In September it would be full of tents and pavilions for the Fall Fair. There were some low bleachers on the north side and across the grounds on the south side there was a hill. Locals called it the mound. It was covered with trees and bushes. Tony was over there somewhere.

When we got into the fairgrounds, the police car had its spotlight trained on the mound. Sergeant Porky was on the radio phone. Another policeman crouched beside the car with his gun drawn. Porky got off the phone. "What in the name of holy snuff-coloured, fucking Christ is this, Crook?" His round face was beet red in the moonlight. Sweat ran down his double chins.

I shrugged. "Seems Tony is fighting the war again." I realized that sounded like the beer talking but I meant it. We'd all had a few too many and that had roused up Tony's demons.

"Is that who that little shit is? That wheelchair came out of the back of your truck like a rocket. Hit the street wheels turning. I damn near ran him over. Should've ran him over."

Blam! Blam!

We all hit the ground as the top row of the bleachers shattered into splinters.

"Holy fuck," Porky said, "I never been shot at before."

"He isn't shooting at you Porky. You'd know if he was."

"Should we rush him, Pork?" the constable said.

"Yes. No. In a minute. Maybe. Jesus. I got to think this through. Maybe I should call Victoria. Herman's coming over with the paddy wagon. Still that's only three of us."

"I'd suggest you just wait," I said, "he'll run out of ammo."

"How much has he got?"

"I think he's got five shells left. He started with twelve. That right, Sammy?"

"Sounds right. He used up five on the street. Two more in here. Oh, yeah. Another one for the gate lock. Four left."

"Let me talk to him, Porky."

"Ok."

"Tony," I yelled, "this is Crook. You hear me?"

Silence.

"Listen Tony, I want to come over and talk to you. OK?"

"Don't come, Sergeant. That's no-man's land. The Huns are dug in."

Shit. Now he's fighting the first war.

Blam!

More shattered bleachers.

"I guess that's your answer, Porky. We should just wait him out."

"Ok. Yeah. When I get my hands on that fuckin' asshole, I'll lock him up forever."

Sam stood up and turned to Porky. "You gonna put him in jail?"

"Of course, what the hell d'you think I'm gonna do with him? Send him on vacation? Yeah, to the crowbar hotel."

Sammy stepped back and looked at me. "They're gonna put him in jail, Crook."

"What's the matter with you Samson?" Porky said. "Don't you understand? You think we're livin' on Mars or somethin'? Jesus!"

Right Porky, he doesn't understand. You wouldn't either. Because to Sam there are places that are worse than death.

"Captain," Sam yelled, "this is Corporal White. Remember the Lamone River, Captain? Remember what happened? I'm comin' to get you, Captain. Hold your fire!"

And Sam was gone, sprinting across no-man's land to the spot at the base of the mound where the blasts were coming from. We heard a thrashing sound and Tony say, "This is insubordination Corporal!" and then silence.

We waited for them to appear. The three cops still had their revolvers out and the spotlight trained on the mound. But I was looking farther over to the left where the mound slopes down to the railway tracks. Presently I saw a form, like a blob with two legs under it, come out of the bush and slide down the bank to the tracks. I figured Sam would head up along the tracks, carrying Tony on his back, like a sack full of hammers, toward the river. Sammy knew where to hide.

"Where the hell are they?" Porky said.

"They're gone," I said. "They're not coming out."

I explained it to him. About the other river. The Lamone, in Italy.

"They're crazy," he said.

"You're right, Porky. They're crazy."

Our outfit crossed the Lamone River on our way to liberate Ravenna. We were attached to a squadron of the Princess Louise Dragoon Guards. The officer was Major Douglas Burke. We called him Black Douglas. We did some crazy stuff with him. He was one tough soldier. There was heavy fighting at the Lamone and we got in behind the Germans and established a position on the river. Our company was the rear guard. We held the Germans back as the brigade waded across. Then Tony ordered the rest of us out into the river. He was last. There was a lull. Then the Germans opened fire again. Sam and I made it to cover on the far side, but a couple of guys were still in the water and were hit.

As Tony was starting across, machine guns raked splashes along the river. Like skipping stones, right across Tony's back. He fell face down in the water. Sammy jumped up and ran in. With our Bren guns we pounded the other shore as Sammy waded over and hauled Tony onto his back and brought him to us. One bullet went right through his cheekbone and up into one eye. The other got him in his lower spine. Sammy saved his life. Tony never forgave him for it.

I climbed into the box of the pickup, unfolded Tony's wheelchair and secured it to the cleats. On the porch, Sam reached down and slipped one arm under Tony's legs and gently folded him forward from the shoulders with his other arm. He scooped him up, head slumped, arms and legs dangling and carried him, like he was a rag doll, to the truck and handed him to me. I placed him in the wheelchair. Sam jumped up into the box. Tony was quiet now.

"I'll ride back here with him," Sam said.

We wound our way out off the Reserve. As we pulled into Tony's long curved driveway, I realized that it was almost exactly 24 hours since we'd collected him and set out on our little adventure. We drove back to Sam's place in silence and I dropped him off and went home. I parked the pickup by the river and watched it as it slipped along. Let it ease my mind. The Cowichan River. It flows out of Lake Cowichan and winds its way east for 30 miles until it empties into Cowichan Bay. It drops through Skutz Falls and then flows into flat country around Sahtlam before it hits the canyons and the rapids and pools above Duncan. At Duncan it runs through flat land again, all Indian reserve, right to the estuary. Sam's cabin is about six miles downriver from my place.

In the fall, the river is chock full of salmon, chinooks and cohos, swimming up to spawn. Sam spears them right in front of his house. In the winter, the steelhead are running. The Cowichan is one of the best steelhead rivers in the world. Tony fished it when he could walk. Funny, before the war, both men used the river but they never met. In the summer the water is clear like now. And warm enough to swim in. The river is like time. You can't catch it or hold it. Runs through your fingers.

They found my father about 20 miles west of Bella Bella, in Hecate Strait. The boat was slowly motoring around in a big circle. All the lines were in. Poles up. The hold was full of salmon. He'd had a good outing. He, apparently, had decided to gut a fish and the knife must have slipped. There was a gash near his groin, through his femoral artery. He'd tried to tourniquet it. He bled to death. Alone. That was two years ago, in '46. The war was over and I was on my way home.

Acknowledgements

That Good Cahors Wine: Piet Mondrian (epigraph), Ernest Hemingway, Lindsay Elms, Margaret Horsfield,

Interlude: Dr. Georg Groddeck.

My Former Yugoslavia: Cormac McCarthy, Dr. Basil G. Conway, Mara Popovic, Wendy Keserich, William (Pop) Keserich, Dusko Peresic, Vlasta Subasic, Mark Mazower, Misha Glenny, Robert Kaplan, John Cornwell, Curzio Malaparte, Rebecca West, Milovan Djilas, Avro Manhattan, The Churchill Centre, Count Nikolai Tolstoy, The Pavelic Papers.

Short Haul: Antoine de Saint Exupery (epigraph), Raymond Carver.

Rhymes With Love: John Lomax, Lorna Crozier, The Nanaimo Free Press.

The Shed: Carol Johnson.

Annie Crook: D.H.Lawrence (epigraph), Lynne Bowen.

The Night Tony Shot the Lights Out: Nancy Buan.

Thanks to the readers: Frances Christopherson, Nancy Buan, Norma Dirom, Leanne Engen, Jim Greening, Gillian Hirst, Rosemary Kennedy.

PHOTO CREDITS

Cover: VEMRA, Robert Campbell, Lucas Wald, Peacock Photocopy.

Page 5: The Outbound.

Page 18: Courtesy Alberni Valley Museum pn 803

Page 33: Jeff Downie.

Page 120: Zdenko Radelic.

Page 144: Lloyd Triestino

Page 156: Tim Horton Hockey Photos.

Page 173: Vermont Timberworks.

Page 223: Shedbuilders.

Page 240: CalyKodak

.Page 266: South Wellington Historical Society (Bill Wilson, Helen Tilley)

Page 278: South Wellington Historical Society (Jack Ruckledge, Helen Tilley)

Page 294: Image i-68012, courtesy Royal BC Museum and Archives.

Page 334: Image cpn12047, courtesy Royal BC Museum and Archives.

About the Author

J. Leigh Hirst, BA, BFA, is a retired investment adviser and freelance writer who lives with his wife Gillian in Mill Bay, British Columbia. He has written numerous human interest articles for local publications, including the Victoria newspapers and has, for years, contributed a column to monthly periodicals that serve the area where he lives. In 2012 he wrote "The Tormented Prince", the biography of Mark Holloway, a British writer and denizen of London's Soho district during the 1940s and 1950s.

CPSIA information can be obtained at www.ICGtesting.com
Printed in the USA
LVOW11s2129270816

502101LV00003B/9/P

9 781460 286623